Dean's Dilemma

Wagner Brigade

Book Two

Ashley A Quinn

TCA Publishing LLC

ISBN is 978-1-959943-25-9

PROLOGUE

FIFTEEN YEARS AGO...

"Wendy, please. Don't go. You're too upset." Annabeth Swenson held her older sister's hands as she pleaded with her to stay. "You can talk to him tomorrow. I think you should just try to get some sleep."

Wendy shook free of Annabeth's hold. "Like I'll really be able to sleep. I'll just lie awake, thinking about—" She stopped and shook her head. "No. He can't use me, then dump me like a piece of garbage because I don't fit into his plan. Not now."

"What do you mean? I don't understand. You were ready to dump him just last week!"

"That was then." Wendy picked up her jacket and put it on. "Things have changed."

Annabeth frowned. "They have? How?"

"I can't say. Not yet. But trust me, they have." She pulled her long, toffee-colored locks free of her jacket collar. "I need to find him. Make him see reason."

"Wendy, no." Annabeth blocked the door. "Please, stay here. I'll stay too. We can have a sleepover and just talk. I can get my roommate to cover for me. The dorm monitors will never know." Which was true. It wouldn't be the first time Annabeth had spent the night in her sister's dorm without them knowing. Sneaking things past the women who were supposed to enforce the dormitory rules was ridiculously easy.

"Not tonight, Annie. I really need to talk to Johnathan. It's important. Now, move, please?" Wendy softened her tone and gave Annabeth a sad puppy look with her bright blue-gray eyes.

But Annabeth wouldn't be swayed. "No. I just have a bad feeling about you going out. You're too worked up. I don't want you to do something you'll regret." She loved her sister, but Wendy could have a temper.

Wendy huffed and cocked out a hip, propping one hand on it. "I'm fine. Yes, I'm angry. Seething, in fact. But really, what am I going to do to him besides yell? Stab him?" She rolled her eyes. "Get real. Now, move." Her voice had a harder edge to it, the attempt at charm now long forgotten.

Annabeth crossed her arms. "No."

Wendy's eyes took on a glint Annabeth hadn't seen before. A shiver of unease went down her spine.

"Listen, you little brat. I don't need you to look out for me. I'm a grown-up, and in a week, I'll be completely on my own. Out of this damn school and in a place of my own. With Johnathan. He is my future. Nothing you or he says will change that. Now either you move or I'll move you."

Wendy and Johnathan were moving in together? Annabeth stared at her sister in shock. That was news to her.

"Annie," Wendy growled.

Annabeth searched her sister's eyes, but all she saw was steadfast determination. She would indeed move Annabeth out of her way to get what she wanted.

"Fine." Annabeth stepped to the side, getting angry now. She hated it when Wendy treated her like a little kid. She might be three years younger, but she wasn't as naïve as Wendy thought. "But please don't do anything stupid."

Wendy gave a mirthless laugh as she opened the door. "Too late, little sister. Much, much too late." She closed the door.

Frowning, Annabeth stared at the wooden door. What did she mean by that? What had she done?

With a sigh, Annabeth tipped her head back and stared at the ceiling for a long moment, then shook her head. Whatever it was, Wendy would tell her when she was ready. Letting out a soft, frustrated growl, Annabeth grabbed her backpack off the floor by the desk and shoved her books inside. One thing was for sure—she wasn't going to sit here and wait for her to come back. Or make excuses with the dorm monitor about where she was. Wendy could explain that when she got back. She might have a week until she graduated, but until then, she still had to abide by the school's rules or face the consequences. And considering how much of a bitch she'd just been, Annabeth hoped she did get in trouble.

Slamming the door behind her, she strode down the hall and outside, crossing the courtyard to her own dorm. She swiped her key card through the reader and yanked the door open, then ran upstairs, using her card again to get into her room.

Her roommate, Olivia, looked up as she entered. "Hey—whoa. What happened?"

"My sister's a bitch and an idiot, that's what." Annabeth threw her bookbag down, then sank onto her bed with a huff. "She's off chasing after Johnathan. Says she won't let him dump her."

Olivia frowned. "Didn't she hate his guts last week because she thought he was cheating on her and wanted to dump him?"

"Yep." She flopped back on her mattress and sighed. "I'm

done trying to figure it out, though. If she wants to screw up her life and stay with that cheating asshole, then fine. But I'm not wasting anymore breath trying to convince her not to." She sat up. Her feet hit the floor, and she stood, moving to her armoire. "I'm going to take a shower and go to bed."

"You sure? We can stay up and talk if you want?"

"No. It'll just make me angrier. I don't want to put any more energy into it. I'm going to shower, put my headphones on and just"—she fluttered a hand—"try to think about something else." She grabbed clean clothes and shut the door.

"If you're sure..." Olivia's voice trailed off.

"I am." Annabeth offered her a soft smile. "Thanks, though."

"Of course. You're my friend. I don't like seeing you upset."

"You're the best, Liv."

Olivia grinned. "Don't forget it."

Chuckling, and feeling a little less angry, Annabeth grabbed her shower caddy, then left the room and went down the hall to their shared bathroom. She picked her favorite shower room and shut the door, then drew back the curtain and turned the water on to boiling. She'd let the water erase the rest of her anger. Stripping out of her clothes, she stepped into the spray and shut the curtain.

Twenty minutes later, feeling like a boiled lobster, she figured she should leave some water for the others and shut off the tap. Drying off, she put her pajamas on and went back to her room.

"Feel better?" Olivia asked. She got up and picked up her shower things.

"I do."

"Good."

Annabeth offered her a smile and picked up her headphones as her roommate left. She scrolled through her iPod and found the playlist she wanted, then turned off the lights and scooted under her covers. Liv had left on her small bedside lamp, so Annabeth didn't feel bad about plunging the room into darkness. She wouldn't kick any furniture coming in with that little light on.

Yanking her comforter up, Annabeth buried herself and closed her eyes. Wendy's face popped into her head. With a growl, she snuggled deeper and focused on the music.

Think about something else. Like your finals tomorrow. She had to get through the next couple of days and Wendy's graduation, then she could go back to the Vineyard with her parents and spend the summer on the beach.

But no matter what she did, her mind kept going back to Wendy, and it wasn't until well after midnight that she drifted off.

The next morning, one glance out the window was all it took to bring last night's argument back. Her sister's dorm was right across the courtyard. Grimacing, Annabeth moved away from the window and got ready for the day. She had a few minutes before she needed to head to breakfast, so she'd go check on Wendy. See if she was doing all right.

God, she was so stupid. Why was she even bothering? Wendy hadn't cared that she was upset last night. Why should Annabeth care if she was okay this morning?

But her feet still carried her across the courtyard and into Wendy's building. She hurried down the hall to her sister's room and knocked. No one answered, so she knocked again. "Wendy, it's me."

"She's not there."

Annabeth glanced back and saw Wendy's roommate, Stella, coming out of the bathroom. "Oh. I guess I'll wait until she's done." She nodded toward the door from which Stella emerged.

"She's not there, either."

"What? Did she leave already?"

Stella walked closer. "I haven't seen her. She was gone when I got in last night and still gone—or gone again—when I got up."

Annabeth frowned. "Okay. I guess I'll check the mess hall. If you see her, tell her to find me?"

"Sure." Stella swiped her key card and entered her room, leaving Annabeth standing in the hall.

Turning, she headed for the door. She had to eat anyway, so hopefully, she could kill two birds with one stone. As she neared the exit, the dorm monitor's door opened and a police officer emerged. Annabeth slowed and moved closer to the wall to edge past.

"Oh! Annabeth! There, officer, that's her sister." The dorm monitor's voice carried through the doorway.

Dread punched Annabeth in the stomach. She stopped and looked at the policeman.

"You're Wendy Swenson's sister?"

Annabeth licked her lips and nodded. "Yes. What's this about?"

"Oh, honey." The matronly woman the school employed for Wendy's dorm, Miss Blumenthal, pushed past the officer and came toward Annabeth with her arms outstretched. "I'm so sorry." Her red-rimmed eyes registered in Annabeth's mind a moment before the woman enveloped her in a hug.

"Miss, I'm sorry to inform you; your sister's been killed in a car accident."

The man's words echoed through her brain like a shout in an empty hall. It bounced off every corner of her mind and made her ears ring. "W-Wendy's dead?"

Miss Blumenthal nodded and hugged her tighter.

No. It couldn't be. She sucked in a sharp breath. "You're —" Her voice broke. She cleared it, swallowing hard, and tried again. "You're sure it was Wendy?"

"Yes." The officer nodded. "The woman in the car matches the driver's license we found with her. I'm sorry."

Pressure mounted in her face, and tears welled in her eyes. "No," she whispered. Annabeth sniffed hard. She couldn't lose it. Not here. "Um, was she alone?"

The officer's gaze sharpened. "Was she supposed to be?"

"Maybe. She left here looking for her boyfriend, Johnathan Cassidy."

Miss Blumenthal straightened and wiped her face. "I knew that boy was a good-for-nothing waste of her time."

The officer cast a glance at her, then looked at Annabeth again. "She was alone, yes. Whether she talked to him, we don't know, but we'll track him down. Maybe he can give us some insight into her mental state. We're not sure how the accident happened. Her car was the only one involved."

The need to cry hit Annabeth with renewed vigor. She choked back a sob and pushed away from Miss Blumenthal. "Excuse me." Pressing the back of her hand to her mouth, she dashed out of the building. One thought played on repeat in her mind: she should have tried harder to stop Wendy from leaving.

ONE

PRESENT DAY...

Dean Adler shoved the laptop away and stood. Walking to the window in his hotel room, he nudged the curtain aside with one finger and looked out. Cars whizzed by on the highway just beyond the parking lot; thick glass and the brick building muffled the noise.

Pensive, he glanced back at his computer. He'd just finished going over everything he'd learned about Johnathan and Will Cassidy again. It was enough to give the police leverage in their investigation into the brothers, but something still bugged him. He'd only had his private investigator's license a year—and it was a part-time gig—but there was a reason Ford talked him into getting the license; Dean had good instincts.

When Asher sent him back to the States to dig up dirt on the man terrorizing the woman Ezra brought down to Costa Rica, Dean figured he'd find a history of cheating. Maybe some palm greasing to encourage the authorities to look the other way here and there. And he'd found both those things.

But Johnathan Cassidy's misdeeds went back much further than just the last couple of years; and they involved his younger brother, Will.

He moved away from the window and back to the desk, staring down at the laptop screen. Smiling gray-blue eyes stared back at him from the grainy online newspaper photo. The young woman, Wendy Swenson, had been Johnathan's high school girlfriend. She'd died in a car accident a week before they graduated. And she'd been pregnant. After what Dean had learned about the Cassidys, he had his suspicions about what happened. At first glance, it sounded like what it was—a tragic accident. But something about it didn't sit right with him. How did a young woman lose control of her car on a clear night on a road she'd traveled many times before? He supposed the police's theory that she was angry and distracted was plausible, but Dean just didn't buy it.

Glancing away, he drummed his fingers on the desk. He had a decision to make. Go home or stay and dig into Wendy Swenson's death. His head told him to go home. It had been a week since he sent the information to Asher, and his investigation here had stalled. Remaining in the U.S. and looking into Wendy's accident would lead him on a path to nowhere, he had a feeling. But still, his gut told him to stay.

Dean sighed and scrubbed a hand over his face. If he went home, this case would haunt him, and he'd regret not pursuing it. "Dammit." He reached for his phone. His boss, Sam Brackley, wouldn't like that he'd be down a bartender longer than expected, but he'd understand. Bringing down Cassidy was a team effort. He dialed Sam's number.

The thump of a heavy beat came over the line, almost drowning out Sam's voice. "Brackley."

"Sam, it's Dean. Listen. You know all that information I sent to Asher on Cassidy?"

"Yeah?"

"Something I uncovered—it just doesn't sit right. I'm staying here a little while longer to look into it."

"What? Hang on." The noise receded to a dull roar. "Okay, that's better. What are you talking about? What did you find?"

"Cassidy's high school girlfriend died in a car accident right before they graduated. Autopsy said she was pregnant. Something doesn't feel right."

"You thinking it wasn't an accident?"

"Maybe. On paper it looks like one, but after what I've learned about Johnathan Cassidy, I'm not so sure. The man's a real piece of work. I want to stay a little longer. See what I can find out."

"After all this time? Dean, there can't be any evidence left."

"Probably not, but I need to try."

Sam let out a long sigh. "All right, fine. Martina was asking if she could work some extra shifts, anyway."

"Good. I'm glad it'll work out."

Sam scoffed. "Yeah. Just don't stay too long. I don't think she meant indefinitely."

"Copy that. Thanks, Sam."

"Yep."

"How are things down there with Ford?" The pseudo-boss of their unofficial protection agency was out on a boat with Johnathan Cassidy's fiancée, keeping her safe after she overheard him planning to murder members of her family.

"Fine for now. I haven't talked to him, but he calls Asher every night. They're out on the far side of the Osa Peninsula, just waiting. Hopefully, the information you sent will be enough to end things."

"I hope so too. Okay. I'll stay in touch. Let you know what I find out."

"Sounds good. Be careful, Dean. The Cassidys have a lot

of money. They might not like you digging around in their son's life."

Probably not. "Will do. Talk to you soon."

"Bye."

The line clicked in Dean's ear, and he lowered the phone. His gaze went to Wendy Swenson again. It didn't matter whether the Cassidys would like his actions. Or what they tried to do to stop him. If she was murdered, he couldn't let her death go unpunished. Dean tapped the computer screen. "I will find out what he did to you. I promise."

Two

Dean drummed his fingers on his knee and tried his best not to fidget. He glanced at the clock and wondered how much longer the police chief here in Medina, Virginia would make him wait. He'd driven up yesterday from Asheville after he talked to Sam, figuring the best place to start was at the source. And he was in luck. The officer first on the scene of Wendy's crash, Tim Wage, was now the police chief.

He drummed his fingers again, then crossed his arms. This was getting ridiculous. He'd been here nearly thirty minutes. He couldn't help but wonder if the chief was putting him off.

The door on the wall to Dean's right opened. He glanced over.

"Mr. Adler?" A man stood in the doorway, a dip in between his brows as he looked at Dean.

"Chief Wage?" Standing, Dean ran an assessing gaze over the man. Fit and trim, with close-cropped dark hair, he appeared to be around forty.

"Yes. Sorry to keep you waiting. I was on call with the mayor, going over budget reports." He rolled his eyes. "My sergeant's note that you were waiting gave me the incentive to wrap things up as fast as possible. Come on back." He motioned for Dean to follow.

They went through the door, and the chief led him down a hallway to his office.

"Have a seat." Chief Wage gestured to a chair in front of the desk.

"Thank you for seeing me."

"Of course. Sergeant Childers said you wanted to talk about Wendy Swenson? That's a name I haven't heard in a long time. But what is it you want to know? She died in an accident."

Dean studied the man as he talked, looking for any sign he was nervous or reluctant to talk. So far, he just looked genuinely curious.

"First, let me introduce myself. I'm Dean Adler, a private investigator from Golfito, Costa Rica."

"Costa Rica? You're a long way from home." He squinted. "And decidedly without an accent."

Dean flashed a quick smile. "I moved down there when I left the Navy. A case that's come my way brought me back here."

"Involving Wendy Swenson?"

"Yes. Do you remember her boyfriend? Johnathan Cassidy?"

Wage's brow dipped slightly, then he nodded. "I didn't talk to him regarding her accident, but I remember the name. Why?"

"He's currently on a yacht off the Pacific coast of Costa Rica, trying to track down his fiancée, who overheard him and his brother talking about murdering members of her family to take over a company."

Wage's eyes widened, and he cleared his throat. "Well. Okay. I can't see how I can help with that, but I'll do what I can."

"I'm actually not here about his fiancée. I'm here about Wendy. In gathering information on Mr. Cassidy to give to the authorities, I came across the report on her accident. Something just doesn't feel right about it. Can you tell me what sort of investigation was done?"

The chief tipped his head, studying Dean. "Not right how?"

"Like the lack of skid marks. And where she was going. I looked at a map. In the direction she was traveling, that intersection is away from both her school and her boyfriend's supposed location."

"You think Johnathan Cassidy had something to do with her death?"

"I don't know what to think."

Wage sat back and crossed his arms. For several long moments, he stared at Dean. Dean held his gaze.

"That case never sat right with me, either. I'm glad you're curious."

It was Dean's turn to frown. "You are?"

"Yes. I was the one who had to deliver the news to her sister." The chief shook his head, his jaw working. "I'll never get her face out of my mind. She was devastated. When I heard the autopsy showed Wendy was pregnant—" He broke off and pressed his lips together, then started again. "I've run across many kids from that school in my day. They all have bright futures—if they can keep their noses clean. I doubt he was happy about the baby; it would have derailed his plans, I'm sure."

Dean agreed. "I'm surprised you remember so much."

"Like I said, her sister's expression stuck with me. It was also the first death notification I ever gave."

Ah. That explained a lot. "It sticks with you, doesn't it?" He'd given one once. Unofficially. To his platoon mates, after an IED took out his Humvee and two others on the way back to base. Two of his friends didn't make it.

"They all do." Wage took a deep breath. "Anyway, what can I do to help?"

"I'd like access to the police and autopsy reports. I want to get a better sense of what was done during the investigation and how the officer in charge came to the conclusion it was an accident."

"Well, that was my sergeant. We didn't have a detective on the force back then. He's long since retired. I'm not even sure if he still lives in the area. But I can get you copies of everything." He picked up a pen and slid a pad of sticky notes closer. "What's your contact info?"

Dean rattled off his phone number and the name of the hotel where he was staying. "How come the accident was handled in-house? Wouldn't it go to a bigger agency since there was a fatality?"

Wage lifted his hand, still holding the pen, and shook a finger at him. "And that right there is why the accident still bothers me—other than the sister's expression. But I was a lowly rookie at the time. No one wanted to hear what I had to say. And, I guess, their explanation made sense to me then."

"What did they say?"

"That the family wanted to wrap it all up and move on."

"Hers or Cassidy's?"

Wage hummed. "Good question."

"Can you tell me about the scene?"

Wage sat back and looked out the window for a moment. "I was the first there. I'd been on patrol by myself for four months. The call came in, and I was only about a mile away. I was there in just over a minute."

"Did you pass anyone?"

"Yes, but no one who stuck out."

"Okay. What about when you arrived? Was there any sign of another person?"

"Not that I recall. There are pictures in the report. But I was focused on her. She was alive when I got there."

"What?" That was news to Dean. The newspaper articles just said she died at the scene.

"Yeah. She wasn't conscious, but she had a pulse. I couldn't get her out of the vehicle, though, even if I wanted to. It was too mangled. She was trapped. The fire department got there about five minutes after me and started working to free her, but they weren't fast enough. She died before they could get her out."

"Nothing stood out to you about the car or the scene?"

"Not really." Wage paused as he thought. "Maybe the lack of skid marks. I don't remember much else. After the firefighters arrived, they took over her care, then my boss put me on traffic control. We went to the school to notify them of the accident at the end of my shift. I walked down with the assistant dean to talk to the dorm manager. Her sister showed up looking for her while we were talking. That was the end of my association with the case."

Dean pursed his lips, processing all that, then nodded. "Okay. Is there anything else you can tell me or that you think I should know?"

The chief paused, staring at nothing over Dean's shoulder, then shook his head. "No. Like I said, I was a rookie." He tipped his head again, a thoughtful look crossing his face. "You could talk to the sister, though. I remember now she asked me if Wendy was alone in the car. Said the reason Wendy left was to go see Cassidy. She might know more about what happened later."

"All right. Do you know where I can find her?"

"No. Their family isn't from here, I know that much. I

want to say Martha's Vineyard, maybe. The Hamptons? Some place ritzy."

Dean nodded. "I'll track her down."

"I'm sure you'll put those P.I. skills to use and do just fine." Wage smiled and pushed back from his desk. "I'll get my secretary to print those files for you and be in touch soon."

"I appreciate it, Chief." Dean held out a hand.

"You're welcome. Keep me apprised of what you find? I'd like to know if we got it wrong."

"I will." Lifting a hand in farewell, he turned and left the office. His thoughts churned. Now more than ever, he felt like Johnathan was involved. Sure, Wendy could have been upset as she went looking for Johnathan and crashed her car on accident. But with what he knew about Johnathan Cassidy, he didn't think so. The question was, how did he cause the crash, and could Dean prove it after all this time?

THREE

Yawning, Dean stared at Annabeth Swenson's house, waiting for her to leave for work. He'd stayed up too late, researching Wendy's accident. He should be sleeping, but he'd wanted to get eyes on Annabeth and feel her out a bit before he approached her. It had been two days since he talked to Chief Wage, and only one since he received the files on her sister's accident. He'd used the other day to track her down. She was a pediatrician in Ohio. Once he had the police reports in hand, he'd checked out of his hotel, turned in his rental car and boarded a plane to Columbus. Now, he was just outside the city in a quiet upper-middle class neighborhood. He hoped none of the neighbors reported him for loitering. His new rental was nice, but someone might notice that the car didn't belong.

The white garage door on Annabeth's two-story brick house rolled up. Brake lights cast a red glow on the driveway as she started the engine and put the car in gear. She backed out, and Dean slid lower in his seat. He'd parked down the street, away from the direction she would go to get out of the neighborhood, but he didn't want to chance that she'd glance his way and see him. No point in making her think he was stalking her. He was, but not in a bad way. Intelligence gathering was part of his job. He knew nothing about Annabeth Swenson, or what she was like. He also needed a little more time to go through the police reports before he approached her. In case she only agreed to talk to him once, he wanted to get as much out of it as he could. That meant going in informed.

She backed onto the street and drove away. Dean waited until she was at the corner before he followed. It wasn't until they turned onto the main road that he switched his headlights on and dared to get closer.

Several car lengths behind, he stayed with her as she drove to a coffeeshop. To his surprise, she parked and went inside instead of going through the drive-thru. He pulled into the lot and parked a few spaces down. Should he go in? It would make him memorable. But seeing her interact with the employees would also give him an idea of her personality. And that's what this stalking mission was about—learning more about her, so he knew how best to approach her.

Turning off his car, he got out and crossed the lot to enter the shop. The rich scent of coffee assailed him as he stepped inside, perking him up. He didn't need it, but he'd get a cup anyway. With the way he felt, he doubted it would keep him awake.

Dean got in line behind Annabeth and sized her up. She wasn't a tall woman. Not short, either. Just average. And she had a little meat on her bones. Enough to fill out her dress slacks quite nicely. This morning, she'd left her long, toffee-colored hair loose. It flowed in soft waves around her shoulders. An insane urge to touch it hit him, and he stuffed his hands in his pockets.

Sidling closer, he looked up at the menu. "So, what's good here?"

She glanced back, a small frown drawing her eyebrows down over her blue eyes. "I'm sorry?"

He pointed to the menu board. "I'm from out of town. What's good?"

"For breakfast or the coffee?"

"I'm a black coffee kind of man, so food."

"I guess that depends on what you're in the mood for. If you want something savory, I like the egg, feta, sausage, and arugula sandwich. When I want sweet, I get a cinnamon roll."

He hummed, looking up at the board. "That sandwich sounds good. Thank you."

"You're welcome." She offered him a soft smile and turned around.

They shuffled closer to the counter. The person in front of Annabeth completed her order and stepped aside. Dean listened as Annabeth talked to the barista and liked what he heard. She was pleasant and polite. And she'd been nice to him when he asked about the menu. While it didn't mean she wouldn't shut the door in his face when he asked about Wendy, it gave him hope she'd offer up what she remembered if he got over the threshold.

Her order taken, she stepped aside. Dean walked forward and ordered a coffee and the sandwich she recommended. As he paid, one of the workers handed Annabeth a coffee cup and a cinnamon roll. She took them, glancing his way briefly as she turned.

He offered her a quick smile. "Thanks for the recommendations. Have a good day."

Her mouth turned up in that tight but polite smile strangers often gave each other as acknowledgment, and she walked away.

Dean stepped to the side to let the person behind him move forward. The door swung shut behind Annabeth, and he turned away, satisfied she wasn't a prima donna. At least, not on first glance.

Shifting, his gaze traveled over the coffeeshop. Something on the floor between him and the register caught his eye. He bent down to pick up the slip of paper. It was a list of websites—medical ones—with the name of a condition written at the top. "Damn," he muttered under his breath. She probably needed the information.

He looked up at the barista making his drink and held up a hand to get her attention. "Hi. I need to run outside quick. I'll be right back."

The young woman nodded. Dean didn't waste any time and spun on his heel, jogging toward the door. When he emerged from the coffeeshop, Annabeth was at her car, opening the door.

"Ma'am." He waved a hand and jogged toward her.

She looked up, a wary frown on her face. "Yes?"

He held out the paper. "I think you dropped this."

"Oh." She took the paper and glanced at it. "I did. It must have slipped out of my pocket when I took out my keys. Thank you."

"You're welcome." Dean backed away, not wanting to spook her by hanging around. She seemed wary of him. He didn't blame her. He probably looked a little rough around the edges. It had been far too long since he trimmed his beard, and he had circles under his eyes from lack of sleep. Plus, his clothes were rumpled from traveling. "Have a good day."

"You too." Her smile this time was more genuine.

Dean answered with one of his own, then turned and jogged back inside. At the counter, his order was waiting. He grabbed the sack and coffee cup and left again. Annabeth was pulling onto the road as he walked out. Crossing the lot, he was almost at his car when the squeal of tires caught his attention. A black BMW sedan shot out of the empty lot across the street, swerving into traffic. He watched for a moment as the car changed lanes before settling between two vehicles several lengths back from Annabeth.

Instinct had him running to his car and getting in. It could be nothing, but it looked like that car was following her. Considering all that was going on with Cassidy, he wasn't putting anything to chance.

Dean started the engine and backed out of his space as he buckled up. He had to wait an agonizing twenty seconds for traffic to clear so he could pull onto the road safely. But he had an advantage. He knew where she was going. Punching the button on the steering wheel with his thumb to activate the voice controls, he rattled off the address to Annabeth's clinic and tried to close the gap. He didn't want to be that far behind in case whoever was following her tried something when she got out of her car.

Ten minutes and a few questionable yellow lights later, he could see Annabeth's car as she turned into the clinic parking lot. The dark BMW was still behind her. It drove past the entrance to the lot and slowed to a stop, parking on the road.

Dean continued past him and turned onto the first road he came to, then pulled a U-turn and rolled to a stop at the corner. He took out his phone and took a picture of the guy's license plate, then sat back and watched. A man got out, dressed in dark jeans and a sweater. Dean cursed and backed up, parking on the road, then shut off the engine and hopped out. Hurrying across the street, he stuck close to the bushes, staying in the shadows of the trees hanging overhead. Twenty yards away, the man stood at the edge of the parking lot and stared at the clinic. Dean watched him mutter something, kick the ground, then spin and march back to his car.

Turning around, Dean ran back to his rental. He wanted to follow the man. Just as he climbed into his car, the BMW rocketed past. Dean started the engine and pulled out. The car barely slowed at stop signs, and once out on the main road, weaved through traffic. He tried to keep pace, but didn't want to draw attention to himself. BMW guy was doing quite enough of that.

Luckily, the heavy morning traffic kept him from getting too far ahead. When he finally turned off on a side street, Dean was still only about seven cars back and able to follow. They wound through the downtown streets until the BMW turned into a parking garage. Dean saw the sign stating it was for pass holders only and cursed. Slamming a hand on the steering wheel, he drove past. The garage was attached to a high-rise office building. Whoever was behind the wheel could go into any one of those businesses.

"Dammit." Dean's mind raced as he debated what to do. It could be hours before the guy left. Or just minutes. And he couldn't run the plate without law enforcement involved. No crime meant no plate.

He glanced at the coffee and food he bought and wrinkled his nose. "Guess it was a good thing I decided to follow her inside." Sighing, he turned around. There had been some street parking not far from the garage. He'd park and wait. The guy might just be a jilted boyfriend, but with everything going on, Dean couldn't leave it to chance that he was someone else. He couldn't imagine why Cassidy would want anything to do with Annabeth after all this time. But his gut told him there was more at play—now more than ever.

Four

"Oh, God, that feels better." Annabeth wiggled her toes as she kicked off her clogs. The clinic had been hopping today. Some viral bug had hit the local schools, and she'd been swamped. Luckily, none of her cases were serious and all the children would recover within a few days. But she was beat.

Hanging up her purse and jacket, she flipped on the kitchen light and wandered over to the refrigerator. She snagged a cheese stick from the top drawer, then glanced over the fridge's contents. She had no clue what to make for dinner.

Annabeth wrinkled her nose and opened the freezer. Maybe she had a burrito or something she could microwave. She needed to make another batch of freezer meals. There was some spaghetti left, but she'd had that the last couple of nights and wanted something different. For a moment, she debated ordering Indian takeout, but she really didn't want to leave her house, and the restaurant down the road didn't deliver.

The trill of her phone interrupted her foraging. She

glanced back at her purse, debating whether to ignore it, but it could be a patient. Sighing, she shut the freezer and hurried over to her bag. Annabeth pulled the phone from the side pocket and looked at the screen. It wasn't a patient. It was her best friend, Margot Gaultier.

Smiling, she answered. "Hey, girl. I just got home. What's up?"

"You need to turn on the news right now."

Annabeth's smile turned down. "What? Why?" She headed for the living room.

"Just do it."

"What channel?"

Margot named a major news network. Annabeth picked up the remote and turned on the TV, then punched in the number for the station. The face of a man she hadn't seen in almost fifteen years stared back at her from the picture in the corner. Her knees went weak as the blood drained from her head, and she stumbled to the sofa to sit down. "Holy crap."

"Yeah. I couldn't believe it, either. The creep finally messed up. I doubt it will make the police reopen your sister's case, but at least he won't be able to hurt anyone else now."

Annabeth blinked as she listened to the anchor give the details on Johnathan Cassidy's arrest for embezzlement and conspiracy to commit murder.

"They said just a little while ago his brother was also arrested."

"Will? Seriously?" She'd always felt sorry for him. Johnathan treated him like the dirt beneath his shoes, but Will just wanted his big brother's approval, so he let him do whatever. Even helped him out on his misdeeds. Apparently, little had changed since they were kids. "What else have they said?"

"Pretty much just what they're saying now. He tried to murder his fiancée after she overheard him plotting her father's and grandfather's deaths so he could take over their company. And that while she was on the run, the authorities discovered he'd embezzled millions. I feel bad for that woman, but at least she got out before she married him."

"Yeah. Maybe I should try to contact her. See if he ever said anything about Wendy." She still didn't believe her sister's car accident was an accident. When she'd tried to tell the police to look deeper, they'd brushed her off. Even her parents hadn't wanted to investigate. Her dad said it was too difficult on her mom; they just wanted to bury Wendy and move on. They'd moved on, all right. They pretended like Wendy never existed. It had led to an even more strained relationship than Annabeth already had with them. She rarely visited and only called on holidays and birthdays. She'd even moved far away, preferring to be nowhere near them, and now called central Ohio home.

"No. Annabeth, you leave it alone. You don't need to go down that hole. I know you believe your sister's death wasn't an accident, but there's no evidence to look at anymore. Nothing to help you prove he was responsible. It'll just tie you up in knots and bring back all the pain from when she died. Don't do that to yourself."

Annabeth sighed. "You're right. But—"

"No buts. Promise me you'll leave it alone."

"Margot—"

"No. The only reason you let it go last time was because you were going to flunk out of med school if you didn't. Think about the life you have now. Your patients. What happens to them if you descend into madness again?"

Annabeth let out a sharp huff, unable to argue with Margot's logic. She remembered how she'd been back then. She'd skated through her undergrad studies with ease, which gave her plenty of time to obsess over finding something to link Johnathan to her sister's death. But then med school hit and the intensity of it left her with a choice: flunk out and keep going on her futile investigation or let it go and focus on her future. Margot had talked her off the ledge back then, for which she was grateful. Apparently, she was going to do it again. "Fine. I promise."

"Good. Look, I have to go. The natives are restless and want their dinner. But if you find yourself tempted to do any digging, you call me so I can talk you out of it, okay?"

Annabeth gave a soft chuckle. "Okay."

"Promise me."

"I promise. Sheesh. Go feed your heathens before they wreck your house." In the background, she could hear Margot's toddler twins yelling.

"Too late." She heaved a sigh. "I'll be glad to go back on night shift next rotation. Let Tad deal with them all day."

Annabeth laughed. "You'd be lost without them." The twins might not have been planned, but for Margot and her husband Tad, they were their world. Annabeth didn't know how they managed two toddlers and the hectic schedules of two doctors in fellowship residency, but they made it work. Annabeth was lucky to keep her house plants alive.

"I would. Doesn't mean they don't drive me up a wall most days." One of the twins shrieked louder. "Okay. I better go. Talk to you later."

"Yep. Give them kisses from me."

"I will. Bye."

"Bye." Smiling Annabeth hung up. Her amusement was short-lived, though, as she caught sight of the television again. They were still talking about Johnathan.

Angry, she picked up the remote and stabbed the off button with her thumb. Drumming her fingers and chewing on the corner of her mouth, she stood up and paced to the kitchen. She might have promised to let it lie, but that didn't mean she could just shove the thoughts away. They were out and racing now.

She gave the freezer door a yank, stared at its contents, then slammed the door shut again. She wasn't hungry anymore.

FIVE

"I'll see you tomorrow."

Annabeth glanced up from locking the clinic door and smiled at her nurse, Kim. "Yep. Relax this evening. You deserve it." Like last Friday, today had been brutal. Even more so, because parents waited to bring their kids in rather than going to an urgent care over the weekend. She'd sent two to the hospital for further evaluation. It wasn't a good day.

"You too, Doc." Kim tipped a finger at her, then waved.

She waved back, then turned and headed in the opposite direction to her car. Key fob in hand, she pressed the unlock button when she was a few feet away.

"Are you Dr. Annabeth Swenson?"

Annabeth paused, looking to her left. A young man dressed in a suit walked toward her. He offered her a friendly smile.

"I am. Can I help you?" She prayed he wasn't a representative from the courts here to serve her with a subpoena. She'd heard horror stories about doctors being sued and this sort of thing happening. Not that she'd done anything to get sued for, but some people liked to be greedy and lie.

He held out a hand. "Noah Reitman. I'm a reporter with the Dispatch."

She eyed his hand, then wrapped both of hers around her purse strap on her shoulder and frowned. "What can I do for you, Mr. Reitman?" As a rule, she didn't trust reporters. They'd been like sharks when Wendy died and left a sour taste in her mouth.

The man's smile faded, and he dropped his hand. "I wanted to ask you a few questions about Johnathan Cassidy and—"

Annabeth waved her hand. "No. I have nothing to say about him or my sister." She'd been right not to trust him. Disgusted, she shook her head. It certainly hadn't taken long for the press to dig up Johnathan's past.

"So you think he's responsible for her death." It wasn't a question. He shifted, moving between her and her car.

"What?" Annabeth's eyes widened. That was a wild leap from her simple statement. He acted like it was a foregone conclusion that she believed Johnathan Cassidy murdered her sister. She did, but he didn't know that. And she wasn't about to admit it, either. "No comment. Please move so I can leave."

Reitman glanced back at her silver SUV. "Oh, is that your car?" When he looked at her again, she could see in his eyes that he knew exactly where he stood and that he'd positioned himself there purposefully. So long as he stood in her way, he could continue to ask her questions and increase the possibility she'd give him something he could quote.

"It is, but you knew that." Angry at being ambushed, she walked forward. He'd either move, or she'd run into him. Either way, she'd get to her car.

He took a step back and leaned against the driver's door. Annabeth stopped and blinked, mouth hanging open slightly at his nerve.

"You have three seconds to move, or I'm calling the police. One—"

He waved a hand. "I have every right to ask you questions."

"But you don't have the right to harass me. Two—" If he thought she was bluffing, he was in for a rude awakening.

"They'll just ask me to leave. And, lucky for me, you parked on the street today, not clinic property. I can't be trespassed."

Maybe not, but it would show a pattern and make it a whole lot easier for her to do just that the moment he stepped onto the clinic's grounds. And she would now make it a point to park in the lot, even if she had to walk from the far corner. She'd run out to get lunch, and when she returned, it was the closest spot to the door. She reached into her purse for her phone. "Three." She withdrew her phone.

"Calling the police won't be necessary."

Annabeth and Reitman turned at the sound of the deep voice intruding on their conversation.

"He's going to move without arguing."

Whoa. Annabeth blinked at the stranger who emerged from the vehicle parked two cars behind hers. A little over six feet tall, he had a shock of wavy dark hair and a short beard, which set off his tanned skin and icy hazel eyes. A black leather jacket framed his broad shoulders over a blue t-shirt. She frowned. He looked familiar.

"Who are you?" Reitman straightened but didn't move.

"Someone who's going to make you move if you don't get away from her car."

Reitman scoffed. "Try it. Then we'll see who's the one calling the police."

The man hummed as he shut his car door and strode closer. His long, powerful, denim-clad legs ate up the ground.

"Go for it. I'm sure they'd like to know where you've been visiting in the evenings after you leave work."

Some of the color leached from Reitman's face, but he squared his shoulders. "Yes. Delano Café is a treasure. Everyone should try it."

The stranger's head bobbed. "Sounds like it would have good soup, but I was talking about that rundown white house you've been frequenting. Or maybe you'd prefer I tell them about the woman who got in your car last night? The one in the stretchy black pants with the long, fake blonde hair?"

Twin red dots flourished on Reitman's cheeks. He pushed away from Annabeth's car. "I don't know who you are or why you're following me, but I wouldn't make it a habit. Some people might not like it."

"You mean like your drug supplier?" The tall man tipped his head side-to-side. "Probably not, but I'm not too scared."

The action set off a lightbulb in her brain. He was the man from the coffeeshop! But why was he here?

All the levity left the stranger's face, and his expression took on a hard edge. Annabeth backed up a step. Whoever this man was, there was a menacing air about him that said, "Don't mess with me."

The man took another step toward Reitman. "Leave."

Glaring daggers at him, Reitman glanced at Annabeth. "We'll chat another time, Dr. Swenson."

"No. We won't." If she ever saw him approach her again, she'd be on the phone to the police before he could open his mouth.

He held her gaze for another moment before he turned and loped away toward a black BMW sedan down the block. Annabeth watched until he climbed in and drove away before she turned to the stranger. "Thank you for your help."

"You're welcome." He held out a hand. "Dean Adler."

She eyed him just as warily as she did Reitman and ignored

his hand. "Annabeth Swenson. Why were you following him?" She tipped her head toward the now long-gone Noah Reitman.

"I wasn't. I was following you. Well, mostly." He dropped his hand.

Trepidation—and the anger from moments ago—surged through her body. "What?"

"Sorry. I'm not being too clear, am I? Could we go somewhere and talk?"

"No. Look, I appreciate you running that reporter off, but I don't know you. Or even what you want. And you admitted to following me." What was going on? She narrowed her eyes. "Are you a reporter too?"

"God, no. I'm a private investigator."

"And you've been following me? How long? Was meeting me at the coffeeshop deliberate?"

He nodded.

"Who hired you to do that?" She searched her memory for anyone who would have reason to have her tailed, but she couldn't think of anyone. She led the most boring life on the planet. If she wasn't at work, she was at home. She didn't date, didn't go out with friends much. Her life consisted of her patients and her books. And she liked it that way. It was safe.

"No one did, but I suppose if you want to get technical, I'm here because of Brooke McGinty."

Annabeth's eyes narrowed further. "Johnathan Cassidy's fiancée?"

"Yes. It's complicated. Look, I'm hungry, and I bet you are too. How about we go down to that restaurant near your house? The Indian place? I'll buy you dinner and explain everything. I promise I'm not here to harm you. I want to help."

"With what?"

He pressed his lips together and glanced away. Annabeth

crossed her arms, willing to wait him out. The only reason she was even giving him a chance to explain is because he ran off that rude reporter.

"I don't think your sister's death was an accident. I want you to help me prove it."

The air whooshed from Annabeth's lungs. She gaped at him, then waved her hands. "No. No, no, no. I'm not getting into this. Not again."

"Dr. Swenson—"

"No!" She pointed at him, backing away. "Leave me alone." Eyeing him, she walked to her car. Yanking on the doorhandle, she slid inside and started the engine. She refused to get sucked back into her sister's case. She would honor her promise to Margot. And save her sanity in the process.

Six

Dean propped his hands on his hips and watched Annabeth drive away. That did not go well. No doubt because of the asshole reporter following her. He should have intervened sooner, but he'd been hopeful Reitman would leave when asked. He should have known the man wouldn't be that cooperative. When he'd camped outside Reitman's office on Friday, then followed him, he'd uncovered much more than he bargained for. The man was desperate for a story to save his job. His habits had put him on the outs with his co-workers and his boss. Dean had overheard him on the phone at one point, reassuring his editor he was working on something big and to give him another couple weeks before making a final decision.

Dean assumed that something big was Wendy's death. He wanted to know what Reitman had discovered—if anything, because he could be bluffing to save his ass—but first, he needed to get into Annabeth's good graces. He needed to know what she knew. If anyone could shed light on Johnathan's activities fifteen years ago, it would be her. His brother, Will, refused to talk to anyone about anything, and

Dean had seen little luck in tracking down Johnathan's friends from back then; he didn't have enough information about who they might be. He needed her help.

Blowing out a breath and running a hand through his hair, he debated what to do. He could let her go home and come back tomorrow during business hours. She might make less of a fuss with patients around. But he didn't want to put her in that position. Scare tactics with victims weren't his thing. Suspects, yes. Victims and witnesses, no.

His other option was to get food and take it to her house. Try to talk his way inside. He'd seen the weariness on her face. A surprise meal she didn't have to cook might be just the ticket to get her to open up.

Decision made, he hopped into his car and headed for the Indian restaurant near her house. He'd seen her stop there Saturday, so he knew she liked it. On the way, he did a quick drive by her home to make sure she was there. The garage door was closing as he went past. Turning at the corner, he went around the block. At the restaurant, he parked and went inside.

"Hello." A woman smiled at him from the hostess stand. "Just one?"

"Actually, I'd like to place a carry-out order."

"Oh, of course. Follow me." She led him to the bar and went behind it to the register. "What can I get for you?"

Dean picked up a menu, glancing at it quickly, and gave her his order.

"Is that all?"

"No. I promised my girlfriend I'd bring her dinner, but I can't remember what it is she usually gets here. Her name is Annabeth Swenson. Do you happen to know what she typically orders?" He took a chance Annabeth ordered from here often enough the staff would remember her.

"Dr. Swenson? Of course. She likes the chicken korma.

Sometimes she orders the butter chicken. Which would you prefer?"

"Korma." Might as well get something he liked, too, in case she refused to let him in.

"Okay. Would you like naan?"

He nodded.

She finished inputting his order and read off his total. Dean handed her enough cash to cover it, plus a generous tip. Ten minutes later, he had his food and was back in his car and on his way to Annabeth's.

He didn't bother to hide his presence. Parking in her driveway, he got out and walked up the sidewalk to the door, eyeing the entranceway with caution. The door was sunk back into a little alcove, casting shadows deep enough to hide anyone standing there. It needed security lighting. He didn't like that she lived here alone and didn't have any. Or any other security, from what he could tell. That surprised him. She came from a wealthy family. Security should be second-nature to someone like her.

Ringing the bell, he stepped back and waited. The outside light flipped on. Two seconds later, it went off. Dean rapped his knuckles on the door. "Dr. Swenson, please open the door. I just want to talk." When she didn't open the door, he held up the food. "I brought dinner. Chicken korma." Still, the door stayed closed.

Dean sighed and dropped his arm, letting the plastic food bag dangle from his fingers. "Look, I know you don't want to relive what happened to Wendy. But Johnathan's current predicament is going to stir up the past. You've already seen it with that reporter. He's not going away. I just want to help. Please open the door and talk to me."

He stared at the wooden door and waited. This time, he heard the lock turn. The door cracked open, and her pretty face appeared in the slit.

"Hi." He smiled and lifted the food bag. "Hungry?"

She eyed the food, then looked him in the eye. "How do I know you're different from Noah Reitman? You want information about Wendy, just like he does. And it felt like he'd do anything to get it."

That was a good question. Dean decided to be honest. "You're right. You don't. I can give you nothing but my word that I'm one of the good guys. If you want, we can go somewhere public and eat our dinner." There was a park nearby, though he hoped she picked an indoor option. He'd been living in the tropics too long and his blood was thin. Late September evenings in Ohio were frigid compared to what he was used to.

She stared at him for another moment, then brought her phone up and took his picture. Before he could process what she'd done, she closed the door in his face.

"What the hell?" he muttered. He knocked on the door. "Dr. Swenson?"

Several seconds went by. He raised his hand, but the door swung open before he could knock again.

"Just so you know, I sent your picture to my friend and told her why you're here. If I don't call her soon, she's calling the police." Moving back, she motioned him in.

"Well, I'm glad you didn't tell her you would just text her. That's easy to fake." He stepped over the threshold.

"I'm not stupid. Although, letting a strange man into my house is pretty dumb."

He paused in front of her, looking her in the eye. "Then why are you?"

"Because it's bugged me for fifteen years how Wendy died. I want to know what you know."

He nodded once. "Let's eat first. Or talk while we eat. I don't particularly care. So long as there's food involved."

Her stomach rumbled, making him smile.

Her face softened. "That sounds good. I'm starving."

Seven

irl, what are you doing? Annabeth eyed her handsome houseguest out of the corner of her eye as she fished silverware out of the drawer. Yes, he'd been her knight-in-shining-armor earlier, but that didn't make him trustworthy. She didn't know anything about him other than his profession, and that didn't particularly endear her to him. The only private investigators she knew worked for her dad, and they dug up dirt on people he wanted to muscle out of a location so he could buy up their property. That was another reason she never went home. She really didn't care for her dad's business practices, no matter how much money it made her family. To her, it was dirty money, and she refused to touch what was in her trust fund. She'd paid for college and med school with the money left to her by her maternal grandparents.

Her phone trilled from her pocket. She pulled it out and glanced at the screen. It was Margot. Annabeth sighed and glanced at Dean. "Excuse me." She slid her thumb over the screen and turned away, walking several steps to the other side of the kitchen as she put the phone to her ear. "I told you I'd call you in a bit."

"What the hell do you think you're doing?" Margot demanded, ignoring Annabeth's words. "You promised you would leave Wendy's accident alone. And yet here you are inviting some strange man—though exceedingly handsome—into your house to talk about it."

"I know. But there's more to it than just that. I was accosted earlier by a reporter. He wanted information about Wendy." She glanced at Dean. He stood where she left him, opening food containers as he tried to look uninterested in her conversation. "Dean intervened. I just want to hear what he has to say. That's all."

Margot huffed. "You say that, but this is the beginning, Beth. Before long, you'll be taking time off work to investigate."

"No, I won't. I meant what I said. I'm not getting involved. He can investigate all on his own."

"Mmm-hmm. Right. Just try to keep your wits about you this time, please? Don't let it destroy your life again."

"I won't." And she wouldn't. Older and wiser now, she understood losing herself in the case wouldn't bring Wendy back. Neither would getting justice. She wasn't even sure it would make her feel better.

"Call me later, or so help me, I will be on the first plane out there, babies and all."

That made Annabeth smile. "I know, and I love you for it. I'll talk to you soon."

"You better." Margot hung up.

Annabeth turned off the screen and pocketed the phone.

"Good friends like that are hard to come by. You're lucky."

She looked at Dean, not surprised he'd heard every word. Margot hadn't exactly been quiet.

"Come eat." He nudged a plate toward her.

Taking a cleansing breath to reset her mind, she walked

forward and picked up her dinner. It smelled delicious and instantly put her in a better mood. "Thank you for dinner."

"You're welcome. I hope it's as good as it smells. I haven't had Indian food in a long time."

Annabeth led him to the small table in her breakfast nook. "Why not?"

"Not much Indian food in Costa Rica. At least not where I live." He set his plate down and slid out a chair.

"Costa Rica?" She paused, frowning at him. "Isn't that where Johnathan was caught?"

He nodded. "I'll explain it all, I promise. Sit, please."

More curious now than ever, she sat. "You said you were involved because of his fiancée. Brooke McGinty?"

"Yes." He scooped up a bite of his food and ate it before elaborating. "Mmm, that's good. So, I should probably start at the beginning."

"That would be nice." She followed his lead and took a bite of her korma. Flavors burst over her tongue, soothing her nerves a fraction. This was comfort food for her.

"So, I was in the Navy—the SEALs. During one of my tours, I met a man named Sam Brackley. Long story short, when I got out, I needed a breather from—everything." He waved a hand. "Sam left the service about a year before me and moved down to Costa Rica near a former commander of his, Ford Wagner. I thought, why not?" He shrugged. "Sam owns a bar, and he offered me a job while I was there, so I went."

Annabeth frowned. "I thought you were a private investigator."

"I am. You're jumping the gun. I'm getting there."

She lifted her hand, still holding her spoon, and spread her fingers. "Sorry. Please, continue."

His full lips twitched, and a hint of a dimple showed above his beard. "Anyway, Ford's some sort of wunderkind when it comes to helping people out of a jam. For whatever reason, people just gravitate toward him. He and his friends have put together a team of sorts that helps people. My association with Sam got me involved. I got my private investigator's license about a year ago, not long after I left the service. I'm licensed in the U.S. and in Costa Rica. I do the grunt work and track down information when I'm not tending bar for Sam."

"Which led you here?"

He nodded. "Some guy Ford knows from the military brought him his boss—Brooke. Our tech guy, Asher, sent me to North Carolina, where Brooke lives, to gather information."

"On her?"

"And Johnathan, yes. Which is how I found out about your sister."

"I don't understand why you think her death was anything but an accident, though. That's what all the reports say."

Dean tipped his head and studied her for a long moment. "Probably for the same reason you don't. I learned enough about him to wonder what he was capable of. Something just felt—off."

Annabeth looked down at her food, stirring the chicken and rice around with her fork. Emotions swirled through her brain, making her heart thud and a lump form in her throat. She swallowed hard and looked at Dean. "I tried to tell the police that something wasn't right. That he was involved somehow, but they wouldn't believe me. Wrote me off as a fifteen-year-old girl, mourning the loss of her sister. But it wasn't that. I knew when Wendy left that night she was upset, but she's not reckless. She wouldn't have missed that turn. Not unless she was distracted." She looked down at her food again. "But they didn't find any signs of anyone else in the car." She lifted a shoulder, the same hopeless feeling she'd had for years about her sister's death settling over her again. "So, I don't know."

"You know what else they didn't find?"

She shook her head.

"Skid marks."

Annabeth looked up. "What?"

"She didn't try to stop."

"So—" She broke off and blinked, then frowned. "What are you saying? That she crashed deliberately?"

"No. Though that is a possibility. I know they said there wasn't anyone else in the car, but—" He shook his head. "I don't know." He shifted in his seat. "I talked to Medina's chief of police, who was also a responding officer to your sister's accident. He said he was the one to first talk to you at the school. Do you remember him? Tim Wage?"

Annabeth looked away. She didn't want to let her mind go to that awful day; it always upset her. But she did remember the officer. "Yes. I asked him if she was alone in the car. He said yes." Swallowing hard and beating back the memories, she looked at Dean. "What did he tell you? Is that how you found out about the skid marks?"

"Yes. He gave me copies of the case file. I've been going over it. It tells me how the accident happened, but none of the background about why she was out. You said she was upset when she left. Do you know why?"

Annabeth shook her head. "No. She wouldn't tell me. Just that it would all come out soon. After the autopsy revealed she was pregnant, I figured that's what she was talking about. It's why I thought Johnathan might be involved in her accident. He wouldn't have been happy about the baby."

"You're sure?"

She scoffed. "Yes. Johnathan was the poster boy for a spoiled rich kid. He was only out for himself. If it didn't benefit him in some capacity, he didn't want anything to do with it. Having a child at eighteen would have messed up all his future plans. And when Wendy left, she said she'd make Johnathan see that their future was together." She shook her head.

"You sound like that surprises you. That she'd want a future with him."

"At the time she said it, it did. The week before, she was ready to dump him. He cheated on her. Then she did a one-eighty, and I couldn't figure out why. Not until after—" She broke off and swallowed. "I'm sorry."

"Don't be. I know this is hard. I've never lost a sibling, but I've lost friends. I prefer not to rehash those times, either."

Annabeth nodded, looking down. She swirled her spoon in the korma sauce on her plate, her appetite waning. "I was so happy when she told me she was breaking up with him. I'd tried several times to convince her he was a worthless jerk, but they were like a power couple on campus. It wasn't until it came out that he cheated on her—and everyone knew—that she wanted to end things." She glanced up at Dean. "It helped that it was the end of her senior year. She could frame it as her moving on since they were graduating and going to different schools." Annabeth pressed her lips together. "I just wish she'd ended things sooner. Before she got pregnant."

"If you don't mind me asking, why did she keep the baby? Why not have an abortion?"

Annabeth lifted a shoulder and swiped her spoon through her food. Lifting a piece of chicken, she put it down again. "It certainly wasn't because we were raised to believe it was wrong. If our parents had known before the accident, they might have marched Wendy to an abortion clinic themselves. I think it had more to do with the status that would come with being married to him. Of being the mother of his child. Where we're from, the Cassidys are a big deal. So is my family, but the

Cassidys are old money. They've been involved in the shipping industry on the East Coast for generations."

Dean nodded, a thoughtful crease forming on his forehead. "I dug into them. Johnathan and Will's cousin, Ted, is the CEO of their family corporation."

Annabeth nodded. "He's the oldest son of the oldest son. Johnathan was always jealous of Ted. He never said it outright, but the way he'd talk about him and the rest of their family sometimes made it clear he didn't like that he wasn't the one who would inherit the top position. I'm not surprised he tried to take over his fiancée's family company."

"That tracks with what I've learned about him. He's a vindictive, manipulative man."

"Very much so." She stirred her food again, still not taking a bite. "So, where does that leave us?"

"I need to talk to some of his friends from back then. See if any of them know anything about where he was that night or what he was up to. I got ahold of a yearbook from your sister's senior year, but it didn't give me much indication who he hung out with."

Annabeth scoffed. "There weren't many. Johnathan was popular, but he didn't have many close friends. He was too narcissistic and mean. There was Will, of course."

Dean nodded.

A furrow formed between her eyebrows as she thought. "And a guy named Jacob Torrence. He was Johnathan's roommate." She shook her head. "The school must have had some special process to match weak-minded people up with strong-willed ones. Jacob followed Johnathan around like a puppy. Just like Will."

"Okay." Dean took his phone from his pocket and opened a note app, typing in the name. "What about Will's friends?"

"Will?"

He nodded. "We already know Johnathan involved his

brother in most things. He might have told Will what happened. Or even asked him to help. Will could have talked to someone else. Who was he close to?"

Annabeth's frown deepened. "No one, really. He spent most of his time with his brother. You could try his roommate, though. Jeff Westin."

"What about your sister's friends? Who would she talk to?"

"Oh. Um, probably her roommate, Stella Scarsborough. There was Gina Martinelli too. They were the ones Wendy spent the most time with. I doubt she'd confide in anyone else."

"Do you know where any of these people live now?"

Annabeth shook her head. "No. I didn't keep in touch with any of them once they graduated. I did see Gina at my friend Olivia's wedding, though, a few years ago. They're cousins."

"Olivia?"

"She was my roommate. Olivia Martinelli. It's Nero now."

His head bobbed as he typed the name into his phone. "This is good. I'll track them down." He looked up. "Did your sister have a diary?"

"She did, but I'm not sure where it is. I have a few of her things that I kept, and it's not in there. Everything else got shipped back to my parents' house. I don't know what they did with it all." Her expression soured. "Probably threw it all away. They wanted to forget."

Dean studied her for a moment. Annabeth tried not to fidget under his scrutiny.

"Do you think they'd talk to me?"

"No." She didn't have to think about that. He'd never get past the front door.

"Would they talk to you?"

Annabeth shifted in her seat, and she looked down at her

cooling food. Whether they would or not wasn't the issue. She didn't want to talk to them. About anything, let alone Wendy.

Warm fingers grazed the side of her hand, and she looked up.

"You don't have to. I understand if the subject is too painful."

She let out a long breath. "It's not that. I don't have the best relationship with them. And Wendy's death is a touchy subject to begin with." She looked at a point over his shoulder, frowning, before she met his gaze again. "Do you think it would help? To have her diary?"

"I don't know. It will depend on what she wrote. At the very least, it might prove motive if she told him about the baby and then wrote about his reaction."

"But can we prove that he murdered her?"

"Honestly? After all this time, I'm not sure. The evidence isn't there, and her car has long since been destroyed. This case is a long shot, but it will haunt me if I don't try. I know it already haunts you."

It did. Annabeth glanced away. Her promise to Margot echoed through her mind. She could not let this consume her. But could she just walk away now? Again?

Her sister's face popped into her head, smiling. Those blue-gray eyes, so like her own, shone with mirth. Annabeth's heart clenched. No. Her sister deserved justice if there was justice to be had.

Taking a deep breath, she turned to Dean. "Talk to their friends. If you still need her diary after that—" She stopped, her mouth twisting. "Well, then, I guess I can talk to Mom and Dad."

Intense light hazel eyes met hers. "You're sure?"

"Yes. You're right. It does haunt me. I need to know what happened."

Dean studied her for a long moment. "Okay. I will do my

best to get to the truth. Even if the truth is that it was just an accident."

Annabeth's stomach churned. She hoped he could get to the definitive truth and put all the questions to rest once and for all. They all deserved peace.

EIGHT

F rustration clawed at Dean. He stabbed the end call button on his phone and set the device down with a clatter. Scrubbing his hands over his face, he let out a harsh sigh. No one wanted to talk to him. Over the last few days, he'd been able to find all the people Annabeth mentioned, but no one wanted to return his calls. It honestly didn't surprise him. He was sure Wendy's friends would rather forget, and Johnathan's probably didn't want to be associated with him right now.

The phone buzzed, skittering over the table. Dean picked it up, brows dipping in curiosity as he saw Asher's name. He swiped his thumb over the screen. "Hello?"

"Will Cassidy made bail."

Dean sat up straight. "What? How?"

"Money talks."

"Were there conditions for his release?"

"Yeah. He's been sent home—to his parents' home in Massachusetts, not his—and told not to leave town."

"Does Ford know?"

"Yes." Asher's voice was tight. "Told me to keep an eye on Brooke, then hung up. Damn, stubborn man."

"Huh? What's going on with Ford?"

"He's in love with Brooke McGinty, but is too stubborn to admit it. And he's being a pain in the ass because of it. He never should have let her leave. Or he should have gone with her." Asher sighed. "Surly Ford is no fun. He keeps saying he's angry because of his boat." He scoffed. "No. But, anyway, I thought you should know Will's out roaming around. He's in Martha's Vineyard."

A jolt went through Dean. "Really?"

"Yes. Why? I can hear the wheels turning from here."

Dean shifted in his chair. Settling his forearm on the desk, he leaned forward. "You know why I'm still here. That's where the Swensons live. And a lot of the people Wendy Swenson and Johnathan Cassidy went to school with live in the area. There are several in Boston and New York. They all have family homes on the Vineyard still. Maybe I should take a trip." It wasn't a bad idea. He was getting nowhere with phone calls. And maybe he could convince Annabeth to go and talk to her parents. See if they could track down Wendy's diary.

"Just be careful. Will might be more mild-mannered, but he's still in this up to his eyeballs."

"I know. But there's more to all this. I can feel it."

"And that's why I sent you there. Your gut instincts are unrivaled. Okay. Watch yourself. Call me if you need anything." He chuckled. "Maybe I'll convince the boss he needs a vacation and send him to you."

Dean smiled and rolled his eyes. "Yes, he'll be so helpful."

"He can be your muscle. I'm sure he's ready to beat some-one. Especially anyone named Cassidy."

"He'll need to get in line if my suspicions are correct." Dean's smile faded, and his voice hardened.

"I'm sure. Okay. Keep us posted."

"Will do. Bye."

Asher echoed Dean's sign-off, and they hung up.

Drumming his fingers on the desk, Dean turned his head to stare out the window. Could he convince Annabeth to go? He could go on his own, but having her there would get him further. And not just with her parents. Everyone else would be more willing to talk to her than him.

He glanced at his watch. Four-thirty. She'd be off work soon. Maybe he could ply her with dinner again.

Getting up, he snagged his jacket off the back of the chair and grabbed his car keys. He had to try.

NINE

The warm breeze hit Annabeth in the face as she walked out of the clinic. It felt nice after being cooped up inside all day and was a welcome change from last week's weather. She wasn't quite ready to give up the seventies yet and was glad they were sticking around a little longer.

Rounding the corner of the building, her steps slowed when she noticed the tall figure leaning against the car parked several spaces down from hers. It was Dean. Arms and ankles crossed, he stared out at the street. Her eyes caught on the sinewy muscles of his forearms before the wind ruffled his dark hair and drew her attention.

Warmth curled low in her belly. Her fingers itched to put the mussed strands back in place and then touch the rough, thick scruff covering his angled jaw.

Annabeth slammed a lid on those thoughts. She didn't need to get involved with Dean. It wouldn't last, and she didn't need the distraction.

He turned his head. Seeing her, he dropped his arms and straightened, smiling.

The warmth turned into a heated tingle. *But, oh, what a distraction it would be.*

Annabeth told her subconscious to shut up and strode toward him. "Hi. What's up?"

Some of the levity left his eyes at her all-business tone. "We need to talk. Can I take you to dinner?"

"No." The last thing she wanted was more people. "But we can do Indian at my house again."

He nodded once. "I'll get it and meet you there. You want korma again?"

"Sure. But get some samosas this time."

Again, he nodded. Stepping back, he opened his car door. "See you in a few."

It was Annabeth's turn to nod. She unlocked her car and got in as he started his and pulled away.

Her mind whirled as she drove home. What could he have to tell her? Had he talked to Wendy and Johnathan's friends? Did they have some bombshell revelation that would point the finger squarely in Johnathan Cassidy's face? Or did he have nothing and wanted her to talk to her parents now?

One thing was certain—she needed more than Indian food for this conversation. Pulling into the convenience store on her route home, she parked by the door and went inside to the freezer section. She made a beeline for the ice cream and opened the door to grab a pint of mint chocolate chip. For half a second, she debated getting a second one for Dean— because he wasn't getting any of hers—but she didn't know if he even liked ice cream or what kind he would want. She let the door close and stepped back. He could get his own after he left her house if he wanted it that badly.

Spinning on her heel, she walked up front to check out. Her shoulders drooped when she saw the line. That wasn't there a moment ago. Where did all these people come from? Resigned to waiting, she tapped her toe, shuffling forward as the patrons in front of her paid for their purchases and left. Finally, it was her turn. She thrust a ten-dollar bill at the clerk after he rang up her ice cream, then accepted her change and the small sack and left the store. Tossing the bag on the passenger seat along with her purse, she pulled out of the lot and drove the rest of the way home.

Pensive and annoyed now, she didn't see the black sedan pull into the driveway behind her until she glanced up to close the garage door and saw a man standing behind her car. It wasn't Dean.

Heart thundering, she hit the button to lock her car doors —which had unlocked when she put the vehicle in park—but she was too slow. The back door opened, and the man slid inside. Annabeth shrieked and reached for her door handle.

A hand landed on her shoulder. "I just want to talk, Dr. Swenson."

She froze, looking back. Her fear turned to anger as she recognized the man sitting in her backseat. "Go away, Mr. Reitman." She shrugged off his hand and reached for her phone in the cupholder. "I'm calling the police."

"I just want to talk, Annabeth. Can I call you Annabeth?"

She scoffed and opened her phone app. "No."

"Let's not do that." He plucked the phone from her hands.

"Hey! Give that back."

"Not until you hear me out."

"I have no interest in talking to you." She thrust her hand through the strap on her purse, picked up the bag with her ice cream, and opened her door, getting out. He could keep the phone. She just needed to get inside and lock the door. Dean would be here soon.

"Annabeth."

She slammed the door. The rear door opened, and she heard the scuff of his feet on the garage floor.

"Annabeth!" He ran around in front of her, making her stop short.

She backed away, not wanting to get too close. From the corner of her eye, she glimpsed the open garage door. She could make a dash for it. Try to get to the neighbor's house and hide out there until Dean showed up. And the cops. Because she was definitely calling the police on Reitman this time.

"I'm sorry to do it like this, but you're a hard woman to get alone. If you're not at work, you're here, or that friend of yours is hanging around. I just want to help you get to the bottom of your sister's death."

"No, you don't. You just want your story. Please move out of my way and get out of my garage."

He crossed his arms and stayed put. "Tell me what your sister's relationship with Johnathan Cassidy was like."

"No."

"Was it tumultuous?"

"No comment."

"Did he ever hit her?"

"No comment." She glared at him, balling her fists.

"He cheated on her, though, didn't he?"

"No comment." Her voice came out as more of a growl through her now clenched teeth.

"I mean, a man like that, who thinks he can have anything he wants whenever he wants, wouldn't think much of fidelity, would he?"

Annabeth stayed silent, still glaring at Reitman.

"You have to have something to say on the matter. There probably isn't a soul alive, except his brother, who knows more about him and his relationship with your sister than you."

"Get. Out."

"I already told you." A slow smile spread over his face.

"I'm not going anywhere until you talk to me." He shifted, moving away from the door, but the move put him at the point of a triangle between the interior door and the garage door. He extended a hand toward the door to the house. "How about we have some coffee and chat?" He reached for the button on the wall and closed the garage door.

Annabeth's gaze darted toward the rapidly closing door. She'd missed her chance to run out. This was not good.

Come on, Dean. Where are you?

TEN

Dean turned the corner onto Annabeth's street. The warm, rich scent of their dinner made his stomach grumble. He didn't care that he ate the same thing from the same place less than a week ago. It was damn tasty.

Nearing her house, the black car in the drive caught his attention. "Oh, that better not be who I think it is." Expression tight, Dean angled his car over to the curb and parked. He left the food on the seat and climbed out. Jogging across the road, he glanced at the BMW's license plate. It was Reitman's car.

He rounded the vehicle, assessing the house as he headed for the front door. No lights were on inside. Not even a hint of a glow. Annabeth should be here.

Dean brought up a hand and knocked on the door. "Annabeth? It's Dean." He stepped back, wishing there were more windows on the front of the house than the skinny ones surrounding the door and the one around the corner.

When she didn't answer, he walked around front. She had the curtains drawn, so there was no looking in. Not that it would matter. He was pretty sure that window went into her study. Her living room was at the rear of the house.

Continuing around the side, he glanced at the street, then the neighbors, looking for anyone watching. Stillness met his gaze. He turned back to the six-foot wooden fence and tried the gate latch. It was locked, which surprised him with her lack of other security measures. With another quick glance around, he hooked his hands over the top and climbed over.

Landing with a thud in the grass, he jogged toward the windows, peering through the glass to the living room. It was dark. He could just make out the outline of her furniture, but nothing moved. Stepping back, he wandered to the back door and knocked. "Annabeth?" He tried the knob, but it wouldn't budge. Where the hell was she?

Dean reached into his back pocket and withdrew his phone. Maybe she was stuck in traffic. She would have had to have taken a different route, though. He hadn't had a problem getting to her neighborhood. And if she wasn't just late getting here, where was Reitman?

Finding her name in his contacts, he tapped it, then brought the phone to his ear as he returned to the back door. It rang several times, then went to her voicemail. With a growl, he hung up. "Annabeth!" He banged on the back door. She had to be inside. With Reitman.

Eleven

Annabeth's heart leaped into her throat when she heard Dean's muffled voice out back. Her phone rang from inside the car, then Dean called her name again.

She took a step toward the door that led to the backyard. "Dean!"

"Oh, no. You're staying here." Reitman moved with a swiftness Annabeth hadn't expected. Before she could take more than a couple steps, he wrapped an arm around her and slapped a hand over her mouth.

She squealed and clawed at his hand, struggling in his grip.

"What the hell is he doing here? I waited and made sure he didn't follow you home. He's not supposed to be here."

Annabeth tried to talk, to tell him they made plans to meet, but her words came out muffled. It didn't matter, anyway. He wasn't paying attention to her. His focus was on the man outside.

Think, Annabeth! She paused, taking a deep breath through her nose, and tried to remember the self-defense class she took years ago. It basically taught her to use every body part she could. Starting with her feet.

Thankful she had decided to wear heels instead of her clogs today, she lifted her leg and slammed the pointy end of her shoe down on the top of his foot. Reitman howled, and his grip loosened. Annabeth twisted her head away and leaned to the side, bringing her elbow up and back, nailing him in the nose.

"Oh!" Stumbling back, he let her go and grabbed his face.

She ran for the door, hitting it with a thud, and grappled with the lock. She flipped it and reached for the knob.

"Bitch! I just want to talk!"

Annabeth's head snapped back as he grabbed a fistful of her hair and yanked. Letting out a yelp, she grabbed her hair above his hand, trying to take the pressure off. "Let go!"

The back door flew open, hitting the opposite wall with a bang. Dean stepped into the doorway, looking like some badass biker warrior in his form-fitting black t-shirt, tight jeans, and boots. Those icy hazel eyes that drew her in had a silver glint to them that said Reitman was a dead man.

The grip on her hair loosened, but Reitman held on.

"What the hell do you think you're doing, Reitman?" Dean stalked closer. "Let her go. Now."

"I just want to talk. She needs to tell me what she knows. I need this story."

"I don't know anything. Please, let me go." She stood on her toes as he tightened his grip on her hair. Her eyes watered, and she clenched her teeth.

"Reitman, there's nowhere for you to run. Even if you try to open the garage and get out, I'll tackle you before you take more than a few steps. Just let her go." Dean edged closer.

The reporter glanced at the door behind Dean, then turned to look at the closed overhead door.

Annabeth felt the breeze as Dean dashed past her and slammed into Reitman. Pain lanced through her head and they all landed in a heap on the floor. She rolled free from Reitman's grip and got out of the way so Dean could handle the man. Scrambling to her feet, she stumbled to her car and wrenched open the back door, searching for her phone. It lay on the back seat. With trembling hands, she picked it up and unlocked the screen to dial 911.

"Ow! That's my arm!" Reitman's screech had her turning to look as the phone rang in her ear.

"Buddy, you're lucky I'm not doing more than twisting it to hold you. A little higher and it'll break. Keep it up and you're going to find out how that feels."

Part of her hoped Dean broke the reporter's arm. She'd never been so terrified.

"Franklin County Sheriff's Office. How may I direct your call?"

Annabeth looked away as the dispatcher's voice sounded in her ear. "Um, I need the police at my house. A man just accosted me in my garage."

"What's your address?"

Annabeth gave it to her.

"Is the intruder still on the premises?"

"Yes. My friend has him detained."

"Is anyone injured?"

"Not badly. Just scrapes, I think."

"All right. Do you think anyone needs medical attention for those?"

"No. I think we're all okay. At least, there's nothing seriously wrong with anyone."

"Okay. The police are on the way. Did he have a weapon?"

"Not that I know of. He just surprised me and backed me into a corner, so I couldn't get away."

Annabeth heard clacking as the dispatcher typed.

"Okay. Stay on the line with me. Help will be there soon."

Annabeth ran a hand over her forehead, trying to calm her nerves. The back of her head pulsed from where Reitman pulled her hair, reminding her how differently things could have turned out.

Her gaze went to Dean. How would this have turned out if he hadn't arrived?

Twelve

Sirens sounded in the distance, growing closer. Reitman struggled against Dean's hold at the sound, but he just tightened his grip.

"Let me go, man. I just wanted to talk to her. I need this story." Reitman jerked his shoulders, then winced and stopped.

"Holding her hostage in her garage is not the way to get it. Now you're going to jail. I'm also turning over every picture I took of you to make sure you stay there." With the trouble the reporter caused, Dean wasn't holding back. He'd just get in the way of the investigation and cause Annabeth stress she didn't need.

Reitman sagged into the floor with a moan.

The sirens grew louder, entering Annabeth's neighborhood now. Within moments, they were on her street. The noise cut out as the police car came to a halt out front.

"Annabeth, go out and greet them. Tell them I'm not the bad guy." Dean tipped his chin toward the closed garage door.

She stood, pushing the button to open the overhead door,

then walked out of the garage, leaving Dean to frown after her. He didn't like that she was so quiet. But until they handled this situation, he couldn't really talk to her and help her past the shock.

The murmur of voices reached him, coming nearer as she led the officer into the garage.

"Hello." The man stepped inside. "I'm Officer Bowman." He stopped and frowned, tipping his head to look at the man Dean had pressed to the floor. "Noah Reitman?"

"You know this guy?" Dean rose, hauling Reitman to his feet.

"Yeah, unfortunately. He's an ambulance chaser and likes to stir up trouble at press conferences by asking politically charged questions. My boss hates him. I see we've crossed a different line now." He looked between Dean and Reitman and Annabeth. "Someone fill me in. What happened?"

"I want to press charges!" Reitman jerked against Dean's hold. "This man attacked me and has been holding me against my will."

Dean rolled his eyes. "Yep. That's exactly what happened." He looked at the officer. "Annabeth and I made plans for dinner. When I arrived, she was nowhere to be found, but his car was in the driveway. And I couldn't find him, either. I walked around the house, heard noises in the garage, and when I opened the door, he had her by the hair." He nodded toward the strands of toffee-colored hair on the ground. There wasn't much, but it was enough her scalp had to hurt.

The officer glanced down, then looked at Annabeth. "Can you tell me what happened prior to that?"

Annabeth took a deep breath, fluttering a hand through the hair by her face. "I pulled into my garage, but before I could shut the door, he ran inside. I couldn't get the car doors locked again before he got in. He said he wanted to talk about my sister—"

"Your sister? Are they dating or something?"

"No. She's dead. My name is Annabeth Swenson. My sister Wendy was Johnathan Cassidy's girlfriend fifteen years ago."

"Cassidy? The man on the news?"

She nodded. "She died in a car accident a week before they graduated. Mr. Reitman said he wanted to talk to me about her death. He's trying to write some sensationalized piece on how Johnathan murdered her."

Officer Bowman frowned. "Did he?"

"I'm not sure. But I'm not going to speculate about it to a reporter."

"I also have some evidence to offer up on things Mr. Reitman's been doing outside of work." Dean bared his teeth in a mirthless smile.

"Come on, man. You don't have to do that." Reitman's shoulders slumped.

"Evidence?" Officer Bowman frowned at Dean. "What's your connection to him? And to her?" He pointed at Annabeth.

"I'm a private investigator working on Cassidy's case on behalf of his ex-fiancée, Brooke McGinty. It led me here to Dr. Swenson. Mr. Reitman piqued my interest when I caught him following her around, so I followed him. Got some interesting things on film. I intended to eventually turn over my photographs and notes to the police, but he's forced my hand, so we'll do it now."

"What's in the pictures?"

"Drug deals, drug use. Prostitutes."

Officer Bowman's eyebrows went up. "You've been a busy boy, Noah." He shook his head and reached for his handcuffs. "Turn around. Right now, you're under arrest for terrorizing this woman."

Chin jutting out and his jaw clenched, Reitman looked at

the garage ceiling as Officer Bowman put the cuffs on him. Dean relinquished his hold and watched as the officer led him down the drive to his cruiser. Annabeth stood stoically next to her car, arms crossed over her middle.

"Hey." He touched her arm gently. "Are you okay?"

She turned away from the retreating duo to look at him. Her head bobbed. "Yeah. I'm okay. Shook up a bit, but—" She stopped and pressed her lips together, shaking her head. "I'm all right." Her voice faded to a whisper at the end.

Dean didn't stop to think. He stepped closer and wrapped an arm around her shoulders, tugging her into his chest. She leaned into him, tipping her head into the hollow of his neck. Her hands came up, and she clutched his shirt. Warm breath tickled his face.

"Thank you." She tipped her head back to look at him.

He raised an eyebrow. "For comforting you?"

"No. For showing up when you did. He was pretty insistent I talk to him. I wasn't sure what he was going to do to make me talk."

"I'm glad I showed up when I did too. How did you not notice him, though? He pulled in right behind you."

A sheepish look crossed her face and her cheeks reddened. She pushed out of his arms to retreat to her spot against her car. "I was distracted by the conversation you wanted to have. My mind wouldn't stop cycling through all the possibilities."

"Ah, crap. I'm sorry." Dean ran a hand through his hair. "I should have given you an idea of what I wanted to talk about."

She waved a hand. "It's not your fault. I still would have been distracted. My brain just would have gone through every possible way the conversation could have gone."

"Well, next time, I'll just show up some place we can talk right away." He offered her a small smile to lighten the mood.

An answering tilt of her lips put some of the sparkle back in her eyes.

"Are you sure you're okay?"

She hugged herself again, then raised a hand to the back of her head. "Yeah." She winced as she touched her hair. "My scalp is a little tender, but it'll be fine."

"Let me see." He swirled a finger, asking her to turn around.

"Really, I'm okay."

"Humor me." He'd seen people bleed from getting hair ripped out.

With a huff, she pushed away from the car and whirled around. "I'm really fine, Dean."

"I just want to make sure you don't have any spots that are bleeding. You'll need to keep an eye on them so they don't get infected. You're a doctor. You know how dirty the scalp can be."

She let out another soft huff, but didn't protest. Carefully, Dean parted her hair, running his fingertips gently over her scalp. The silky toffee tresses were cool on his skin, and the floral scent of her shampoo wafted toward him. Goosebumps erupted on the back of his neck. Gritting his teeth, he made quick work of inspecting her scalp, only finding a couple of spots that were raw.

"Um." He cleared his throat and dropped his hand. "You've got a couple places you might want to watch, but nothing terrible."

She turned around, tucking a lock of hair behind her ear. "I figured. It stings."

He nodded, stuffing his hands in his pockets. His fingers itched to feel her hair again. While he buried his nose in it as well. The doctor was getting under his skin with her soft vulnerability and pretty eyes. He needed to remember she was more or less a client. That meant hands off.

Luckily, Officer Bowman came back to take their formal statements, saving Dean from himself. But his reprieve didn't last. Once the technicalities were taken care of, he and Annabeth were once again alone.

THIRTEEN

The trashcan lid banged as Annabeth stepped on the pedal to open it. She dropped the sack with her melted ice cream inside and lifted her foot. The soft closure of the lid did not match her feelings. She wanted to throw things and scream, then flop onto her bed and have a good cry.

But first, she wanted to hear what Dean had to say.

The interior garage door opened, and he stepped in carrying the bag with their now cold supper and a black leather jacket. She heard the overhead door whir as he pressed the button to close it. The sound cut off as he shut the kitchen door.

"I'm glad this stuff reheats well." He lifted the bag, setting it on the island.

"Me too." Annabeth opened a cabinet and withdrew a couple of plates. After a quick reheat, they were sitting down at the breakfast nook table to eat.

The first few bites were in silence. Annabeth's brain was stuck on autopilot. Plus, she was hungry. Her afternoon had been busy, and she'd been on her feet since lunch. It didn't matter that her mind didn't want food now; her body did.

"So, are you up for hearing why I'm here?"

She glanced up from her meal. "Yes."

He stared at her for a long moment. "I tracked down all the people on the list you gave me. Most of them live in the northeast still. Boston, New York. I can't get anyone to call me back, though, so I need to take a trip up that way and try to talk to them in person."

"Okay." She wasn't surprised no one wanted to talk. If she were in their shoes, she wouldn't, either.

"Also, Will Cassidy made bail. He's in Martha's Vineyard."

The food in Annabeth's stomach turned to lead. She set her spoon down and pushed her plate away. "Great."

"There's more."

She steepled her fingers against her forehead and sighed. "What?"

"I want you to go there with me."

"What?" She dropped her hands to stare at him, mouth agape. "No. Why would you ask that?"

"Because I need you. These people—they don't know me. I won't get any more out of them in person than I will on the phone. But you? They know you. They'll sympathize with you and be more willing to talk."

Annabeth sighed and sat back, glancing out the window. She wanted to dispute his logic, but couldn't. It didn't mean she wanted to go, though.

"Someone has to know something. Johnathan Cassidy is a narcissist and probably a sociopath. It would be hard for him to keep things to himself."

"Which is why he probably told Will. But Will won't talk to anyone. He's too loyal to Johnathan."

"Right, but that doesn't mean Johnathan didn't let something slip to someone else. It doesn't even have to be a full confession. Just some comment that would make you go"—he cocked his head—"'that was odd.' And what do we really know about Will Cassidy? He's been overshadowed by his big brother his entire life. He could have friends we don't know about because no one ever thought to look."

She pressed her lips together; her resolve to stay out of things wavering.

"Annabeth, I wouldn't ask you to go if I didn't think your presence wouldn't make a difference. Me going alone is pointless. I might as well just go back to Costa Rica."

Her heart stuttered at the thought, giving her a bit of a wake-up call. She wanted to know for sure what happened to Wendy. Going back to the status quo wasn't an option anymore. It would haunt her if she let this drop now. More than it ever had.

Groaning, she propped her elbows on the table and covered her face. "I don't want to go, but you're right." Scrubbing her face, she dropped her hands to look at him. "When were you thinking?"

"This weekend? We could try to get a flight out after you get off work Friday."

She nodded. "That will work. Can you make the arrangements? I'll pay you for my flight. I just don't have the energy to think about this tonight. It's all just so—" Annabeth covered her mouth and blinked furiously as moisture gathered in her eyes. She waved her hand. "I'm sorry." What happened earlier, and knowing they could uncover some truly terrible things about what happened to her sister—well, it was all just hitting her full-force. She wanted to be alone now. And she really wished she had her ice cream.

"Don't apologize. You're definitely allowed to be upset." He paused, studying her. "Do you want to talk about it?"

Annabeth shook her head. "No. I think I'd like to be alone. Would you mind?"

"No, of course not." He pushed his chair back and stood. "I'll just scrape this back into the box and eat it at my hotel."

Turning away, he walked to where they'd left the containers on the counter by the sink.

Barely holding back her tears, she absently toyed with her spoon in the korma sauce on her plate as Dean dumped the remnants of his dinner into the to-go box. In seconds, he was closing the lid and ready to go.

"I'll call you tomorrow with details on our trip." He stopped beside her and picked up his jacket from where he'd draped it over the chair. "If you need anything, I'm only a phone call away."

Looking up at him, she nodded. "Thank you."

The soft, understanding smile he gave her brought the tears closer to falling. She clenched her teeth and blinked to keep them away.

He laid a hand on her shoulder. "I'll see you soon. Get some rest." With a quick squeeze, he let go and walked away.

Annabeth's eyes tracked his progress until he turned the corner. A moment later, the front door opened and closed. The silence that descended was so absolute and deafening, she almost got up and went after him. But her desire not to let anyone—especially uber-handsome and confident Dean Adler —see her fall apart, kept her in her chair.

Inhaling a shaky breath, a tear tracked down her face. She sniffed and dashed it away with the back of her hand. What was she doing? Crying over getting pushed around a little bit? She was tougher than that.

Wendy's face popped into her head. Her heart lurched and her breath caught. It wasn't her encounter with Noah Reitman that had her all out of sorts.

No longer hungry, she got up and put her food away. Wetting a rag, she wiped down the counter, then rinsed Dean's plate and put it in the dishwasher. A ding sounded from her phone on the island. Annabeth dried her hands and walked over to pick it up. A curious frown creased her forehead when she saw a text from Dean. Clicking on it, she read the message.

I saw the ruined ice cream. Check your porch. Sleep well, Annabeth.

She looked up, turning to look toward the front of her house. He brought her ice cream?

Putting the phone down, she left the kitchen, walking down the short, open hall to the front door. Annabeth flipped on the outside light and turned the doorknob lock Dean had flipped when he left and opened the door. On her welcome mat was a pint of mint chocolate chip ice cream.

A smile spread over her face and some of her melancholy disappeared.

He brought her ice cream.

FOURTEEN

Humming along to the radio, Annabeth turned onto her street, trying to hold her heart back from galloping out of her chest. Today was the day. She and Dean were leaving for Martha's Vineyard. He should be waiting when she pulled up.

Over the last day and a half, she'd asked herself multiple times if she'd lost her mind. It was one thing to answer Dean's questions; it was quite another to go ask the questions of other people. After getting on a plane with a man she barely knew. Margot would kill her if she knew what Annabeth was up to. She really would get on a plane with her twin toddlers to shake some sense into her. Thankfully, Margot had been too busy to keep tabs on Annabeth's new foray into her sister's death.

But she would be right about one thing, though. Annabeth needed to verify Dean's identity before they left. She'd taken him at his word he was who he said he was. She was determined they weren't going anywhere until she saw some ID.

Passing the neighbor's large oak tree, her driveway came into view. Dean was parked on the far side of the drive. She could see him sitting in the car. Annabeth reached up and pushed the button to open her garage, then turned into the driveway and drove in. Turning off the engine, she heard his car door shut, then saw him walking toward her. She opened her door and got out.

"How was your day?"

"Long." She opened the backseat and withdrew her briefcase and purse, then shut the door and looked at him. "I was thinking."

"Uh-oh. Your tone doesn't sound good. You aren't backing out on me, are you?"

"No. Well, probably not."

"What?"

She pressed her lips together and frowned. "I don't know you. I mean, I know who you say you are, but you've never actually proven you're Dean Adler, former military man and current private investigator."

"Oh. That's easy enough to fix." He reached into his hip pocket and pulled out a thin wallet, opening it up. "Here's my driver's license." He handed her the plastic card. "And my P.I. licenses for here and for Costa Rica, and my veteran's military ID." He passed her three more.

Annabeth looked at each one. If they were forgeries, they were good ones. All of them looked legit. Not that she'd know how to spot a fake, but they definitely weren't obviously forged. She handed them back. "I guess your name and profession check out, at least."

"You can trust me, Annabeth. I'm not here to do you any harm."

She rolled her lips and bobbed her head. "It's not your intentions I'm worried about. It's our actions. All this is bringing back bad memories." She waved a hand. "But I want to put it to rest. For good."

"Does that mean you're ready to hit the road?"

"Yes. Let me dump this stuff inside and grab my suitcase. I'll be back out in a couple minutes."

He nodded, and she walked away, going inside.

In the stillness of her quiet house, she paused at the island and leaned her hands on it, taking a deep breath. She felt better, confirming his identity, but she was still nervous. Could she go on and have a normal life if they went to Martha's Vineyard and only ended up with more questions they could never answer? Could she live with herself if they didn't go?

That was a hearty no. Now that it was all back in the forefront of her mind, she couldn't let it go until she had answers. She had to see it through.

With that thought in mind, she pushed away from the counter and retrieved her little rolling carryon from where she left it by the back door, leaving her briefcase on the island. Purse in hand, she exited the house.

Dean stood near his car, looking at his phone.

"I'm ready."

He glanced up. "Good. Our plane's still on time." He waved the phone, then put it in his pocket. "Let's roll."

Squaring her shoulders, Annabeth stiffened her spine, pulling her resolve around herself like a cloak. It was time to find out what really happened to Wendy.

Fifteen

Darkness surrounded them, broken by the occasional streetlight as Dean drove away from the ferry terminal in their new rental car. He'd booked them into a hotel in Edgartown, one that didn't break the bank. He had no doubt Annabeth could afford whatever hotel she wanted, but he couldn't. Brooke was paying for some of his investigation, but not all of it. The majority of this side quest was on him. If he figured out what happened to Wendy Swenson, though—even if her wreck really was an accident—the hit to his savings would be worth it.

He glanced at Annabeth. She stared out the window, but from the vacant look in her eyes, he doubt she saw any of it. She'd been quiet since they left her house. Even on the plane ride, she hadn't talked much. He knew she was struggling with this, but he didn't know how to help except to push on and find out what happened to her sister. He was glad she was along. It would make doing that easier.

The ride to Edgartown was a quick one. Dean steered the car through the downtown to the hotel on the seaside. He pulled into the lot, searching for a parking space.

"Why is it so dark?"

"What?" He cast a quick look at her.

"The hotel." She pointed at the building. "There aren't any lights on."

Dean stopped, staring at the building. She was right. None of the lights inside were on. "Well, crap." He pulled forward, stopping under the portico. "Let me go in and see what's up."

"I'm coming with you."

He didn't argue; just shut off the engine and got out. Annabeth trailed him inside. They didn't even make it inside before he noticed the water on the ground. When he opened the door and stepped into the building, water sloshed at his feet.

A flashlight bobbed, landing on his face.

"Sir, I'm sorry. We're closed." A young man waded through the ankle-deep water toward them in rain boots.

"We had a reservation."

"Oh. I'm sorry. We've had a massive water leak, as you can see." He gestured to the floor, inches deep in water. "It's short-circuited our electrical too. I can't check you in or give you a refund at this time. I can take your name, though. Once we get back into our system, we'll refund any deposit you made."

"Okay. Where are you sending guests in the meantime?" Dean pinned the man with a stare.

"Down the street, but they're full now. All that's left are the small, private establishments, but I don't have a list of the ones that have rooms left. All I can give you are a list of names and numbers the chamber of commerce supplied for us."

Dean sighed and glanced at Annabeth. Weariness shone in the lines of her face. This was not the welcome she'd needed. But it seemed they didn't have any other choice. "I guess we'll take the list. Thank you."

The man nodded. "Give me one moment. I'll get a copy. I think there are still some left." He turned and waded away.

Dean looked at Annabeth again. "I'm sorry."

"It's not your fault."

"I know, but you don't exactly want to be here, and you've put in a long day at work. Searching for a new place to stay probably wasn't at the top of your list of things to do once we got here."

"No, but it is what it is. Just don't expect me to hang out once we find a new hotel. I'm going to crash."

"Noted." He nodded, turning his attention to the hotel employee as he sloshed back through the water toward them.

"Here you go." He held out a single sheet of paper. "I'm sorry for the inconvenience. I hope you can find something suitable on the list."

Dean took the paper. "Thank you."

The man offered them a tired smile. "Have a good night."

Dean nodded, refraining from wishing the same for the man. He knew he wouldn't. Placing a hand on Annabeth's back, he ushered her outside to the car.

"Let me see that list."

He handed it to her, then got in as she walked around to the passenger side. Settling into the driver's seat, he flipped on the overhead light. "Anything look promising?"

"Maybe. I know a couple of these places are really pricey." She pointed to several. "But there are a few we can try that aren't too bad."

Dean lifted his hip and took out his phone. "Read off the first phone number."

She recited the number. He input it, then lifted the phone to his ear. A woman answered, and after a quick conversation, where he learned they were full, he moved on to the next. Three inns later, they still didn't have a place to stay.

Annabeth sighed and put the list down. "The rest are in different towns. You know what? Let's just go to my parents' house."

Slowly, he lowered his hand holding the phone and turned to look at her. "You're sure? They'll want to know why you're here."

"I know. And it's not like I wasn't planning on telling them, anyway. Eventually." She shrugged. "It'll just be a little sooner than I thought. But I'm tired, Dean. I just want to go to bed."

It was the droop to her face and the fatigue in her voice that convinced him. "Okay." He set his phone in the center console. "Point the way."

Sixteen

I really have lost my mind.

Annabeth stared out the window, waiting for her parents' house to emerge from the trees as Dean drove up the long driveway. This was a bad idea, but she was too tired to continue to look for a room. She hadn't slept much this week, and the worry about what they would find added to her fatigue. She just wanted to lie down in a comfortable bed and pass out for a few hours. Her parents' house was as good as any other place for that. And they could get a jump on their inquiries in the morning.

The drive opened up and her family home came into view. It stood against the night sky like a hulking shadow in the moonlight. Annabeth's gut tightened.

"Whoa. Not what I was expecting."

She knew what Dean saw. With its cedar shake and board and batten façade, the house looked like a quintessential New England home. But it was super-sized. Three stories, it boasted a cupola on top that hosted a widow's walk. She'd spent many hours sitting up there with a book, staring out at the sea. It was her favorite place in the entire house.

"You can park in front of the far bay." She pointed at the garage.

Dean angled the car, pulling to a stop. He turned off the engine and looked at her. "You ready to go in?"

"Yes." She yanked on her door handle. "I want to go to bed." Not waiting on him, she got out and slammed the door. Wind whipped her hair around her face, obscuring her vision. She raised a hand and pulled it away, turning her face into the wind. The scent of the ocean beyond the house assailed her, but it had an earthier undertone tonight. Rain was coming.

Annabeth heard Dean's door open, then the trunk lid a second later as he pulled the lever to pop the hatch. His door closed, then he met her behind the car. He lifted their bags out, and she took her suitcase before walking away, leading him to the front door. With a steadying breath, she reached out and poked the doorbell. Chimes sounded inside. Stepping back, she wrapped her hands over her suitcase handle and waited.

Several long moments went by with no answer. She poked the bell again. "I hope someone answers. It's a little late. They might be in bed."

A moment later, a light came on in the rear of the house, then another in the hallway. A silhouette of a woman moved toward them. Her mom.

The porch light came on, then the lock clicked and the door swung open.

"Annabeth?" Katrina Swenson stepped into the doorway, her wide brown eyes landing on her daughter.

"Hi, Mom." Annabeth bared her teeth in a tired smile. She only needed to get through the next few minutes, then she could sink into bed and let the world and all her worries fade away for the night.

"What are you doing here? And so late?" Her gaze traveled past Annabeth to Dean. "Who's this?"

"Can we come in?" She did not want to have this conversation in the doorway.

"Oh, yes, of course." Katrina stepped back and motioned them inside. "Your father's not home. He's in London on a business trip. Is everything all right? It's not Christmas or Easter, so I'm not sure why you're here. Although, it's not like you come home then, either..." Her voice trailed off and she raised a questioning eyebrow.

"It's complicated. We need a place to stay, at least for tonight. Our hotel is flooded."

"Well, of course you can stay here. I just—"

Annabeth waved a hand. "I know you have questions. I promise to answer them. In the morning. I'd really like to just go to bed." She didn't bother to hide the fatigue in her voice. Everything was finally catching up with her.

"Oh. Well, all right. Do I at least get to know who your friend is, though?"

Annabeth looked at Dean. A smile erupted on his face and he stepped forward, hand outstretched.

"Hello, Mrs. Swenson. I'm Dean Adler. It's nice to meet you."

Katrina smiled back, some color coming to her cheeks. Annabeth fought not to roll her eyes. She hadn't known Dean long, but it had only taken her a few minutes to see his charm. He was laying it on thick tonight.

"You too. Call me Katrina, please. Are you Annabeth's boyfriend?"

"He's a friend, mother. And now that you've officially been introduced, we're heading to bed. Is it all right if I sleep in my old room and Dean takes the one next to it?"

Some of the charmed look eroded from Katrina's face. She nodded. "Yes. You'll have to make up the beds. Linens are in the hall closet, like always."

"Okay. Thank you, Mom."

"You're welcome, honey." Katrina stepped forward, enveloping Annabeth in a quick but hard hug. When she stepped back, a bright smile sat on her pretty face. "I'm so glad to see you."

Annabeth forced a smile, a bit confused by her mother's behavior. Katrina Swenson was normally friendly, but not quite so—hands-on. "It's good to see you, too, Mom. You'll be around in the morning?"

"Yes. I'm supposed to have brunch with my ladies' group, but they can do without me for one day."

"You can go. We can talk after."

Katrina waved a hand. "No. They'll understand. I'd rather be here."

"If you're sure..." Annabeth let the sentence trail off.

"I am. You two go get some sleep." She shooed them toward the hallway. "I'll make breakfast in the morning and we can talk."

Annabeth's smile turned more genuine. She hadn't known what to expect, just dropping in like this and appreciated her mom's effort to be welcoming. She hoped things didn't swing wildly the other way once Katrina found out why they were here. "That sounds good."

Looking at Dean, Annabeth tipped her head, indicating he should follow her. With a quick goodnight to her mom, they wandered deeper into the house. She hung a left just outside the kitchen and went down another hallway to the staircase.

"She seemed pleased to see you. I thought you said you guys didn't get along."

Annabeth sighed, glancing back at Dean as they climbed. "It's not so much that. Well, not with her, anyway. If Dad comes home while we're here, you'll understand more. He's a force to be reckoned with. Mom always bows to his wishes.

It's created tension between all of us. My mom is kind. She's just very submissive."

A furrow formed between Dean's eyebrows. "He's not physically abusive, is he?"

"I don't think he's ever hit her. At least, not that Wendy or I ever saw. I know they argue sometimes. I've heard him yelling at her. But I've never seen any marks. It's always just been verbal abuse."

Dean snorted softly. "That can be just as bad."

Annabeth's mouth flattened. "Yeah." She stopped and looked down the hall, her jaw working. She did not want to talk about her parents' relationship, or her dad's attitude. "I learned a long time ago nothing I said made any difference, though. She just lets him run roughshod all over her." She turned away again and pointed at a door. "That's your room. Mine's next to it." She gestured to the door just past it.

He nodded. "Where are the sheets your mom mentioned?"

Annabeth walked down the hall to a door on the left. She opened it and removed two sets of sheets. "Grab a couple blankets, would you? And some pillowcases?" She stepped back so he could reach inside. A wave of his pure male scent hit her nostrils, sending a shiver of awareness down her spine. It hit harder than she would have thought, her fatigue making her more susceptible to his magnetism.

She rolled her eyes at herself behind his back. Who was she kidding? Dean Adler could make a nun sit up and take notice. She refused to give the attraction any more space in her brain, though. Her life was complicated enough without adding a man into the mix, no matter how nice he seemed or how good looking he was.

Spinning around, she left her suitcase in the hallway and marched down the hall to his room, depositing his sheets on the bed. He walked in behind her. When Annabeth turned around to leave, she saw the frown on his face. "What?"

"I thought it wasn't made up." He nodded to the bed.

"It's not. They just throw the duvet over the mattress to make it look made up." She reached out and peeled back the cover, showing him the mattress encased in a mattress protector.

"Ah. Makes sense." He stepped forward and put the blankets and pillowcases down on the bed.

Annabeth grabbed a set of pillowcases and a blanket. "Make sure you change your pillowcases. The ones on the bed are probably a little dusty." She stepped back, heading for the door. "Have a good night."

"You too."

Giving him a tight smile, she retreated with her armload of bedding. Back in the hallway, thoughts of why she was standing in her parents' house returned. She paused outside her bedroom door and glanced across the hall. That was Wendy's room. She hadn't been in there in years. Not since her mom caught her in it one summer afternoon not long after Wendy's death. It was the one and only time Annabeth had been scared of her mother. Red-faced and screaming at Annabeth to get out and not to ever touch anything in the room, Katrina shoved her into the hallway and slammed the door.

Annabeth frowned and turned around, staring at her bedroom door. She'd forgotten about that memory. Her frown deepened. What else had she forgotten?

Huffing out a harsh breath, she opened the door. She didn't want to think about it any more tonight. Sleep. That's what she wanted. Because it meant for a few hours, at least, she could forget.

SEVENTEEN

Wind rattled the window and rain pelted the glass with a dull tink. Annabeth glared at it, then flipped over, pulling a pillow over her head. Why were New England storms so much louder than Ohio ones? She never had any problems sleeping through them at home. But here?

A roll of thunder shook the house. Annabeth growled and sat up, glancing at the clock. Six-seventeen. She might as well start her day.

Throwing back the covers, she got up. Lightning flashed and another rumble of thunder rolled through her room. She padded across the rug covering the hardwood floors and turned on the light, then rummaged through her suitcase for clothes. After a quick shower, she dressed and left her room.

She stared at Wendy's door. It would be so easy to cross the hall and go inside. The lock on the door was flimsy. Only meant to deter. It had appeared the day after her foray into the room fifteen years ago. Annabeth went out with a friend for a day at the beach, and when she came home, a handyman had been around and installed a new knob. Annabeth had respected the boundary, but now she had no such qualms. She could wiggle that open in seconds. A handy skill she'd picked up from a colleague in med school. He'd been an inner-city kid who'd run with a rough crowd before a caring teacher convinced him he was worth more than a life of crime. But he was still rough around the edges and had liked to show off some of his more questionable skills. She'd become quite adept at picking locks—and rather quickly. Her mom wouldn't come looking for her. Not for hours. She could be in and out long before that happened. She'd never know.

But did she want to set that kind of tone for this visit? She wanted her mom to cooperate with them. And if Annabeth snuck around behind her back and Katrina found out, it would lead to the opposite.

With a final look at her sister's room, Annabeth walked away, heading for the stairs. She needed coffee.

Her steps were light going down the treads in her socks. At the bottom, she rounded the banister and wandered down the hall to the kitchen. To her surprise, her mom was already awake.

Katrina looked up as she entered, smiling. "Well, good morning. I didn't expect to see you for at least another hour. You looked ready to drop last night."

Annabeth nodded and crossed the tile floor to the cabinet that held the coffee mugs. She took one down and reached for the full pot on the counter below. "Yeah. It was a long week. Traveling did not help."

"You're up early, though."

"Storm." Annabeth pointed up, indicating the weather raging outside.

Katrina looked out the window over the kitchen sink. "It's quite the tempest out there, that's for sure. I hope you didn't have outdoor plans this morning."

"Subtle, Mom."

"What?" Katrina turned a wide, innocent look on her.

"Don't be coy. Just ask what you want to ask."

Katrina sighed. "It still never ceases to amaze me how blunt you are. You never used to be that way."

"I learned I had to be, to be taken seriously in med school and residency." Really, all she'd done was lose her give-a-damn filter. With it gone, she was more direct. It saved time, and sometimes, that time was critical.

"Yes, well, there's something to be said for the art of subtlety. You can learn a lot that way."

"I can learn a lot by being direct too." She took a drink of her coffee, letting her words—and the look she pinned her mother with—do the talking for her.

Katrina huffed. "Fine. Why are you here?"

Annabeth clenched her teeth, then forced herself to relax. This had to be done. "You've heard about the legal trouble Johnathan Cassidy is in, yes?"

Her expression closing, Katrina nodded. "I saw something about that."

"The man who's with me is a private investigator. He's working with Johnathan's former fiancée. During the course of his investigation, he discovered Wendy's accident."

Some of Katrina's ambivalence disappeared. "What does that have to do with what's happening now?"

"Nothing. But Dean thought the circumstances of Wendy's accident seemed suspicious, so he dug deeper."

Katrina moved to the sink, features pinched, and picked up a dishcloth. She wiped at the sparkling countertop. "Wendy's death was an accident. There's no need to dig up ancient history. I can't believe you brought a stranger here to dig into our family's past." She turned an angry stare on Annabeth; red colored her cheeks. "I mean, really, Annabeth. What were you thinking?"

Righteous anger welled in Annabeth's chest, straightening her spine. How could her mother—Wendy's mother—not want to know the truth? "I was thinking what I've always thought. That Johnathan had something to do with Wendy's death. I could never prove it, but I was just a kid, and I didn't have access to the resources he does. And I'm not the only one looking into her wreck. A reporter accosted me at work and at home, trying to get details on what happened. I'm sure he won't be the only one once media scrutiny around Johnathan heats up. More will crawl out of the woodwork. I'd rather have Dean digging into things and uncovering the truth than some lowlife who only sees ratings points and dollar signs in his eyes."

A little of the fight left her as her mom's breathing grew shallow and a touch of panic entered her eyes. "We can't hide from it, Mom. And we owe it to Wendy to find out what really happened."

"She crashed because of the idiotic choices she made. And I don't want any part of whatever it is you aim to do."

Annabeth pressed her lips together, unable to argue with her mother's statement. Wendy's actions were a factor, for sure. "I'm not asking you to get involved."

"Then what do you want?"

"Let me look in Wendy's room."

Katrina's eyes widened. "Why? There's nothing there."

"I just want to go through things. See if there was anything that was missed. The police didn't do a very good job investigating."

"No, honey, you don't understand. There's nothing in her room. Literally nothing. We sold or donated all her things years ago."

Eighteen

The sound of the rain hitting the roof grew louder as Dean climbed the stairs to the widow's walk. When he left his bedroom this morning, he'd gone down to the kitchen expecting to find Annabeth and her mother there. But neither woman was anywhere to be found. Annabeth's room was empty when he passed it, and he saw no sign of Katrina. He'd gone through the public rooms downstairs without finding Annabeth. The widow's walk was the last place he could think to look. If she wasn't up there, she'd gone for a walk; in the current weather conditions, he couldn't see that happening.

Dean crested the top of the stairs and glanced around the square room. On the bench that lined three sides of the room beneath the windows, Annabeth sat with her knees drawn up and her arms around them, looking out at the angry sea. "There you are."

She didn't look away from the windows. "Hi."

Uh-oh. Dean stepped off the landing and walked toward her. Apparently, sleep hadn't improved her outlook. He sat down at the other end of the bench. "What's wrong? Or is it just more of the same that's got you down?"

"No." She looked at him. "I talked to Mom this morning."

A hollow pit opened up in Dean's stomach at the bleak look in her eyes. This wouldn't be good.

"She said they sold or donated all of Wendy's belongings years ago. There's nothing here for us to look at."

His mouth worked, and he turned to look out the window as he digested that information. "Well, we still have all their friends to talk to. And Will, if we can get him to talk to us."

"This is all pointless. Without any of her stuff, we can't prove anything. I can't believe I let you talk me into coming here. Into ripping out the stitches that sealed the wound all those years ago." She glared at him through narrowed eyes before glancing out the window again.

"There was no guarantee we'd find anything in her stuff, anyway. You knew that. What we need is for one of their friends to tell us that Johnathan confided in them or that he left something stashed somewhere and we can go find it. That's the real reason we're here. Why you're here. They won't talk to me; but they might talk to you. Also, did your mom actually show you that the room was empty?"

She turned to him, the glare from before now a frown. "No. Why?"

"Because maybe she said that so you wouldn't look."

"Why wouldn't she want me to look?"

He shrugged. "Maybe it's too painful for her. It could be she wants to keep it all locked up for herself. Everyone deals with grief differently. Is she still here?"

"No. After we argued, she went to her brunch thing with her ladies' group."

"Perfect." Dean popped to his feet and held out a hand. "Let's go."

Annabeth's frown deepened. She eyed his hand, then looked up. "Go where?"

"To see if she was telling the truth."

NINETEEN

Annabeth stared at Dean's hand. Her heart thumped as she debated his proposal. She wanted to believe her mother hadn't lied to her, but she remembered the way Katrina reacted all those years ago when she snuck into Wendy's room. Dean was right. It was possible she just didn't want to let anyone into the shrine she'd built for Wendy.

She glanced up and met Dean's gaze. "All right. But let's make it quick. I'm not sure how long she'll be gone." Unfolding her legs, she took his hand and let him help her up. He gave her fingers a quick squeeze after he pulled her to her feet and then let go.

Together, they filed down the steep stairs to the third floor, then down the hall to the main staircase. In moments, they were standing outside Wendy's bedroom.

Annabeth tried the knob. "It's locked." She hadn't expected any less.

"Do you know where she might keep the key?"

"No. But we can pick it." She backed away. "I just need a couple things." Turning, she headed for her room.

"What?"

She glanced back as she reached her door. He had his hands propped on his hips, eyes fixed on her. For a moment, she forgot what she was after. No one should be allowed to look that good. Ever. That cream henley hugged his chest, and the pushed-up sleeves showed off tan, muscular forearms dusted with dark hair. Annabeth bit her lip and dragged her eyes back to his face. It did little to quell the swirl of heat forming in her belly. Dean's face was as beautiful as the rest of him. She cleared her throat. "I need a couple hairpins to pick the lock."

His dark brows dipped lower over his eyes. "You know how to pick locks?"

"Learned it in college. I'll be right back." Needing to escape for a moment and gather herself, she twisted the doorknob and stepped into her room. Away from his magnetic presence, she took a deep breath and closed her eyes, resetting her mind. She was here to find out what happened to Wendy; not get involved with the handsome investigator.

Blowing out her breath, she crossed to her en suite bathroom and flipped on the light. She always traveled with an assortment of hair stuff; that included hairpins. Annabeth snagged the small blue pouch off the counter and unzipped it, rummaging inside. She pulled out several pins, then retreated to the bedroom. As she neared the door, she steeled herself. Both against Dean's rugged good looks and whatever they might find in Wendy's room.

"Did you find what you needed?" Dean glanced over from his position next to Wendy's door.

"Yes." She held up the pins, crossing to his side. Dropping to her knees, she tipped her head and stared at the lock. "It's been a bit since I've done this. I hope it works."

"If not, I can give it a go."

She didn't look up as she inserted a pin into the lock. "You can pick locks too?"

"Private investigation 101." He chuckled.

"Right." Annabeth poked her tongue out as she concentrated. Sticking a second pin in the lock, she jimmied it, then turned the two pins. The lock clicked. "Got it."

"Damn. That was quick."

She looked up at him with a grin, getting to her feet. "If I ever change careers, I might give you a run for your money."

He returned her smile. "I'll just make you my partner." Dean reached in front of her and turned the knob, then pushed the door open.

Annabeth's smile died as the panel swung inward. Dean stepped into the doorway and flipped the lights on.

"Oh my," Annabeth breathed. "She lied." It was exactly as she remembered, right down to the posters on the walls. Stepping further into the room, she walked to the vanity to her right and skimmed her fingers over the smooth white surface. A soft smile lit her face. "Wendy used to sit here for hours, playing with her hair and makeup. She liked to try new styles and colors." Moisture gathered behind her eyes. She looked away with a quick sniff and a blink and tried to focus on their objective. "If there's anything here to find, it would be in her closet."

Annabeth crossed the room and opened the closet door. Acres of clothes and shoes met her, stopping her in her tracks. She lifted a hand, touching one of Wendy's favorite sweaters. A memory hit her—one of her sister laughing while wearing the sweater—and a tear trickled down her face.

Warm, firm hands curled over her shoulders.

"You don't have to stay." Dean's deep voice was quiet. "I can search on my own."

She sniffed and swiped at her face. "No. I think I need to do this."

He squeezed her shoulders gently, then dropped his hands. "Okay. Where do we start?"

"Back there." Annabeth pointed to the far-left corner.

"A pile of shoes?"

"No. Under them. Wendy pulled up a section of the floor. She didn't want Mom to read her diary. My sister wasn't a bad kid, but she liked to skirt the edge of the law sometimes, and she liked to write down her escapades to relive them later."

"How do you know that? Did you go with her?"

"Sometimes. When she deigned to bring me. But she would tell me about some of the things she did, and that she wrote down the details so she wouldn't forget. I never read what she wrote, though."

"Did she know you knew where her diary was?"

"Yes. But she also knew I'd never tell anyone." Annabeth lifted a shoulder, then sank to her knees in front of the shoes. "It just wasn't in me to get her in trouble. Unless she did something really, really dumb. Like drink and drive." She reached for a pair of boots and moved them out of the way. "That was the only time I ratted her out. Mom took away her car keys for the rest of the summer and told us not to tell Dad." She snorted, moving a pair of tennis shoes. "It's not like he was around enough to do anything about it, anyway."

Dean crouched next to her and helped her remove the shoes. Once they'd cleared the space, Annabeth hooked her fingernails into a crack between two boards and tugged. One board popped up easily.

"I never would have known that was loose."

"I know. She did a good job creating her hidey-hole." Annabeth moved the board out of the way and looked inside. A small light pink journal sat in the hole. Her heart skipped a beat as she reached in to pick it up. The smooth, glossy cover was cool in her hand. "I don't know how much information we'll get out of this. The last time she was here and probably wrote in it was when we were home for spring break. She kept another one at school. I don't know what happened to it." She glanced up at Dean.

He stared at the diary, a curious frown marring his forehead. "What do you think your parents did with her things from school?"

Annabeth sighed, looking away as she thought. "I'm not sure. Dad hired someone to pack her things, then shipped everything home. I never saw it get delivered. But I didn't spend much time here once I came back. Mom was a basket case, Dad still wasn't ever here, and it hurt too much to walk past Wendy's room and know she was never coming back." She stared at the wall, trying to think where they might have put the stuff. "In the attic, maybe? Or in the storage space in the garage? If they kept it, that is. Considering Mom lied about cleaning out Wendy's room and donating everything, I'm betting they did. And I doubt it left the house. I think Mom would want it close. The only other place might be in the master bedroom."

Dean nodded once, then stood. "Okay. Let's go take a look at those spots."

TWENTY

Annabeth's stomach churned as she led Dean down the hallway toward her parents' bedroom. She clutched Wendy's diary in her hands so hard her fingers ached. Would they find her school diary? What would it say? What did the one she held contain? Wendy wrote about everything. She wanted to be an attorney and always said it was important to keep a record of stuff. Annabeth doubted her friends knew that she kept notes on what they did. She wouldn't have had any friends.

They reached the master suite, and Annabeth opened the door, not stopping to think about what she was doing. If she did, she might chicken out. Going through Wendy's room was one thing, but her parents' room? It felt wrong. But since her mom refused to tell the truth, it was necessary.

Annabeth stopped near the bed and looked around.

"Where do we start?" Dean asked.

"No idea. Just start searching. Be careful what you move, though. Mom will notice."

He nodded and walked toward the nightstands.

Annabeth headed for her mom's dresser. If she kept

Wendy's diary, it would be somewhere her dad wouldn't look. And she doubted he would look in her mom's underwear drawer.

The top drawer slid open with a soft rasp of wood on wood. Annabeth rifled through the silky slips, but found nothing and moved on. She glanced at Dean, who was going through her mother's nightstand. "Anything?"

"No. Sleeping pills, some chapstick, other... lady... things." His face turned red, and he shut the drawer.

Annabeth cleared her throat, feeling her own cheeks heat, and went back to the bureau. By the time she was through the third drawer and found nothing, Dean was walking away from the bed and heading for the closet. Opening the fourth drawer, she hit paydirt; her mom's underwear.

Thankful her mom didn't fold her panties and just chucked them in the drawer, Annabeth plunged a hand in and rummaged through. Nothing but satin and lace met her touch.

Uttering a soft curse, she shut the drawer, then opened the last one; it was full of socks and hose, but no diary.

A little deflated, Annabeth closed the drawer and turned, looking around the room. There weren't many other places to hide things. Even though she doubted he would have it, she searched her dad's dresser just to be thorough. Like her mother's, it was empty of Wendy's things.

Dean reappeared. "There's nothing in the closet. Not that I could tell, anyway. A few shoeboxes on your mom's side with pictures, but it looked like it was mostly filled with pictures of you and Wendy when you were little." He grinned. "You were a cute kid."

Annabeth's cheeks heated. She hoped he didn't look too closely at those pictures. There were a few of her in the bathtub as a toddler with a soapsud beard and hat. "Thanks."

She looked away and gestured to the room. "I don't think there's anything here. Let's go check the attic."

"Sounds good." He swept an arm toward the door. "Lead the way."

She led him into the hall and upstairs, stopping at a door opposite the one leading to the widow's walk. She opened the door to reveal a steep staircase. Holding onto the handrail, she ascended. Her shoes and Dean's heavy boots thudded on the treads as they made their way up. At the top of the stairs, she found the string that turned on the attic lights and gave it a yank. Dim yellow light flooded the space, illuminating old furniture and boxes. And dust. Lots and lots of dust.

Annabeth wandered deeper. "There's a lot more stuff up here than I remember."

"That could be good. Maybe some of it is Wendy's." Dean stopped at a stack of boxes and opened the top one.

"Maybe." Annabeth went to another stack and lifted the flaps on the first box. It was full of papers. A quick leaf through them, and she realized they were from her dad's business. Wrinkling her nose, she shut the box and moved it to the side. All of these were probably his, but she had to make sure.

Steadily, she and Dean worked their way through the attic. Near the back, she opened a box and saw Wendy's favorite sweatshirt on top.

"Dean." She pushed the sweatshirt aside and dug deeper. It was full of Wendy's clothes from school.

"Did you find something?" Dean's boots scuffed across the floor as he walked over.

"Yeah. These are her clothes from school."

"You're sure?"

She nodded, digging deeper into the box. "I recognize the sweatshirt. I remember because I borrowed it when I was at her dorm one night a couple weeks before she died. I'd only brought it back to her the day before her death."

"These must all be from her dorm, then, yes?"

She glanced at him and saw him surveying the stacks of boxes. "Probably." Her heartbeat quickened. That diary had to be here somewhere.

A half hour later, they'd looked in every box and found nothing except more clothes and her bedding. Her diary and a handful of her favorite room decorations were missing.

Annabeth let out a frustrated huff as she shut the last box.

"There's still the storage area in the garage," Dean said.

"Yeah." Shoulders curled in slightly, she headed for the stairs. She doubted they'd find anything there. Not when the rest of it was in the attic.

"You don't think we'll find anything there, do you?"

"No. I don't know what they did with the rest of her stuff, but I'm starting to doubt it's here. I can't see Mom storing it in the garage. It would be some place... nicer? Especially since it's been separated from her other things." Annabeth put a hand on the rail and started down the steep stairs.

"What about an empty room in the house?"

"Maybe. I just don't know which one." She scrunched her face. "I need to get Mom to talk to me. Now that I know she lied, I can use that knowledge; she might break and tell me where the rest of it is."

"Or she'll clam up and kick us out."

He wasn't wrong. Katrina Swenson had a tendency to hide from things she didn't like. "Well, if we don't find anything in the garage, I don't know as if we'll have a choice. I can't search the house when she's home without risking her finding out. It's the weekend and Dad's out of town, so there's likely no party for her to go to. Maybe a dinner for one of her charities or with a friend, but that will only last a couple of hours."

"You know her best, so whatever you think we should do, I'll back you."

She was glad. She didn't want to fight with him anymore than she wanted to with her mom.

Reaching the ground floor, they walked down the hall to the kitchen, then out the door to the garage. Annabeth flipped on the lights, then headed for the door tucked into the wall to her right. She grabbed the knob and turned it as she walked forward and nearly took her nose out as she slammed into the still closed door. "Ow." She stepped back and glanced at Dean.

"Are you okay?" He touched her shoulder with a gentle hand.

"Yeah." She rubbed her forehead where she'd smacked it. "It's locked." She reached into her jeans pocket and withdrew the hairpins she'd used on Wendy's door. Bending down, she inserted them into the lock, and in moments, had the door open. "Come on." She waved Dean into the room, then flipped on the lights. "We need to make this quick. Mom's been gone almost two hours. She'll be home any time."

He nodded and waded deeper into the room.

Annabeth looked around in despair. There wasn't really anything here. It was tools, a couple of bikes, and some lawn stuff. The sole stack of boxes against the far corner was the only place something of Wendy's could be.

Dean spotted them, too, and headed that way. Annabeth followed at a slower pace, already knowing this was a dead end. He opened the top one, then grimaced. "Old spray paint cans. Rusty ones." Picking up the box, he set it to the side, then repeated the process with the remaining three. It was all just junk.

She sighed, running a hand over her hair. "So, what now?"

"We talk to people. You fancy a trip into Boston? I found several of Wendy and Johnathan's classmates living there."

Annabeth glanced at her watch. It wasn't even eleven yet. "Sure. The next ferry leaves at noon. We could grab a quick lunch on our way to the marina."

"Works for me." He spun on his heel and headed for the door.

Annabeth followed, but with less enthusiasm. Frustration clawed at her. And anger. Why did her mom lie? And how was she supposed to get her to tell the truth?

Twenty-One

Dean pushed the doorbell on the three-story brownstone where Wendy's roommate, Stella, now lived, then stepped back. A moment later, the intercom crackled to life and a woman's voice came over the speaker. "Yes?"

"Hi. I'm Dean Adler. I called several days ago to talk to Stella Scarsborough." He shifted, glancing at Annabeth. "I have Annabeth Swenson with me."

A long pause followed his words. Dean made eye contact with Annabeth, then mouthed, "Was that her?"

She nodded.

"Did you say Annabeth Swenson?" The voice came through the speaker again, this time more hesitant and curious.

"Stella, please let us in." Annabeth stepped closer. "We just want to ask you a few questions."

Silence met them. Twenty seconds passed. Dean's mouth flattened, and he looked at Annabeth. "I don't think—"

The inner door opened, and he turned to see a pretty blonde a few years older than Annabeth step into the doorway.

She pushed open the storm door and pinned Annabeth with a wide-eyed look. "It really is you."

Annabeth lifted a hand and offered the woman a soft smile. "Hi, Stella."

"I knew when I saw Johnathan's name in the news it would bring up questions about Wendy." She pushed the door open wider, then tipped her head toward the brownstone's interior. "I'm just glad it's you who's here and not some reporter. Come in."

Dean followed Annabeth inside, glancing around at the home's interior. The cream walls, rich wood moldings, and gleaming hardwood floors were what he expected from a Beacon Hill brownstone. It looked polished, clean, and understated.

Stella led them into the living room and gestured to the couch. "Have a seat, please."

Dean waited for Annabeth and Stella to sit, then sank onto the cushion beside Annabeth.

"So, since you're here, I take it you still think Johnathan had something to do with Wendy's accident?" Stella asked. She looked relaxed in the overstuffed reading chair, but Dean could see a deep curiosity in her eyes.

"Don't you?" Annabeth countered. "He knew she was pregnant. She was determined to make him be a father to their baby. Then she wrecks her car, and no one knows how?" She shook her head. "It doesn't add up, Stella."

"When you put it that way, I guess it doesn't." She tucked a strand of hair behind her ear, then propped her chin in her hand and rested her elbow on the chair's armrest. "But I don't know how I can help you prove it."

"Did she say anything to you about how he reacted when she told him she was pregnant?" Dean asked.

"No. I didn't know about the baby. I found out when everyone else did. I knew she was upset about something, and that she was pissed at Johnathan, but that's all. And I remember finding it odd that she changed her mind so abruptly after being ready to throw him from the dormitory roof. And they weren't happy for a long time before that, so it surprised me that she'd want to continue seeing him."

"She told you nothing?" Annabeth asked.

Dean resisted the urge to take her hand and squeeze it. The despondency in her voice tugged at his heart. She wanted answers, and it was wearing on her to not get any.

"No. The last few weeks before graduation, she was really secretive and just not herself. When she was in our room, if she wasn't studying for finals, she had headphones on and was writing in her journal. We didn't talk much the last few weeks of school."

Dean glanced at Annabeth. They needed to find that notebook.

"Do you know what happened to her journal?" Annabeth asked.

A small frown formed between Stella's eyebrows. "It wasn't with all her other stuff the movers your parents sent packed up?"

"Not that I've seen. I was hoping you might have seen it in her stuff, so I know for sure it made it home."

Stella shook her head. "No. I didn't want to be in the way while they packed everything up, so I spent the day with Gina."

Annabeth grimaced and glanced away.

Dean spared her a quick glance, then turned his attention to Stella. "Tell us what you remember about the last time you saw Wendy."

"There isn't much, really. It was the day before she died. We had breakfast together. I asked her if she was ready for her chemistry final, and she said yes." Her brow wrinkled. "I'm not sure she was telling the truth, though. It felt like she was just giving me the answer she thought I wanted to hear. She was a little—absent all through breakfast. Kept watching the doors while we ate. Knowing what I know now, she was probably watching for Johnathan."

"Did you ask her what was wrong?"

"Not then. She'd been distracted for a few days. Every time I asked about it, she just said she was worried about finals. That she'd be fine. Eventually, I quit asking."

"And that's the last time you saw her?" Dean asked.

Stella nodded. "I don't know what else I can tell you. I really don't know anything."

"Do you think he could have done it?" Annabeth asked. "Could he have pulled that off?"

Stella tipped her head and worried her bottom lip between her teeth. "Maybe. He's certainly smart enough. And evil enough." She shuddered slightly. "I was glad when it looked like Wendy was going to break things off with him. I never liked him. He and his brother both give me the creeps."

Dean frowned. "Why does Will give you the creeps?"

Stella lifted one shoulder. "He's just—weird—you know?" She looked at Annabeth. "You know what I mean, right? He's quiet, but he has this intense stare that he pins you with, and you feel like he's reading your deepest thoughts. A lot of people thought Will was sweet. That he was the nice Cassidy brother." She shook her head. "In some ways, I found him creepier and scarier than Johnathan."

"Is that how you felt, Annabeth?" Dean looked at her.

She pressed her lips together and tipped her head. "A little. He was definitely nicer than Johnathan, but still, like Stella said, weird."

"Would he have helped Johnathan commit murder?" Dean directed the question to Stella.

"Absolutely." She didn't hesitate. "He followed his brother

around like a lost puppy and worshipped the ground he walked on."

"He did," Annabeth said. "And he was Johnathan's alibi for the time of Wendy's crash. They were supposedly studying at an all-night diner across town."

"That was in the police report I read. A waitress at the diner, Donna Taggart, confirms they were there, but she couldn't remember what time they left."

Stella let out a snort. "Donna knows exactly when they left. That woman is the biggest busybody that's ever lived. She's also greedy. If she says she can't remember, you can bet Johnathan paid her not to."

Dean arched an eyebrow. "Really?"

"Yes. Sometimes, she'd overhear things kids said—stuff they wouldn't want getting back to the school administration or to their parents, so she'd offer to keep her mouth shut for a price. Usually, it was a hundred bucks or so. She knew what type of kid went to that school and that they could afford a little hush money. I even paid her once when she caught me smoking at a park in town."

Sitting back, Dean looked at Annabeth. Why did no one talk to this woman and ask these questions when Wendy died? She potentially just blew a hole in Johnathan's alibi. He turned to Stella. "It was Murphy's Diner, right?"

"Yes," Annabeth said.

Stella nodded and tipped a finger. "That's the one." She let her hand fall into her lap. "Find her and ask if she saw Wendy that night."

"Do you really think she'll talk?" Annabeth asked.

Stella smiled and looked at Dean. "All he'll have to do is smile."

Dean bared his teeth, making her grin.

"Yep. She'll sing like a bird." She looked at Annabeth.

"How'd you find this one? And are you keeping him? I would." Her grin widened. "I like the one I have, though."

Annabeth chuckled, her cheeks reddening. "He found me. And I'm glad you're happy."

A twinkle lit Stella's eyes. Her gaze darted to Dean, then back to Annabeth. He knew she'd noticed that Annabeth avoided her advice to hang on to him. Not wanting to make Annabeth more uncomfortable, he pushed to his feet. "Stella, you've been very helpful." He reached into his inside jacket pocket and removed a business card. "If you think of anything else that might be useful, give me a call."

She took the card, standing. "I will. I hope you nail the bastard. I'm glad he's already in custody, at least."

Annabeth stood next to Dean. "Me too."

Twenty-Two

Annabeth sucked in a breath, letting the crisp October air fill her lungs and clear her head. Stella's revelations put a hope in her heart that she was finding difficult to tamp down. Just because Johnathan's alibi had a hole didn't mean they could prove he was there or that he murdered Wendy. It would take more than a blown alibi to do that. She looked at Dean. "Now where?"

He stared out at the busy street for a moment, then glanced down at her. "How about we see if Will's roommate is available? He's got office hours this afternoon, if I remember right. I want to know if he has a similar impression of Will that Stella does."

"Office hours? Today? It's Saturday."

Dean shrugged. "I guess he doesn't care. That or he knows his students need a little more access to him. He's an assistant professor of physics at Harvard."

"Whoa. Okay. I guess that sounds good, then." She remembered Jeff being smart, but never imagined he would end up a physics professor. Especially not at Harvard.

Dean stepped off the curb to get in the car, and Annabeth

followed. Soon, they were making their way across the Charles River to the university. Once on campus, Dean pulled into a parking garage, squeezing his rental into a space.

A soft bang went through the garage as they closed their doors. With a beep, the doors locked behind them as they walked toward the stairs.

Annabeth squinted as they exited the dim building into the sun. It wasn't raining here, like on the Vineyard. She glanced to the east. Buildings obscured her view, but she knew just beyond, dark clouds trained over the island, the outer fringe of a tropical system well-offshore. It had almost missed them entirely.

It was a ten-minute walk to the science buildings and Jeff's office. Annabeth was even happier it wasn't raining. And that it wasn't colder.

Eventually, they stopped outside a four-story, late-1800s brick building. Dean held the door open for her, and she preceded him inside. An elevator ride later, they meandered down a long hallway, glancing at nameplates as they went.

"There." Dean pointed to a closed door fifteen feet away.

"Is he here?"

Dean tapped the schedule taped to the door. "Should be any time."

Annabeth sighed and stepped back to lean against the opposite wall. She crossed her ankles and her arms, then turned her head to watch for Jeff. The hair on the right side of her body raised as Dean settled against the wall next to her. She'd thought she was too preoccupied with their quest to notice him. She'd certainly been distracted on the way here from Stella's. All she'd done was stare out the window, thinking. But now, here in this quiet hallway, that insane attraction she had to him was back. She wanted to lean to the right and let him hold her up.

She bit the corner of her lip, holding back the emotions

that wanted to make her cry. Why hadn't the police investigated more? Why were they so quick to rule Wendy's death as an accident? With one conversation, they'd already poked a hole in the story of that night's events. What else would they learn?

Her phone rang, startling her. Straightening, she took it from her purse and glanced at the screen. A groan slid free before she could stop it. Margot. Oh, she would have a field day with this. Annabeth sent a quick glance at Dean. "I need to take this. Excuse me." She slid her finger over the screen and stepped away. "Hello?"

"Hey, friend. Tad told me he's taking over bath and bedtime for the twins tonight since it's my evening off. I desperately need a break. You want to FaceTime me and we can watch a movie?"

A smile broke out on Annabeth's face. Movie nights with Margot were some of her favorite memories, even though they now had them via a computer screen instead of in person. "I wish I could. I'm busy, though." She left it at that and hoped Margot would too.

"Doing what?"

Annabeth sighed. "Stuff."

A beat of silence passed. "You're working on your sister's case, aren't you?"

"Maybe."

It was Margot's turn to sigh. "Girl... At least tell me you're getting somewhere. Is Mr. Hottie still helping you?"

"Yes, Dean's still with me."

"With you? Wait. Where are you?"

Annabeth bit back a curse. Leave it to Margot to pick up on her wording. "Boston."

"Boston? Why are you in—Oh, Beth. You went home, didn't you?"

"Yes. We weren't getting anywhere in Ohio."

"And are you now?"

"Actually, yes."

Dean moved, and Annabeth glanced down the hall. A man had just turned the corner and was headed their way.

"Margot, I need to go. I'll call you later."

"What? Beth, you can't say that and just leave me hanging."

"I'm sorry. I'll call you tonight." Annabeth hung up with a wince over her friend's protests. She would get an earful later. Hopefully, she'd have more information to report, which would make up for hanging up on her.

The man neared, slowing a bit as he noted them waiting. "Hello."

Annabeth smiled, seeing vestiges of the boy she knew. "Hi, Jeff. Remember me?"

He paused and squinted, studying her face. It only took a moment before his eyes widened. "Annabeth Swenson?"

She nodded. "Yep. Do you have a minute? We have some questions for you." She tipped her head toward Dean.

Jeff cast a quick glance at the tall man at her side, wary. "What's this about?"

"My sister."

His wary frown deepened, and he looked at Dean again. "Are you the one who called and left a message?"

"I am."

Jeff pressed his lips into a flat line, then nodded. "Okay. But only a few minutes. I have students coming by."

"Of course," Annabeth said. "We'll be quick."

Metal clinked as Jeff unlocked his office door. He walked in, leaving it open. "Have a seat." He dropped his bag behind his desk and sat down.

Annabeth perched in a chair opposite him. Dean sat next to her.

"So, what can I do for you?"

"Tell us about your roommate, Will Cassidy," Dean said.

"Will?" He frowned, then his expression smoothed out, and he shrugged. "He was quiet. Spent a lot of time with his brother."

"We know that," Annabeth said. "What was he like? Other than quiet."

Jeff's frown returned. "What do you mean?"

"Did anything seem strange about him? I mean, you probably knew him better than anyone besides Johnathan. What was he like?"

"I told you. He was quiet."

"Right, but did you ever get an idea there was more there? That he was hiding something about himself?"

"What? Like he was a psychopath, or something?" Jeff chuckled, then sobered when they didn't laugh with him. "You can't be serious."

Dean sat forward. "Stella Scarsborough mentioned that he had this quirk about him, where he would just stare. She said it made her feel like he could see her deepest thoughts. You ever get that feeling?"

Jeff shifted in his seat and looked away for a moment. "I don't know. Maybe. Yeah, some days, he freaked me out a bit. He wouldn't say much, but I could tell he was thinking when he looked at me. Judging." He shook his head. "I got the feeling there were times he thought I was an idiot."

Annabeth raised an eyebrow. "You?" She glanced around at the stuffed bookcases and diplomas on the walls.

He chuckled. "I know, right?" His smile faded. "But that's what it felt like. I think it was more that he thought my social endeavors were dumb. Like when I asked Olivia to the winter formal our freshman year. I told him about it, and he just looked at me like he couldn't comprehend that I would make a fool of myself for a girl."

Annabeth smiled, remembering. He'd written a message

on a piece of poster board, strapped it to himself and worn it around school. It had worked, though; she said yes.

"And there were other things, I guess. Why are you asking this?"

"Just trying to get a feel for the brothers' relationship," Dean answered. "Stella also said Will followed Johnathan around like a puppy. That true?"

Jeff let out a soft snort. "Yes. He'd jump to do his brother's bidding. I called him out on it once, and he told me to shut up. That I didn't understand." He shook his head again. "There was such vehemence in his words I never said anything about it again."

"What about after Johnathan graduated? How did Will act then?"

"Mostly like he did before. He was just more focused on school without Johnathan around to pull him away from his studies."

Voices coming down the hall drew his attention. "That's probably my students."

Dean nodded and shifted to get up. Annabeth stood, then frowned as Dean stayed seated.

"One last question, then we'll get out of your hair." Dean paused. "Would Will help Johnathan commit murder?"

Jeff's eyes widened. "What? Whose?" His gaze went to Annabeth. "Wait. You think Wendy was murdered? That Johnathan did it?"

"I do. Their alibi for that night is shaky. And the details about her crash don't add up."

Jeff blew out a breath. "I—" He stopped and shook his head, bringing a hand up to run along his jaw. "I mean, I guess? He'd certainly do just about anything Johnathan asked, I think. I never saw him say no to him."

"Okay." Dean stood. "Thank you for your time, Dr. Westin."

Jeff nodded, staring at nothing. "Yeah, sure."

Dean laid a hand on Annabeth's back, ushering her to the door. Two students stopped in the doorway, their conversation ceasing and smiles disappearing as they caught sight of them. The girl's eyes went to Dean and widened. She knew how the girl felt. He'd rendered her momentarily stupid, too, when she first saw him.

"Excuse us," she murmured, stepping out of the office. Tucking her head, she hurried down the hall. When they were out of earshot, she looked at Dean. He looked calm and collected, but she could see the thoughts churning in his eyes. "You think Will knows, don't you?"

He nodded once. "I also think we need to track down Donna Taggart and talk to her. Confirm our suspicions." One side of his mouth lifted. "See if my smile works as well as Stella thinks."

Annabeth's heart stuttered. It was certainly working on her.

TWENTY-THREE

The sun sank low in the sky as the ferry headed east out of Woods Hole; the bright orb descended behind clouds and then the horizon as the ship churned through the water on its way back to the Vineyard. The weather had cleared, paving the way for a spectacular sunset.

Annabeth watched the now shadowed island rise into view. Lights popped on, illuminating the shoreline. She didn't really see it, though. Her mind was stuck in a spin cycle of hope and pessimism. She wanted to believe they had a solid lead, but experience told her Johnathan Cassidy was a slick son-of-a-bitch.

The scuff of boots on the deck growing closer alerted her to Dean's presence. She stiffened as he came up beside her to lean on his forearms on the railing. He did something to her insides whenever he was near. It made her uncomfortable, because she didn't know how to deal with it. Although, it wasn't entirely unwelcome right now. She needed the distraction from her current thoughts.

"You doing okay?" He leaned closer so he wouldn't have to shout over the sound of the engine and the churning water.

Annabeth nodded, sucking in a lungful of his spicy male scent. It was a mix of leather, soap, and man. *Damn. He should bottle that and sell it.* She turned her face away and took another breath, needing the salty sea air to clear her head. "I'm fine." When she glanced back, he had one eyebrow raised.

A smile crossed her face. "I am. I'm just thinking."

"About?"

"What this all means? Even if we've caught Johnathan in a lie, can we prove he murdered my sister?"

Dean straightened, wrapping his hands around the railing. "I'm not sure. If we had her car, probably. Or if the autopsy was more thorough. The only reason they knew she was pregnant was because they did a standard blood panel to check for drugs. There was no full autopsy done."

Annabeth straightened, a frown creasing her forehead. "Wait. The M.E. didn't do a formal autopsy?"

"No. It was just a blood panel."

"Why not?" Autopsies were standard practice in suspicious deaths.

"It was quickly ruled an accident. She was alone, it was late, and she was upset. The authorities deemed there was no need."

Annabeth ground her molars together. *No need.* Bullshit! She clenched her fist, propping it on the railing. Briefly, she wondered what it would take to get Wendy's body exhumed, but quickly discounted the idea. Her parents would fight her on that. If she didn't have solid evidence to take to the police and reopen the investigation, she'd never get a judge to side with her.

Tears gathered in her eyes. This was so frustrating.

"Hey." Dean's hand landed on her shoulder. "We're not out of this yet. We haven't found her diary, and I want to talk to Will. Medina's police chief seemed like he'd be on our side if I could bring him something decent. I just need one piece of solid evidence to take to him to reopen things. It would be enough to start asking Johnathan formal questions. Don't lose hope, okay?"

His hand moved to the back of her neck. Annabeth let the warmth from it seep deeper. She wanted to believe him, wanted to think that Wendy would get justice. But there was so much they didn't know.

A tear leaked out. Dean tugged, and she turned, wrapping her arms around his waist. Hugging him was a bad idea; it would only encourage the feelings that produced butterflies in her belly.

"I'm not going anywhere, Annabeth. Not until you tell me to."

The deep timber of his voice rumbled through the ear she had pressed to his chest. The butterflies flapped harder. She sniffed and looked up. "I appreciate that." Her gaze caught on his. Those light jade eyes flecked with brown held compassion —and something else that sent her butterflies into a tizzy.

She cleared her throat and pushed back, needing a bit of space. Swiping at the wetness on her face, she stared at the lights on the Vineyard that were growing closer. "When you showed up, I wanted nothing to do with your investigation. I'd put all that behind me, I thought." She shook her head. "But I hadn't. I know that now. I still believe Johnathan killed her somehow. I just don't know how we'll prove it." Her voice ended in a whisper. She swallowed and took a deep breath. "But I'm glad you're helping. I couldn't do this alone." She chanced a glance at him, then. He still watched her with the same intensity.

Annabeth looked at the lights again. "What do we do now?"

He settled in beside her. "First, we get some dinner. Then, we go back to your mom and dad's and sit down with your mom. Tell her what we've uncovered."

She let out a soft scoff. "She won't care. She'll clam up and walk away."

"Maybe. But we'll have planted the seed. That's all we can hope for at this point."

Annabeth grimaced. "I just wish I knew what they did with the rest of her stuff. I can't believe it's not in the house."

"Where else would they put it? A storage unit?"

"Maybe." A thought hit her. She bolted upright. "Wait." She looked at Dean with wide eyes. "Grandma and Grandpa's."

He frowned. "What?"

"My mom's parents. They're dead, but she never sold their land. Mom and Dad rent the house out to tourists. It has some outbuildings, though, and it's on the Vineyard."

"You think they'd have stored the stuff there?"

"Quite possibly, yes. In the beginning, it was probably too difficult for them, especially Mom, to have Wendy's things from school in the house. She probably didn't even want to deal with it. I think that's why her room is still the same. She didn't want to pack it up. She couldn't. But the stuff from school? That was already packed. It might have gone straight to Grandma and Grandpa's. They were alive then. Mom could have asked them to store it. Maybe when they died, stuff got moved back, but not all of it made it home."

A slow smile bloomed over Dean's face. "Okay. Tomorrow, before we leave, we'll go over there."

The hope growing inside Annabeth's heart swelled, pushing back the pessimism. Maybe they had more of a chance than she thought.

Twenty-Four

Heat and the din of a large crowd hit Dean the moment he opened the door to the restaurant they'd chosen for dinner. Holding the heavy door, he waited for Annabeth to cross the threshold, then followed her inside. A hostess greeted them, then led them to a table near the window.

"What can I get you to drink?" The woman handed them menus, then took out a notebook.

"Just water, please," Annabeth said.

"Same." Dean opened his menu.

"Okay. Your server will be over in a moment." The young woman smiled and left.

"So." Dean glanced through the menu, then at Annabeth. "What's good here?" One corner of his mouth kicked up.

She smiled back. "Sadly, not the cinnamon rolls. They don't have any. But if you like lobster, they make a great lobster roll."

He hummed. Actually, he was in the mood for something hot. The ferry ride had been chilly. "How about their chowder? Is that any good?"

"It's passable."

"Works for me." He set the menu down, then raised his hands to blow on his fingers.

She chuckled. "You're still cold?"

"Yes." His smile turned self-deprecating. "I don't like the cold."

"Where did you grow up?"

"Arizona."

"Do you have any family?"

His head bobbed. "My mom and sister still live there. My dad lives in Nevada now. He's a park ranger in Death Valley."

Her eyebrows shot up. "Really?"

"Yep. And he loves it."

"Well, that's good, I suppose. I know that much heat would bug me. Summers in Ohio are bad enough."

"You don't like the heat?"

She lifted a shoulder, glancing at her menu. "It's okay. I'm just more used to the Vineyard. We get a strong sea breeze. Some days in Ohio, the air is so stagnant and thick I feel like I could slice it, you know?"

"Yeah. It's like that in the rain forest down in Costa Rica. You get in amongst those trees and the ocean breeze disappears. In the summer, it's nasty."

Annabeth wrinkled her nose. "No, thank you." She smiled and looked at him. "So, why didn't you go back to Arizona when you left the Navy? You have a U.S. private investigator's license. And for that state. You showed it to me."

A bit of his mood soured. She was digging deep enough to make him uncomfortable. But, seeing as he'd dug up her past, he felt he owed her an answer. "Going home—" He paused and shook his head, blowing out a breath. "Mom would have just fawned all over me, trying to cheer me up. And my sister, she'd have understood that I needed space, but it still would have put a strain on things. I just needed time."

Annabeth's eyebrows knit together. "I take it something bad happened?"

"I'm a SEAL. Of course it did. It wasn't any worse than others have seen or done. But it takes time to come to grips with it. And with being a civilian again. Going down to Costa Rica let me do that without feeling pressured to be the old me. I'm not the same man I was when I joined the military. I'm okay with that now."

"Have you been home to see your family since you left the Navy?"

He nodded. "A couple months ago, actually. The guys thought it would be a good idea for me to get a P.I. license in the States, too, so I went home to do that. And to visit. It was time."

"Did it go well?"

"Yeah. Yeah, it did. I'd adjusted by that point, so I was more confident in the new civilian me. We had a good visit."

"Well, good. I'm glad." She smiled. "I have a question, though. How come you left the SEALs so young? We're practically the same age. Don't you guys stay in until you reach retirement age, or even longer?"

He was saved from having to answer right away by the arrival of their server. The girl set two water glasses down, then took their orders. When she walked away, Annabeth leaned forward on her arms.

"Well? Why did you leave?"

Dean sighed, sitting back. He fiddled with his straw wrapper, staring at it. "I joined the SEALs because I wanted to be one of the best. I wanted to go on the missions that made the world safer. To be part of something bigger than myself."

"But?"

He looked up. She watched him with curious, but sympathetic, eyes. He sat forward, leaning on his arms. "But the mission felt never-ending. There was always another terrorist cell to root out. Always another bad guy waiting in the wings. It just felt futile, you know?"

She said nothing, letting him talk.

"Anyway, one of the senior chiefs I worked with a lot—the guy I mentioned before, Sam?" When she nodded, he continued. "He retired because of an injury and went down to Costa Rica. When I was thinking about getting out, he suggested I come down there with them for a bit. Just to get my bearings. It's been just over a year, and I don't have any plans to leave."

She toyed with the straw in her drink. "I can see how you —how any soldier—could have trouble assimilating into normal society after what you've seen. I'm glad you found what you needed."

"Me too."

"And your friend—the one you followed down there—is he doing all right?"

"He is. He bought a bar, and now he serves liquor and loud music to tourists." Dean grinned. "We have a lot of fun."

"We?"

"I tend bar when I'm not doing private investigation work, remember?"

"Oh, right. Is there not enough of that to keep you busy?"

"It's not that. I got the license to help some of our other friends. We've formed an unofficial protection agency, I guess. The guy who's helping Cassidy's fiancée, he's our 'leader.'" Dean made air quotes. "We're all down there in some way because of him."

"How many of you are there?"

Dean glanced up, counting. "Including me, six." He tipped his head. "Maybe seven if you count Ford's pilot friend, Ezra. He doesn't live down there, though." He looked at her. "It's nice, having military friends close by. And it helped me adjust. I didn't leave everything about the military behind. I know I have people there to back me up if I need it."

"Like now?" Her voice was quiet.

"Yes. If I need help, or you do, they'll do everything they can." For which he was glad. This case had the potential to explode in his face.

Their food arrived, putting an end to their conversation while they ate. Dean watched, amused, as Annabeth tried not to lose most of her sandwich every time she took a bite.

"Stop laughing." She swiped at her face with a napkin.

He grinned. "I'm not."

"You are. Maybe not out loud, but it's in your eyes."

He chuckled.

"See?"

He laughed harder, then held up his hands. "Sorry. At least you get your money's worth. That's some sandwich."

She picked up a fork and stabbed a piece of lobster that had fallen onto her plate. "Yeah. And it's yummy. I can't get this in Ohio."

Dean started to reply, but something across the room caught his attention. He paused, glancing over, and his eyes widened. "What's he doing here?"

Annabeth's gaze followed his. "Oh my goodness. Shouldn't he be under house arrest?"

"I don't know. But I'm glad he's not." He looked at her with banked excitement. "I think we need to have a chat with Mr. Will Cassidy. Finish your food." He raised a hand and flagged down their server.

TWENTY-FIVE

Heart thudding in her ears, Annabeth followed Dean as he walked away from their table toward the bar. Will Cassidy stood in a corner, staring at his phone screen. It looked like he was waiting for an order. The bartender called Will's name, and he looked up, then moved toward the bar to take the bag the man held out.

"He's leaving," she hissed at Dean.

"Yep. Come on." He grabbed her hand and pulled her toward the door behind Will, who was back to looking at his phone. When they exited the restaurant, the other man was several yards ahead.

"Mr. Cassidy!"

Will paused and glanced back at Dean's shout. He frowned, then turned around, lowering his phone, and started walking faster.

Annabeth bit back a growl. She couldn't blame him for not wanting to talk to a stranger. Reporters probably hounded him. But they couldn't let him leave yet.

Dean picked up his pace, towing Annabeth along. She broke into a jog to keep up.

"Mr. Cassidy." Dean tried again as they closed in.

Will glanced back once more, tripping over his feet as he caught sight of Annabeth. His eyes widened, and he stopped.

They came to a halt several feet away. Annabeth offered him a tight smile. "Hi, Will."

"Annabeth." He swallowed. "How are you?"

"Fine. I'd ask you the same, but, well…" Her voice trailed away, and she flipped a hand in the air.

"Yeah. It's a mess. But my lawyer is working on it."

"Oh, I'm sure. So, I have a question for you."

"I can't talk about Ms. McGinty or the case." He took a step back and glanced toward the parking lot.

"It's not about that. Did you have a late-night study session with Johnathan the night Wendy died?"

Will blinked, then frowned. "What?"

"Were the two of you studying the night Wendy died?"

"Um, I think so. That was a long time ago."

Annabeth clenched her teeth at the brush-off tone in his voice. "Fifteen years, yes. Where were you?"

"Where was I?"

"Yes." She resisted the urge to roll her eyes. It was a simple question.

"I don't remember."

"Think."

"No." Will backed up another step, anger darkening his face. "I don't have to talk to you. Or anyone. About anything."

Annabeth clutched Dean's hand, letting out a bit of her frustration. He squeezed it back.

"Just one more question, Mr. Cassidy," Dean said.

Will glanced back. "Who are you?"

"A friend. Did you know Wendy was pregnant?"

Something flashed in Will's eyes before his mask dropped back into place. Annabeth narrowed her gaze.

"I heard that when the details of the accident came out. Such a shame. Two lives lost that night because she was driving too fast and couldn't stop in time."

Dean squeezed her hand again. Annabeth took it for the warning it was and planted her feet, even though she wanted to step forward and smack the smug look off Will's face.

"Except she didn't," Dean said. "Try to stop, that is. I find that unusual. Don't you?"

Will lifted a shoulder. "She was distraught. Finding out you're pregnant and your boyfriend doesn't want the baby will do that to a girl."

"So, you knew she was pregnant, then?" Dean pinned the man with a stare.

"I didn't say that. And this is all speculation. What other reason could there be for her crash?"

"I don't know. Maybe an animal in the road? She was looking at the radio instead of where she was going. Or maybe her brakes failed." He watched Will closely as he said the last. The man's eyes flashed again with something Dean couldn't read. He'd hit a nerve, though. Will knew something.

"Yes, well, it's a shame we'll never know." Will looked at Annabeth. "I'm sorry for your loss. I don't think I ever got to tell you that."

Annabeth blinked. He actually seemed sincere. She pressed her lips together, uncertain what game he was playing. "Thank you," she muttered.

"I really must go. The marshals don't like it when I'm away from home too long." He lifted his pant leg, revealing an ankle monitor.

Dean raised an eyebrow. "You're under house arrest and not at home?"

"No. Island arrest. I can't leave the Vineyard."

Annabeth's frown deepened. Anyone else would be

confined to their house. She wondered what other leniencies he'd been granted.

"Well, we won't keep you." Dean tugged on Annabeth's hand. "Goodnight."

Will gave them a tight-lipped smile and a nod, then trotted away.

"He's lying." Annabeth stared at his retreating form.

"No doubt." Dean took a step toward their car. "Come on." He tugged on her hand again. "We can't do anything about it now. But I will take great pleasure in wiping that smug look off his face when I prove he had something to do with your sister's death."

Annabeth's heart stuttered in her chest at the conviction in his voice. It was still a long shot that they could prove anything, but he seemed so sure. It gave her more hope than she thought wise.

The ride back to her mom and dad's was short, thankfully. It gave her less time to work herself up over Will's comments. When Dean pulled into the driveway, lights shone downstairs. Her mom was home. She hoped it was just her mom. She didn't want to deal with her dad.

Their shoes scuffed the pavement as they walked up to the front door. Annabeth let them in with her house key. Dean closed the door and locked it. They stowed their coats in the coat closet, then walked deeper into the house. Katrina sat in the living room, reading a book.

"Hi, Mom."

Katrina looked up. "Hello." Her eyes roamed over them, lingering on Dean for a moment before her expression soured. "I suppose you've been out looking into your sister's accident?"

Annabeth's spine straightened as she grew defensive. "We have. And we—"

Dean grabbed her hand. "We're making progress, Mrs. Swenson. But we're tired. Have a good night."

Before Annabeth could say anything more, he spun her around and ushered her down the hall.

"What are you doing? Why didn't you let me tell her what we found out?" She glanced at him over her shoulder.

"She's not going to listen until we have something solid. She might even say something to someone in her anger over it all. That could tip off the wrong people. We keep this to ourselves for now."

Annabeth bit her lip, considering what he said. It made sense, but she didn't like keeping it from her mom. Wendy's death haunted her, and Annabeth thought she deserved to know.

"I promise you can tell her when we know more. But it's just better if we keep it quiet for now."

"Fine." She sighed.

They walked upstairs, stopping in the hallway outside her room. Suddenly, Annabeth felt a little shy and awkward. Like a teenager being dropped off after her first date with the boy she liked. Through her lashes, she looked at Dean, unsure what to do now. It was only seven-thirty. She didn't want to go to bed yet. And she couldn't go downstairs, because he told her mom they were tired.

"I need to make a phone call; check in with the rest of my team in Costa Rica. I need to do some research on that waitress too. Will you be okay by yourself?"

"Oh." Her heart dropped. She'd stupidly hoped they could spend some time together. Maybe watch a movie. Or just talk. She'd enjoyed their conversation at dinner.

It wasn't a date, her subconscious reminded her.

Annabeth clenched her teeth, then forced herself to relax. She nodded. "Yeah, I'll be fine. I packed a book." That was a lie, but she had an e-reader app on her phone. She'd find something. If nothing else, she'd log into her work email and go through that. There were probably test results waiting for some of her patients.

"Okay, good."

She gave him a tight smile. "Well, if you need help researching, let me know. I'm good at that." Inwardly, she rolled her eyes and cringed. *Smooth, Annabeth.*

He didn't seem to notice her awkwardness, though. His expression remained blank. "I will."

Dean stared at her for a long moment, then brought a hand up and pushed a lock of her hair back. Annabeth's skin tingled where his finger skimmed her cheek. Fire erupted down her neck when he traced the shell of her ear.

"I'll see you in the morning." He leaned forward and pressed a kiss to her forehead.

Annabeth closed her eyes and clenched her fists, so she didn't bring her hands up and wrap them in the lapels of his jacket. The damn man needed to stop touching her or just kiss her and put her out of her misery.

He pulled back. "Goodnight, Annabeth."

She avoided his eyes. "Goodnight, Dean." Turning away, she entered her bedroom and shut the door.

Twenty-Six

Annabeth jolted awake as her bedroom door flew open, banging into the wall. She caught a glimpse of a slight figure stalking across the room a moment before her covers were yanked off. Terror flooded her veins, making her pulse pound in her ears and a sick feeling roil in her stomach. A small hand gripped her wrist and pulled.

"How could you?"

Relief coursed through her, but her terror turned to dread. "Mom? What's going on?" She pulled against her mother's hold, breaking free, and sat up.

"You went into Wendy's room! After I told you not to. How could you, Annabeth?"

Annabeth scrubbed her hands over her face, trying to process Katrina's angry words through her sleepy brain. "How did you know that?"

"The shoes. They were moved." She grabbed Annabeth's arms and pulled her to her feet. "Why?"

Katrina gave her a shake, and even in the low light, Annabeth could see the fury in her mother's eyes. The last time she'd seen her this angry was the last time she went into Wendy's room.

"Why would you do that?" She shook Annabeth again.

The fog cleared from Annabeth's mind as her own anger took hold. "Because she's my sister!" She raised her arms, throwing off her mother's hold. "I have every right to her things. To her. You don't get a monopoly on that because you're her mom. I knew her better than you ever did!"

"She's still my daughter. *You're* my daughter. And I asked you not to go in there. You should have listened." Katrina narrowed her eyes to slits and thrust a finger at Annabeth.

"I am an adult, Mother. You can't dictate my life. You never could, because you were never around to do it."

"Just because your father and I wanted you girls to have the best education possible—"

"Oh, cut the crap. You sent us to that school because we got in the way of your social life."

"No, we didn't."

"Yes, you did. Do you think—"

"Your father sent you there! I never wanted you to go." Katrina covered her mouth after her outburst. Tears gathered in her eyes.

"Whoa, what's going on?" Dean's deep voice from the doorway drew their attention.

Annabeth looked at him, noting his mussed hair and naked chest. And the tattoos. *Holy crap.*

Katrina's broken sob pulled her back to the reason for his presence.

"I'm sorry." Katrina waved a hand, then turned and hurried from the room.

Dean watched her go, then looked at Annabeth. "What was that all about?"

"She's mad that we went into Wendy's room. I need to go talk to her." That bombshell about why she and Wendy went to private school in Virginia reverberated through her brain. "Excuse me." She slipped past him, avoiding the wide expanse of his tattooed chest. She knew it would feature in her dreams tonight, but right now, she had other concerns.

"Mom?" She hurried down the hallway. Her parents' bedroom door shut. Annabeth jogged toward it, then stopped outside and knocked. "Mom?"

"Go away."

"No. We need to talk." She tried the doorknob, surprised to find it unlocked. "Mom?" She poked her head in, her voice soft.

Katrina looked over, tears streaming down her face. She sniffed and looked away.

Annabeth crossed the room and sat down next to her on the edge of the bed. Taking a deep breath, she laid a hand over her mom's. Emotions rose to clog her throat. She swallowed them back. This conversation was long overdue. "I'm sorry Dean and I went against your wishes. But you know I believe Wendy was murdered. I always have."

"No. I'm sorry. I never should have let your father convince me boarding school was best for the two of you. None of this would have ever happened if I'd insisted you go to school here on the island. I mean, you did all through middle school. But no. He insisted the high school wasn't good enough. That the school in Virginia was the best." She shook her head. "He just didn't want to deal with Wendy and her moods. I tried to tell him it was just her being a teenage girl, but he wasn't having it." She choked back another sob, her voice thick. "I should have said no."

Annabeth felt a twinge of sympathy for the weak-willed woman sitting next to her. She knew her mother had little in the way of a backbone, but she'd never considered how Katrina felt about bowing to her husband's every whim.

She squeezed her mother's hand. "Well, that's in the past

now. And Dad can't send me away to school anymore, so he doesn't have to deal with me. Will you give me your blessing to find out what happened to Wendy? And keep in mind, I'm not stopping, no matter what you say. But I would like you to be on my side."

Katrina looked at her. Something in her mom's eyes gave Annabeth pause. Fear, maybe? And shame?

"I'm sorry, Annabeth." Katrina looked at their entwined hands and laid her other one over top.

Annabeth tipped her head, trying to get a better look at her face. "For what?"

"For not telling you the truth."

"About Wendy's room? It's okay. I understand. Her death was painful for all of us."

"It's not that." Katrina took a deep breath and lifted her head. "I lied about her things. We do have them."

"I know. I found the stuff in the attic."

"Oh. Well, that's not all of it."

Triumph surged through Annabeth. She knew it.

"They're in a barn at your grandparents' place." She pinned Annabeth with a look. "So is her car."

Twenty-Seven

"What?" The word came out as a barely there whisper. Annabeth's eyes widened. "You—you have her car? Why?"

Katrina rolled her lips in and wiped away a tear before responding. "Your father did it. When he talked to the police, he asked if they could ship the car back to us instead of sending it to a scrap yard. He said he'd take care of it himself." She skimmed her fingers over the back of Annabeth's hand as she talked. "I thought it was part of his grieving process. But then he stuck it in the barn at Mom and Dad's and never touched it."

"What did he say when you asked him about it?"

"That it was insurance."

"Insurance? For what? Wait, hang on." She glanced toward the door. "Dean!" She turned back to her mom. "Sorry. He should hear this. Plus, he might think of questions I won't."

Katrina nodded. "So long as he puts on a shirt."

Annabeth smiled at her mom's attempt at levity. "It might help us concentrate, yes."

Dean appeared in the doorway a moment later—wearing a t-shirt. "Hey, what's up?"

"Mom dropped a bombshell," Annabeth said.

He strode into the room, taking up a spot by the window at the head of the bed. "Oh?"

"Yep. They have Wendy's car in the barn at my grandparents' house."

His eyes widened. He looked at Katrina. "Seriously?"

She nodded.

"Why?"

"I don't know. At first, I thought Pierce couldn't bear to part with it. But then he said it was insurance. I don't really know what for. I asked once, and he said it was to make sure the insurance company paid out. I didn't question it."

Dean kneeled in front of her, his expression serious and stoic. "Mrs. Swenson, I need you to think. What was going on in your husband's business at the time of Wendy's death?"

"I—I don't know." Katrina fluttered her free hand, then let it settle on Annabeth's again. "He doesn't share his work with me. Frankly, I don't want to know. I've heard enough over the years to know he doesn't play fair."

Annabeth looked at Dean. "Why would Dad want Wendy's car as insurance? The insurance company angle doesn't make sense. They'd send out an adjustor who would take all kinds of pictures. So, what, or who, was he concerned about?"

His light jade eyes bore into hers for a long moment, then he turned to Katrina. "Has your husband ever had dealings with the Cassidys?"

She blinked, then glanced at Annabeth, then blinked again. "No. No, it can't be." She gripped Annabeth's hand tighter.

Clenching her teeth against the force of her mother's grip, Annabeth covered her hand. "Mom?"

"No. He wouldn't. He just wouldn't." Her voice fell away to a whisper.

Annabeth frowned. "What are you talking about?"

Katrina turned teary eyes on her. "Your father. If—" She stopped and bit her lip, then sniffed. "I don't want to believe that he knew—or at least suspected that Johnathan had something to do with Wendy's death—and didn't make the police investigate further. It was his idea to go with the initial theory that it was just an accident. He talked to the police chief and told him we just wanted to bury our daughter. That it was all just a terrible accident. Why would he do that if he knew?" Anguish laced her voice.

Annabeth wrapped an arm around her shoulders, holding her close as the older woman dissolved into tears. She looked up at Dean. "We need to look at that car."

He nodded.

With a gentle hand, Annabeth sat her mom up and smoothed her hair back. "Mom. Do you have keys to the barn where Wendy's car is?"

Hiccupping, Katrina nodded and swiped at her face. She hiccupped once more, then took a shaky breath. "I made copies. Your dad didn't want me to go there. Told me I didn't need to see the vehicle. That it would just upset me more. I didn't listen. I knew it would be—unpleasant—but I had to see it for myself. So, I took his keys one night when he was passed out drunk and went to that kiosk at the store and copied it. I still don't think he knows."

Annabeth's gaze flicked to Dean. The more her mom talked, the more dread—and anger—filled her. Her dad knew exactly what had happened and had covered it all up.

She looked at Katrina. "Is her diary there too?"

"Diary?"

"Yes. Her school one. I found the one she kept here at home, but she had one at school. Do you have it?"

Katrina sat up and frowned. "No. I knew she kept journals, but I never found any. Where was the one here?"

"She loosened a board in her closet and hid it in the floor. That's why the shoes were moved. I tried to put them back the way I found them, but I guess I didn't do a very good job."

"Do—do you have the diary now?"

Annabeth nodded.

"May I read it?"

Flattening her lips, Annabeth hesitated. Wendy wasn't always kind about what she said about their parents. But she didn't want to deny her mom access to her daughter's innermost thoughts. "I have to warn you, she probably said some mean things about you and Dad. Even when she knew she was in the wrong, she didn't like being punished. And her diary was where she felt safe. She poured every thought and emotion out on the page."

"I know. But I still want to read it."

"Okay."

Dean glanced at the bedside clock. "Would we be bothering anyone if we went to look at Wendy's car now? I'd like to get a jump on it. Annabeth and I have to leave later today."

Swiping at the residual moisture on her face, Katrina shook her head. "There's a rear access road to the property. We can use it. The weekend renters won't know we're there."

"Sounds good." Dean stood. "Should we all go get dressed?"

Annabeth disentangled herself from her mom. "We'll meet you downstairs."

Katrina nodded, tearing up again. Annabeth squeezed her hand, blinking back her own tears, and followed Dean into the hallway.

He caught her eye as they turned to head to their rooms. "You okay?"

"No." Her jaw worked, and her tears dried up as she

processed what her mom said. "Dad's lucky he's not here. Actually, it's me who's probably lucky. I won't end up in the local jail for assault. I can't believe this," she hissed.

He touched her arm. "I'll get to the bottom of it."

"I hope so. And if it turns out he really did cover up what happened, I hope he rots in jail."

TWENTY-EIGHT

The light frost crunched beneath Annabeth's feet as she crossed the grass to the weathered white barn in the trees at her grandparents' farm. Dean walked ahead of her, his long legs eating up the ground. Reaching into his jacket pocket, he removed the key her mother handed him on the way out the door. He glanced back, arching an eyebrow, silently asking if it was all right for him to proceed. When Katrina nodded, he inserted the key into the padlock on the door. With a soft snick, the lock opened. He removed it, then grabbed a handle and pulled.

The big door opened with a creak, revealing a dim interior. Dean pulled a small flashlight from his other pocket and clicked it on. The light bounced off the crumpled front bumper of Wendy's car.

Annabeth tucked one arm around herself and raised her other hand to cover her mouth. She'd never seen Wendy's car. Not even right after the accident. There was a picture in the paper, but she'd never seen it in person. The previously gleaming white Volkswagen Jetta was now covered in a fine layer of dust. Scuffs marred the paint on the side she could see, and bird droppings dotted the hood. The roof was gone; cut away by the firemen on scene to free Wendy from the wreckage. The black leather seats held the same layer of grime as the rest of the vehicle.

Dean walked into the barn and circled the car.

"What are you looking for?" Annabeth asked, stepping closer. She tried to keep her eyes off the driver's seat. One flash of Dean's light had been enough to show the rusty color of dried blood on the leather. She didn't need to see that again.

"Evidence she was hit by another vehicle."

"Wouldn't the Medina police have noticed that?"

"Maybe. But as we've established, they weren't very thorough." He crouched down, shining the light at the rear left tire, then rose again.

Arms crossed, Annabeth huddled near the door with her mom. Their frosty breath mingled as they watched Dean study the car. After several minutes, he reached the front again and lowered his light.

"Well?" Annabeth asked.

"I don't see much. All the damage seems to be on the front end and the driver's side, which is consistent with her going off the road and hitting the tree. The suspension has collapsed, so I can't get underneath it to look at anything." He glanced back at the car for a moment, then looked at Katrina. "Mrs. Swenson? If I hired a transport service, could I have the car shipped to someone who could examine it?"

"Oh." Katrina blinked twice, staring at the car, then looked at Dean. "I'm not sure. I mean, Pierce will be back soon. Someone will say something."

"I can have them here soon. Tomorrow afternoon at the latest. It'll be gone before he knows."

Katrina pulled the corner of her mouth between her teeth and looked away, staring at the mangled car.

"Mom, please? We need to know the truth. Dean can help. He can get us answers."

"But your father—"

"Gets no say in this. He hid this all these years for some reason. There's got to be something here. I don't know why else it would be insurance. Wendy deserves justice. If Johnathan did something, he needs to be held accountable."

For several long moments, Katrina just stared at the car. Finally, she nodded. "Okay. But it has to be gone before Pierce returns. He won't let you remove it from the property if he's here."

"It will be," Dean said. "I'll make some calls when we get back to your house. Now, is there anything else of Wendy's on the property?"

"Over there." Katrina pointed to a stack of boxes at the back of the barn.

Annabeth left her standing where she was and followed Dean. "Do you really think you can figure out what happened by examining the car?" she asked, keeping her voice low.

"I'd say there's a decent chance. No one's really looked at it closely, from what I can tell."

Her head bobbed. She reached for the closest box and lifted the flaps. "What I want to know is where her diary went. If Mom doesn't have it—"

"Yeah. That's a good question. Who took it? And what was in it that they didn't want anyone else to see?"

A dark frown descended over Annabeth's face. It couldn't be good, whatever it was.

She dove into the boxes, coughing as years of dust flew in her face. Despite the hope in her heart, she doubted they'd find anything useful.

Fifteen minutes later, she was proven right as Dean closed the last box and set it with the others. He dusted his hands and stepped back. "Nothing but books, schoolwork, and a few knickknacks. Unless she was in the habit of writing her deepest secrets in the margins of her English homework, there's nothing here."

"Yeah." Annabeth turned to look at her sister's car. "We need to hope her car lends us something to go on. We have a strong theory; we just need proof." She wanted to nail Johnathan Cassidy's ass to the wall.

TWENTY-NINE

Dean watched Annabeth and Katrina walk inside the house. They weren't speaking, but an undercurrent of connection ran between the two women who were united in their grief. Seeing that car had done a number on them both. It had hit him hard too. Especially the bloodstain still visible on the driver's seat. It was a strong reminder of what the stakes were. He had to get this one right.

Turning away, he walked into the yard and headed for the beach. He could use the soft song of the waves to settle his emotions before he called his buddy Jordan for help. He needed to put a call into the others in Costa Rica as well.

Stopping just beyond the reach of the waves, Dean stared out at the rolling sea. The weather had cleared after yesterday's rain and wind. It was still breezy, but the sun shone down, burning off the morning dampness. The sea spray sparkled in the bright sunlight.

Dean removed his phone from his pocket and found his friend Jordan MacDowell's number in his contacts. Touching his name, he lifted the device to his ear.

"Hey, man. How's Costa Rica?" Jordan's cheerful voice came over the line after two rings.

A smile lit Dean's face at the sound of his old friend's voice. "It's good. I'm not there right now, though."

"Oh? Where are you? Are you home? We should go get a beer."

"Not home. I'm in Martha's Vineyard."

"What the hell are you doing there? Never figured you for a ritzy vacation type of guy." Jordan snickered.

Dean chuckled. If anyone would know what he was like, it was his high school best friend. He'd known Jordan since they were five years old. "I'm working. Which is why I'm calling, actually."

"What's up?" Jordan's voice took on a more serious note.

"You fancy a trip to Costa Rica?"

"What? Why?"

"I have a car I need you to take a look at." Jordan was a mechanical genius. If it had gears and/or an engine, he could fix it. Not only did he know cars, there weren't many people Dean trusted more to look at a vehicle like Wendy's.

"You can't ship it here?"

"I need it to go someplace safe."

A short pause met his words. "My garage isn't safe?"

"Not like my friend Max's." Not only was Max's behind a locked and alarmed gate, it was miles away from anyone the Cassidys could easily hire to retrieve the car. "And I don't want to put you in danger without backup."

"Whoa. Hold up. Explain. Whose car is this, and why would it being in my garage put me in danger?"

"It's a long story. Can you get away and go down there? I'm having the car shipped out first thing tomorrow." Even if he had to pay an arm and a leg to do so, that car would be leaving the Vineyard by the end of the day.

Jordan sighed. "I guess. You're lucky. I don't have any big

projects due at work. Will we at least get to have that beer down there?"

"I'm not sure. I need to go to Virginia and interview a witness after the car ships out. Maybe after that." Though he didn't want to leave Annabeth alone in the States. Perhaps he could get her to take a vacation.

"I know that tone. You're not going anywhere. What's going on? What's this about? And don't give me that bullshit about it being a long story."

Dean raised a hand and ran it through his hair. Jordan wouldn't give up until Dean told him the truth. "You know the case in the news about that guy, Johnathan Cassidy, who was arrested in Costa Rica after trying to murder his socialite fiancée?"

"Yeah."

"So, the fiancée landed in my buddy Ford's lap thanks to a friend of his who knows her. When Cassidy came after her, I came back to the U.S. to dig into his life, and I found some things."

"Oh, man. How bad?"

"Bad. His pregnant girlfriend died in a solo car crash a week before they graduated high school fifteen years ago. The investigation into the accident was, well, lackluster at best. Miraculously, her car wasn't destroyed and has been in a barn since the wreck."

"Isn't he still in jail, though?"

"Yes, but his brother isn't. And—this is the really bad part —I'm not sure the girl's dad wasn't involved in covering things up."

"What?" Jordan let out a string of curses. "Okay, count me in."

Dean blew out a sigh of relief. He should have just laid it all out there to begin with. Jordan wasn't one to shy away from something like this. "Awesome. I owe you."

"Nah. I'm getting a beach vacation out of the deal."

Dean chuckled. "That you are. Okay. Once you book your flight, text me the details. I'll make sure someone's there to pick you up. You can stay at my place. They'll let you in."

"Sounds good. Now tell me why you're really staying behind."

A soft curse burst through Dean's lips. "I hate it when you read my mind."

Jordan laughed. "There's no mind reading involved. I just know you. Now, spill. I'm betting it's a woman."

Dean cursed again. Jordan laughed harder.

"Who is she?"

"The girlfriend's sister."

"Oh, I get it now. You're worried about the dad taking it out on her."

"Sort of. He's out of the country right now. She's leaving the Vineyard tonight. She lives in Ohio, and I convinced her to come here for the weekend to talk to a few people. See if we could dig up anything I couldn't get on my own."

"And did you? Other than the car, I mean."

"Plenty. Which is why I want to hang around here. We stirred the pot, and I'm worried someone might try to make Annabeth stop asking questions. I don't want to be too far away if she needs me."

Jordan's laugh started soft, but quickly grew louder.

Dean scowled. "What's so damn funny?"

"You fell for her. The guy who had all the girls following him around in high school, but never dated any of them seriously, has finally fallen like a rock. I'll be sure to tell Alyssa Webber you're off the market the next time she asks me about you." Jordan laughed again.

Dean's scowl deepened. "You do that. Even though I'm *not* off the market, I'm not interested in her." That woman was toxic. He'd gone on one date with her their sophomore year, discovered she was a lunatic, then spent the rest of high school avoiding being alone with her. It wasn't any surprise to him she was still single.

Jordan chuckled. "If you say so."

With a groan, Dean propped a hand on his hip. "I do. I need to go. Text me your flight details."

"Will do. Be careful, Dean. I know danger's your thing, but don't make me come to your funeral. Especially not for this."

"I'll watch my six. Talk to you soon."

"Yep. Bye."

"Bye." Dean hung up, then immediately called Ford.

"Wagner." Ford's gruff voice came over the line. "What's up, Adler?"

"Did Asher or Sam fill you in on what I'm doing in the U.S.?"

"Yeah. Sam said you were staying behind to dig up more dirt on Cassidy. You find something?"

"I did. I'm sending a car to you. It belonged to Wendy Swenson. I'm also sending you a friend of mine. Jordan MacDowell. He's going to look at it and try to tell us if it was tampered with."

"What? Wendy Swenson... isn't that Cassidy's high school girlfriend? How did you get her car? That was fifteen years ago."

"It's been in a barn on her grandparents' property since then. There's a lot in play here. Take that vehicle to Max's and lock it up tight."

Ford groaned. "You delight in complicating my life, don't you? All of you do."

Dean arched a brow. Ford sounded exasperated—and not in a good way. "You all right, man?"

"Fine." The word came out short. "Text me the details when you have them all." He hung up.

Pulling the phone away from his ear, Dean stared at it for a moment, then turned off the screen and stuffed it in his pocket. He shook his head. He didn't know what Ford's issue was, but he was betting it had something to do with Brooke McGinty. When Asher told him Ford was in love with Brooke, but being stubborn about it, he'd shrugged it off. Ford could get surly when something bothered him, but it usually only lasted a day or so. It sounded like this time it was much worse. Dean was glad he was here and not down there.

Hands stuffed in his pockets, he wandered down the shoreline and let his thoughts drift. He knew he needed to get on the phone and find a company to ship Wendy's car, but it was Sunday; he doubted he'd have much luck. Later, he would get online and find local transport companies. He'd start calling first thing tomorrow morning.

When he'd walked about a half mile, he turned around. He didn't want to be gone too long. Besides, he needed to take Annabeth to the airport in a couple of hours. And change his flight.

Nearing the Swenson's house, he noticed a figure on the beach, standing much where he had been fifteen minutes ago. It was Annabeth. Toffee-colored hair whipped around her face in the wind. Her long sweater fluttered in the breeze, held closed by her arms crossed over her chest. She turned her head and spotted him.

Dean stopped a few feet away. "Sorry. I didn't mean for you to come looking for me. I was on my way back."

"You're fine. Mom went to her room to lie down. I needed to move, so I came down here. Did you make your phone calls?"

"Some of them, yes. I still need to get someone to pick up the car, but I won't get anyone to answer until tomorrow."

The wind blew a strand of hair over her eyes. She reached

up and tucked it away behind her ear. "I'm flying back alone, aren't I?"

"I know we didn't talk about it, but yes. Do you think your mom will let me stay tonight without you? If not, I can try the local hotels again, or take the ferry to the mainland."

"I don't think she'll mind. We probably won't see too much of her the rest of today." Annabeth's mouth flattened. "She was pretty upset."

Dean shuffled closer and ran his hands up and down her upper arms. "And you? How are you holding up?"

"I'm fine." The words were quick to come.

He dipped his head and arched an eyebrow, one side of his mouth lifting the slightest bit. "Really?"

She huffed. "Okay, no. I'm pissed!" She uncrossed her arms, but didn't pull away from him. Anger flashed in her blue eyes, turning them silvery. An instant later, they went watery. "And my heart hurts. I never—" Her voice caught, and she swallowed. "I never saw her car before. After the accident, I mean. I just—" She broke off again and shook her head.

Dean tugged. She fell into him and wrapped her arms around his waist. He tucked her close, resting his chin atop her head.

"I'm sorry, honey," he murmured into her hair. His heart hurt, too, for what she was going through. He didn't like seeing her upset and in pain. Something deep inside him wanted to wrap a cage around her and protect her from everything awful in the world.

She sniffed. "How can I want to commit murder and bawl my eyes out at the same time?"

"Because you feel betrayed by someone who should have protected your sister. Defended her."

Her head rolled against his chest as she shook it. "I just want this to be over. I want the truth, and I want it over." She lifted her head. "Why can't it be over?"

Dean leaned back enough to see her face. He raised a hand, framing the side of her head, and traced her cheekbone with his thumb. "It will be soon. I'll get you answers. I promise." He knew better than to make such a promise; there were no guarantees. But he'd move mountains to bring this woman the closure she needed.

Jordan's words echoed in his mind. He wasn't in love, but she'd certainly gotten under his skin. Staring down at her now, he couldn't remember why kissing her would be a bad idea; how it would complicate things. All he could think about was how he wanted to taste her pretty lips and offer her some comfort.

So he did.

Dipping his head, he held her gaze, making sure she understood his intent. Her eyes darted to his mouth, then back up. She licked her lips and stayed put. Dean closed the distance.

The first touch of her mouth on his electrified him. The hair on his neck stood on end and a floaty sensation went through his head. A thread of desire unfurled in his gut and tugged, urging him to pull her closer and to deepen the kiss. He ran his tongue across the seam of her lips, begging entrance. Without hesitation, she opened to him. He plunged inside, sipping from her sweet mouth.

Long moments went by, and Dean got lost in their kiss. The sound of the waves retreated and the cool, salty breeze disappeared as she captivated him. It wasn't until two seagulls streaked overhead, squawking at one another, that he lifted his head.

She blinked up at him, her lips damp and plump from his kiss. He stiffened, forcing himself to take a step back so he wouldn't kiss her again. As much as he wanted to, he was afraid if he pushed too hard, she'd bolt. The intensity of the feelings that kiss provoked were... unexpected.

"Well." Annabeth cleared her throat and uncurled her

fingers from his jacket. "That was, um..." She trailed off and glanced away.

Dean dropped his hands from around her shoulders and put more distance between them. "Yeah." He looked out at the waves, then turned back to her. It was on the tip of his tongue to say more about it. Like, how he didn't regret it and hoped they could do it again sometime, but the look on her face stopped him. With her lips rolled in and pressed tightly together, she stared at the waves with unfocused eyes. It was the look of someone who was overwhelmed.

"Come on." Dean touched her arm. "Let's go back to the house. We could both use some coffee. And some breakfast."

THIRTY

The hard jolt of the plane's wheels touching the ground pulled Annabeth out of her thoughts. She dropped her hand from her lips, doing her best to shove away the memory of how Dean's mouth felt pressed to hers; it had dominated her thoughts the entire flight. That, and his naked chest, would star in her dreams tonight. She wasn't sure she minded the idea, though. She kind of wished she'd gotten a second kiss when he said goodbye to her at the airport. The first one had been one of the best she'd ever had.

She sighed and looked toward the front of the plane as they slowed to a taxi and turned. They were nearing the gate. It was probably for the best he hadn't kissed her again. Nothing could come of it except a quick fling, and she didn't do those.

Her body heated at the thought of falling into bed with Dean, and she shifted in her seat. She might make an exception to her no-fling rule for him, though. It would be spectacular. And heaven knew she could use a good distraction right now. She scoffed at herself. Wasn't it just last week when she didn't want any distractions? Now she'd welcome one.

The plane came to a halt, and the seatbelt sign blinked off. Annabeth stood and patiently waited her turn to get off. Once inside the airport, she booked an Uber on her phone, then headed for the exit. Forty minutes later, her driver rolled to a stop outside her house. She thanked the young woman and got out, clicking through the review and tip portions on the Uber app as she walked up the driveway to her front door.

She let herself into her dark house and left her keys and suitcase by the front door. She'd deal with unpacking later. Right now, she wanted dinner. The flight home hadn't been long enough for meal service, and the airline cookies wore off hours ago; she was starving.

Opening the freezer, she found a container of spaghetti and took it out. It was the last of the big batch she'd made last month to freeze for quick meals. She made a mental note to get supplies to make more. Annabeth lived on pre-cooked, frozen meals. She'd gotten into the habit during med school. It was easier than cooking when she was exhausted or had to study, and healthier than takeout. She'd also quickly learned that she preferred home-cooked options to the store-bought frozen dinners.

Popping the container into the microwave, she set it to reheat, then grabbed a bottle of red wine from the rack on the wall. After rummaging in a drawer for the corkscrew, she opened it and poured herself a hearty glass. One big swig later, she took out her phone to text Dean that she was home. When she opened her messaging app, her gaze landed on Margot's name.

"Crap." Sighing, she sent a quick message to Dean, then called Margot. She'd forgotten all about calling her friend back yesterday. She hoped she was free to talk. Though it might be best if Annabeth left her an update in a message. Then she wouldn't have to hear Margot tell her she was a terrible friend for forgetting about her.

The line rang four times. Annabeth prepared her voice-mail spiel, but before it could ring a fifth time, Margot picked up.

"You know, if we hadn't been friends for as long as we have, I'd think you were blowing me off."

"I'm sorry. I forgot. This weekend was crazy."

"You're forgiven, so long as you tell all right now. I have a few minutes. You're lucky."

Annabeth chuckled. Her mind skipped right to Dean's kiss. That bit she might hold back. Or at least save it until the end. It would help soothe Margot's anger that Annabeth was firmly entrenched in her sister's death investigation again.

She picked up her wine and took another drink, sitting on a barstool. "So, Dean tracked down Wendy's roommate as well as Will's. We talked to them both. Stella gave us a lead that could poke a hole in Johnathan's alibi for the night of Wendy's accident. We also ran into Will on the Vineyard."

Margot gasped. "And?"

"And I'm pretty sure he knows exactly what happened. He didn't say as much, but it was in his posture and his eyes when we asked him about the wreck and about Wendy's pregnancy."

The microwave beeped, and Annabeth got up to stir her food.

"So, where does that leave you?"

"With Will? Where we were before. We can't prove yet that he lied. But there's more." She shut the microwave door and turned it on again. Her food was still a little cold in the middle.

"More?"

"Yep. Seems my dad brought Wendy's car home and stowed it in a barn at my grandparents' farm instead of having it destroyed."

"Oh my gosh! Why? I mean, I don't want to sound callous

or anything, but your dad isn't the sentimental type."

"You're right. He's not. Mom said he put it there as insurance."

"Insurance? For what?"

"Good question. I don't know. But I swear, if he had anything to do with covering up her murder—" Annabeth stopped and clutched her fork until her knuckles turned white.

"Girl, I will help you bury the body."

"Thank you, Margot. Though I'm more likely to dump him at sea and let the sharks eat him," she growled.

"What about your mom? What are her thoughts on all of this? And how did you get her to talk?"

"She figured out that we'd searched Wendy's room after she told us there was nothing there to see. She said they'd sold everything years ago. Dean suggested we look, anyway; so we did. After she found out, she flipped out on me, then spilled the tea. Dad's out of town, so we were able to go look at the car. I'm home now, but Dean stayed behind. He's going to have the car shipped to a friend to have it examined."

"Will that hold up in court?"

The microwave beeped again. Annabeth wedged the phone into her shoulder, then pushed the button to open the door and took out her food. "I don't know. But at this point, it doesn't matter." She set the container down on a plate and waved her hands; it was hot. "The investigation is closed. I'm not sure what it'll take to convince a judge to reopen it."

Margot blew out a long breath. "I do not envy you. This is turning into some crazy story."

"Tell me about it. I just hope we can get some answers. It's been too long, and Wendy deserves it."

"Yeah. You think this guy you've latched on to can do that?"

Annabeth grabbed a fork and stirred the spaghetti. "I do.

He's determined."

Margot gave a soft chuckle. "Is that because he likes to solve mysteries or because of you?"

A quick lancet of need speared Annabeth as an image of Dean's face right before he kissed her went through her mind. She twirled noodles onto her fork and pushed the memory away. "Probably the mystery."

"Uh-huh." Margot's tone told her she didn't believe her. "Please tell me you've kissed him."

"Margot!"

Her friend laughed. "What? I saw the picture you sent me. I might be married, but I'm not dead. He's hot. And you're single. So?"

Annabeth twirled her spaghetti some more and stayed silent.

"Oh, you did!"

"I didn't say that. I didn't say anything."

"Exactly. With you, silence usually means you did."

Rolling her eyes, Annabeth set her fork down. "Fine. Yes."

"And?"

"And it was spectacular. Happy?"

Margot laughed. "Immensely."

"Well, don't get your hopes up. It probably won't happen again. I'm not even sure when I'll see him next. If at all. He might dig up all the information he can and then go back to Costa Rica."

"Oh, please."

Annabeth couldn't stop the smile that bloomed on her face. She could hear Margot's eye roll in those two words.

"If that kiss was as good as you say, he'll be back."

"Maybe."

"No maybes. Yes. You watch. He won't leave the U.S. without seeing you again."

Annabeth wiped at a non-existent speck of spaghetti sauce

on the counter. She wanted him to come back, but she also didn't. It would be easier to forget him if he just went home. But the thought of never seeing him again made her sad. "Well, I'm not going to waste too much brainpower thinking about the what-ifs and maybes. I have plenty of other things to keep me occupied."

Margot sighed again. "Sometimes, I hate your practical side."

Annabeth chuckled. "It's what got your butt through med school. My charts and flashcards saved your bacon."

"No comment," Margot muttered, then laughed. "Fine. Whatever. But mark my words. He'll be back."

"We'll see." It was time to change the subject. She didn't want to think about Dean anymore tonight. "How are Tad and the twins?" Annabeth lifted her fork and took a bite of her dinner.

"Oh, they're fine."

Something in her friend's tone told Annabeth otherwise. She hastily chewed and swallowed. "What's that tone?"

"What tone?"

"Don't be coy. You know what I mean."

"Dammit. I hate your perceptive side too."

"Margot."

Margot huffed. "It's Tad. Something's—off."

"How so?"

"He's been distracted lately." Margot blew out a short breath. "Things haven't been the greatest in the last few months. Since the twins started walking. They've been into everything and everywhere at once. It's exhausting."

"Do you think he's cheating?"

"No," she was quick to say. "Maybe." A hesitant note crept in. "I don't know."

"Okay, start at the beginning. What's going on?" Annabeth took another bite.

"Oh, man, okay. So, he's been working long hours—longer than normal. Which, at first, I thought maybe he was just looking to put himself in a good position with their new chief. But when I asked him about what he's been doing, he just says, 'Oh, it's work. Research.' But he won't tell me what the research is."

"You snooped, didn't you?" She knew Margot well. What some would view as a violation of privacy, Margot would see as finding out what was wrong so she could fix it. "What did you find out?"

"He hasn't brought anything home, but I did talk to the new division chief. I asked him what he's got my husband working so hard on. The man had zero clue what I was talking about. None. And then he said he actually hasn't seen too much of Tad. That he's been leaving as soon as his shift ends, unless he has a patient in need of critical attention."

Annabeth closed her eyes on a long blink. That did not sound good. "Have you talked to Tad about it?"

"No. I want to, but... God! I'm afraid of what he'll say if he tells me the truth. I don't want to be a single mom, Annabeth. But if he's cheating—" She broke off to give a low growl. "Men suck."

"They totally suck." Annabeth stabbed a chunk of sausage with her fork. "I'm sorry. If you need a place to crash, I know I'm way far away from your job, but you're always welcome here."

"Thanks, Beth. And who knows? If my husband turns out to be a total dweeb, I might just move there. Setting up a family practice might be my only option if I have to go the single parent route. We could do it together."

Annabeth made a face. She hated to see Margot give up on her dream of becoming a pediatric pulmonologist. "I'll keep my ear open here. See if there might be a chance of you moving your fellowship."

Margot scoffed. "Yeah, right. That's like asking the sky to not be blue. I appreciate it, though. I'll figure something out. And I could just be worrying over nothing."

"Maybe."

"You're supposed to be convincing, Beth."

Annabeth smiled. "You're worrying over absolutely nothing. He loves you and is working on a surprise that will knock your socks off."

Margot chuckled. "That's better."

"Good."

"All right. I should probably go. I've got some case notes to catch up on before I crash for the night. Keep me posted on your sister's case and on Mr. Hottie."

"I will. Kiss your babies for me."

"You got it. Good night."

"Night." Annabeth hung up, then let out a long breath as she set the phone down. She hoped Margot's problems weren't serious. Tad had never given her cheater vibes. Or liar ones, for that matter. But stress did weird things to people.

She let out an inelegant snort at that thought and shook her head. It certainly did. She'd never contemplated jumping into bed with a total stranger before, but if Dean asked, she'd probably strip naked right then and there. Especially if he kissed her with as much enthusiasm and raw need as he had before.

That burning need she felt earlier crept back in, heating her blood and making her thoughts swirl with memories of their kiss. And the tattoos she'd glimpsed this morning when he appeared in her doorway, shirtless.

Huffing, she picked up her wine and took another healthy sip. If she was going to dream about the man all night, she might as well lower her inhibitions and make the fantasies good ones.

THIRTY-ONE

Dean cut the engine on his rental and got out, walking up the path to the front door of the Swenson's house. He'd just watched the transport company drive away with Wendy's car in a crate. Because of its mangled and deteriorated state, he'd been able to ship it as parts, which meant less red tape. It would be on a plane first thing in the morning and land in Costa Rica tomorrow evening. Max and Edie would pick it up in San Juan and drive it back on a flatbed. Jordan was due to arrive Thursday.

Using the key Katrina gave him yesterday, he let himself inside. A male voice coming from upstairs made him pause. He shut the door and locked it again, listening. Whoever it was sounded angry. The words were low enough Dean couldn't make them out, but the tone was rushed and harsh.

The man paused, and he heard Katrina's softer voice. He couldn't make out anything other than a pleading note.

"I don't care!"

At the man's angry shout, Dean ran for the stairs. Feet slapping on the hardwood floor, he rounded the corner and jetted down the hall to take the steps two at a time. In moments, he was on the second-floor landing.

"Katrina?" He hurried down the hallway toward her logical location. Stopping outside the master bedroom, he peered inside. Katrina stood by the window, tears in her eyes, while a man stood a foot away, a thunderous expression on his face. He turned an angry gaze on Dean.

"Who the hell are you? What are you doing in my house?"

The man's identity clicked. "Mr. Swenson. I'm Dean Adler." He strode into the room, hand outstretched. He doubted the man would take it, but Dean refused to be rude. Yet.

As he'd surmised, Pierce Swenson stared at Dean's hand like it was a poisonous snake. "Is that name supposed to mean something to me?"

Dean dropped his hand. "Not unless your wife has filled you in on what's going on."

Pierce narrowed his eyes. "You're the man who came to the Vineyard with my daughter, aren't you?"

"Yes, sir."

"Where is she?"

"She went home yesterday. I stayed behind to take care of some things."

Pierce spun around. "You let him stay here without Annabeth? What were you thinking? People talk, Katrina. First, I have to hear from Mike Barnaby that Annabeth is here unexpectedly—and with a man. Then, you tell me they're here asking about Wendy. Now I find out you've been alone with him." He pointed at Dean.

"Mr. Swenson—" Dean tried to correct the record, but Swenson cut him off.

"I didn't ask you to speak."

Okay. He was done playing nice. Dean stalked forward, putting himself between Pierce and Katrina.

Pierce blinked, some of his anger turning to confusion.

"I don't take kindly to being talked to like a peasant, Mr. Swenson. Nor do I like watching men berate their wives. Since you seem so concerned about what's going on and want answers, I'll give them to you, but you will not interrupt me. The moment you do, you get nothing, and Katrina and I are leaving. Understand?"

"Dean—" Katrina touched his jacket sleeve, her voice wobbly.

He glanced back at her, silently asking her to trust him. She held his gaze, but stayed quiet. He turned around and arched an eyebrow at Pierce, asking for his agreement to the question.

Holding his gaze for a long moment, Pierce nodded. "Speak."

"I'm a private investigator." Dean dove straight in. "I became aware of your family's association with Johnathan Cassidy through my involvement in the current case against him. I contacted your daughter, and we came here to track down a few people who could possibly shed some insight into Wendy and Johnathan's past. In the process, we discovered a few things. Like a possible hole in Cassidy's alibi for that night. And Wendy's car, which was never properly examined."

Twin pops of color bloomed on Pierce's cheeks. "Yes, it was."

"I doubt that. I think you paid someone to not do their job. What I want to know is why? Why was Wendy's car insurance? Against whom?"

The color on Pierce's cheeks deepened. He looked past Dean to Katrina. "You told them about the car?"

"Yes. I want answers too."

"We know what happened. Wendy got knocked up, got ticked at her baby daddy, then drove into a tree. End of story."

Katrina gasped. Dean's expression soured another level. He understood better now why Annabeth never came home.

"If that's so, Mr. Swenson, why did you keep her car?"

Pierce grasped the hem of his suit jacket and tugged, then fussed with his coat sleeves. "It was a business decision. Our insurance didn't want to pay to destroy the car, so I brought it home."

Dean's eyebrows flew to his hairline. "Seriously? That's the lie you're going with? Scrap yards would pay to come get the vehicle. And I highly doubt you owed any money on that car. What's the true reason you brought the car back here?"

"I'm getting annoyed by you, young man. What I do with my possessions is none of your business. I'd like you to leave my house now."

Before Dean could answer, Katrina pushed her way forward.

"No."

Pierce glared down at her. "Excuse me?"

"You heard me." She stared up at him, looking fiercer than Dean thought she could. "I'm done, Pierce. With the lies, the secrets, you. All of it. For years, I've lived in my grief, not questioning anything you've said or done because it was easier to just shove it all away and not deal with it. But Annabeth—she won't let it go. She knows something happened that night. That Wendy didn't just crash into a tree." She paused and studied her husband's face for a moment before she straightened her spine and locked eyes with him. "I gave them permission to take the car to someone to have it properly analyzed. It's time we got proof that she either just failed to stop or someone made it so she couldn't."

"You what?" Pierce's voice dropped an octave and went deathly quiet.

Dean tensed, ready to jump in if the man tried to lay a hand on Katrina.

"You heard me."

"I forbid it. That car stays right where it is."

Now Dean was doubly glad he'd gotten the car out before Pierce found out. He had a feeling it would have "disappeared" if he hadn't. It also sounded like he didn't know Dean had moved it already. Before Katrina could say more, he laid a gentle hand on her shoulder. "Fine. We won't touch it, Mr. Swenson. Right, Katrina?" She turned to look at him, and he hoped he telegraphed well enough to get his point across that she needed to keep quiet about their plan.

She looked at her husband. "Right. For now, we'll leave it there."

Pierce relaxed a fraction. "Good." He looked at Dean. "I still want you out of my house." His gaze dropped to Katrina. "You and I will talk more later."

"No, we won't."

"What?"

"I'm leaving. I meant what I said. I'm done with you. I only stayed because I was too afraid to leave. I'm not scared anymore."

Pierce laughed mirthlessly. "Where will you go? All your friends are my friends too. And you signed your parents' farm over to me years ago."

She blinked, startled, and her hand flew to her throat to fiddle with the small gold cross she wore. Dean narrowed his eyes, taking mental notes. From her reaction, he didn't think she knew that.

"I'll go stay with Annabeth for now," Katrina said, not contradicting him. "I doubt any of our *friends* would care enough to take me in, anyway."

Dean moved forward, making Pierce back up. "I think you should go now, so your wife can pack."

"This is still my house, and I asked you to leave."

"It's still my house, too, Pierce. I want him to stay. If you want him gone, call the police." She aimed a cold smile at her husband. "I'm sure all our friends would love to hear about who you're kicking out and why."

The red flush crept back up Pierce's cheeks. His jaw flexed, and he stared at her for a long moment, then spun on his heel and marched out of the room.

Katrina wilted the moment he disappeared from sight and sank onto the bed. She dropped her head into her hands.

Dean kneeled in front of her. "Hey." He peeled her hands back to hold them. "Are you okay?"

She offered him a watery smile and nodded. "Yeah." She let out a shaky laugh. "I can't believe I just did that."

"It was a well-deserved thrashing. And a good decision. I don't know how you've stayed this long."

"I didn't lie when I said I was scared. But you—you and Annabeth—gave me strength. I couldn't have done that if you weren't here to back me up. Thank you." Her words ended in a whisper as she teared up again.

"You're welcome." He patted her hands and stood. "I'm going to call Annabeth and book you a flight. Why don't you get to packing?"

She sniffed and nodded. "I will. Thank you."

"Not a problem, Katrina. I'm glad I could be here." And he was. He hated to see someone emotionally abused by their spouse and was ecstatic that he could help her break free of the cycle. Although, he imagined that had more to do with Pierce's decision to hinder their daughter's death investigation than anything Dean had done. Regardless, he was proud of Katrina for standing up for herself.

Leaving the room, he ducked into the hallway and wandered down toward his room, keeping an eye on the master suite in case Pierce came back. With his back propped against the wall and his ankles crossed, he scrolled through the internet app on his phone and booked Katrina a plane ticket.

She could pay him back, or not. He didn't care. He just wanted her out of this situation. Even if Pierce had nothing to do with covering up Wendy's death and had other reasons for holding onto her car, he wanted Katrina out of this situation. Now that she'd opened up more and some of her standoffishness toward Annabeth was gone, the older woman was growing on him. He doubted her newfound openness would make up for years of emotional neglect and ambivalence with Annabeth, but it was a start.

Once her flight was booked, he called Annabeth. The phone rang in his ear, and his heart rate kicked up with each trill.

She picked up on the third ring. "Hello?"

"Hi, Annabeth. It's Dean."

"Hi. I only have a couple minutes. You caught me between patients. Did you get Wendy's car sorted out?"

"I did, but that's not why I'm calling, actually."

"Oh?"

"No." He ran a hand through his hair. "So, your dad's home."

She groaned. "Oh, God. What happened?"

"He wasn't happy to learn we've been here poking around. I came back from shipping off Wendy's car to hear him yelling at your mother."

"Did he hit her?" Annabeth's voice was low.

"No. I'm not sure he would. She didn't seem afraid in that way. Just downtrodden, you know? Anyway, I stepped between them. Apparently, having a champion was what your mom needed. She's decided to leave."

Annabeth gasped. "I bet that went over well."

"Like a bucket of ice water. I got him to back off and leave her alone so she could pack. I'm in the hallway, keeping an eye out. And I've booked her a plane ticket. She's coming to you."

Her soft sigh carried a resigned note. "I had a feeling you

were going to say that. Okay. I'll get one of the spare rooms made up. When does her plane get in?"

"Seven-thirty this evening. I got her out on the flight to Boston with me. We go our separate ways from there."

"Okay. I'm glad you'll be with her that far. I wouldn't put it past Dad to try to convince her not to get on that first flight if you weren't there to support her."

"No, I agree. Though she might have told him to stuff it. I think she's done caring about appearances. He threatened to call the police to kick me out. She told him it was her house, too, and she wanted me to stay, then told him to go ahead and call the cops. That she was sure their friends would love the gossip."

"Oh, seriously? Good for her. I hope she maintains this backbone." A muffled voice sounded in the background, and Annabeth paused for a moment before speaking to him again. "Dean, I need to go. Can I call you tonight?"

"Yeah. But I'll call you. Once I make it to Medina."

"That sounds good. Talk to you then. Bye."

She was gone as his own goodbye left his mouth. He tucked his phone away, then glanced down the hall, listening. It looked like Pierce was honoring his request to leave Katrina alone. Dean decided to chance ducking into his room to pack. They needed to get going; their flight left in just under two hours.

Thirty-Two

Annabeth paced near baggage claim at the airport, waiting for her mother to arrive. Her plane landed fifteen minutes ago, so it shouldn't be long.

She wasn't too sure how she felt about this turn of events. On the one hand, she was happy her mom had broken free of her dad. But on the other, she remembered what it was like to grow up with a mom who bowed to everyone else's direction. There were times when her dad wanted Annabeth and Wendy to do certain things—like go off to boarding school—and her mom disagreed. But she'd been too afraid, too beaten down by his constant emotional and mental abuse to stand up for them. Annabeth loved her mother, but she didn't necessarily like her. She hoped now that Katrina had taken a stand, they could work on their relationship. It certainly couldn't get a whole lot worse than it was.

Taking a turn, Annabeth glanced toward the arrivals area. Behind a businessman in a black polo shirt, her mother emerged, towing a carryon. Annabeth's heart stuttered as reality sank in. Her mother was moving in with her.

Well, nothing to do but do it. She took a deep breath, straightened her shoulders and walked toward Katrina.

"Mom." She waved.

Katrina looked up, and a smile lit her face. Annabeth felt an answering one lift the corners of her mouth.

"Hi, honey." Katrina wrapped her in a tight hug.

"Oh. Hi." Annabeth blinked in surprise at the strength of her embrace.

Katrina pulled back and squeezed Annabeth's arms lightly before letting go. "Thank you for letting me stay."

"It's not a problem. Let's get your bags and get out of this craziness." She motioned to the sea of people walking by.

"Sounds good."

They found Katrina's luggage with ease once the carousel started up. Ten minutes later, they were in Annabeth's car and leaving the airport.

"Did you have a good flight?"

Katrina nodded. "It was fine. A little cramped. I'm not used to flying economy." She lifted a shoulder. "But it was okay. I'm just glad to be away from there." Relief colored her voice.

"Dean said you were pretty fierce." Annabeth merged onto the highway and sped up.

"I don't know about that. I'm just fed up. Covering up Wendy's death was the last straw. I put up with a lot of things from your father over the years, but that—" She propped her elbow on the windowsill and rested her chin on her fingers, staring out at the passing cars. "It broke something inside me."

Annabeth sent a quick glance at her mom. "Well, I'm happy you're out of there. I just wish it hadn't taken this to do it."

Katrina was silent for a long moment. "I am too. And I'm also happy you didn't turn out like me."

A frown wrinkled Annabeth's forehead. She shot another glance at Katrina. "What do you mean?"

"I mean, I'm glad you don't let people walk all over you." She shook her head, still looking outside. "First my father, telling me proper ladies were silent ladies and always shushing me when I tried to speak up; then Pierce, telling me how to do everything else. I even let some of the charity ladies push me around. But no more. I'm done being there for others to use." She turned and looked at Annabeth. "And I want to make it up to you."

"Mom, you don't need to do that." Annabeth really didn't want her mother to fawn all over her in some attempt at an apology. Hearing the words was enough for now. The rest would come with the way Katrina lived her life from here on out.

"I want to. God knows, you deserve a better mother."

"I'm thirty years old, Mom. I don't need to be mothered anymore." She reached over and took her mom's hand. "But I could use a mom. The kind an adult woman has. One who's a friend." She looked at her to see her blink hard.

"I think I'd like that too." Katrina's voice was tight with emotion.

A smile wreathed Annabeth's face. "Good. So, right now, we start over, okay? I know it'll take some time for us to fully come to grips with our new normal, and that we have some things to work through, but I'm willing to give it an honest go."

"Me too." Katrina squeezed her hand.

THIRTY-THREE

The rental car beeped as Dean pushed the button to unlock its doors. He frowned as he opened the trunk and tossed his suitcase inside. This car was smaller than his last one. He wasn't super tall, but at six-foot-two, small cars still felt cramped.

Climbing into the driver's seat, he grunted as he folded up like an accordion. Fumbling along the side, he realized it had a manual adjustment. Face practically in the steering wheel, he reached between his legs and found the bar to adjust the seat, pushing it all the way back. He still felt closed in, but at least now, the steering wheel wasn't wedged into his chest. With the push of a button, the engine roared to life. Dean buckled up and pulled out of the parking lot.

The miles ticked by as he drove down the highway toward Medina. He'd sent a text to the police chief, Tim Wage, when he got off the plane and asked to meet. He wanted to know what the man knew about Donna Taggart, and he'd promised the chief an update. Once he talked to Wage, he'd call Annabeth and make sure she and Katrina were doing okay.

Ninety minutes after he left the airport, he pulled into the

Medina police station. Pole lights lit the parking lot, and he parked beneath one, then headed inside. After signing in, an officer showed him to Wage's office. This time, he didn't have to wait.

"Adler. Good to see you again. Have a seat." Wage smiled from behind his desk and motioned for Dean to sit.

"Thanks for meeting me so late." Dean walked into the office and sat down.

"Not a problem." He nodded to the officer, who showed Dean in. The young man shut the door, leaving them alone.

"So, you said you had an update?" Wage didn't waste time getting to the point.

"I do." Dean was glad they weren't beating around the bush. He was tired and wanted to find a hotel. "Did you know Wendy's car wasn't destroyed? It's been in a barn on Martha's Vineyard since the wreck."

Wage's eyes widened, and he sat forward. "Seriously? I thought a wrecking service removed it from the police lot."

"Nope. Pierce Swenson paid to have it shipped there."

A deep frown creased Wage's face. "Why would he do that?"

"Not sure. It wasn't for sentimental reasons, though. That man doesn't have a sentimental bone in his body." Dean shifted, crossing his ankle over his knee. "I shipped it to a friend who's going to take a good look at it. As much as I don't want him to find anything, I hope he does. Then we'll know for sure what we're dealing with."

"Damn. What else did you find? Anything?"

"Maybe a hole in Johnathan Cassidy's alibi. Do you know a woman named Donna Taggart? Stella Scarsborough said she was a waitress at Murphy's Diner."

Wage rolled his eyes. "She's still a waitress there. Biggest busybody you'll ever meet. She knows everything, because she makes it a point to stick her nose where it doesn't belong." He shook his head. "Drives me nuts. I've had more than one suspect tipped off because my officers go in there to eat and can't keep their mouths shut. Even when they swear she was nowhere close, she knows things."

"Well, then she'll probably be useful. I need to talk to her."

"Why?" Wage gave him a thoughtful look.

"She provided the alibi for the Cassidy brothers. Said they were studying at the diner at the time of the crash."

"That's right." The chief's expression cleared. "She did. She works the breakfast shift most days now. How about we meet in the morning for coffee and eggs? I'd like to hear what she has to say too."

"So long as there are pancakes and bacon involved, sure."

"Good thing Murphy's has both." Wage smiled.

"Sounds good." Dean stood and held out a hand to the chief. "Thanks for your time."

Wage rose and shook Dean's hand. "Of course. I appreciate the update. Keep me posted on that car, and I'll see you tomorrow. Seven o'clock work?"

"It does. See you then."

"Yep."

With a wave, Dean left. Climbing into his car, he headed for the same hotel he stayed at the last time and checked in. Once he was ensconced in his room, he flopped onto the bed and called Annabeth.

She picked up after a couple rings. "Hello?"

Her soft voice sent a hot tremor down his spine. Lying in bed might not be the best place to talk to her. He sat up. "Hey, it's me. I didn't wake you, did I?" He glanced at the clock. It was later than he thought.

"No. I'm in bed, but the lights are still on. I was reading, trying to get sleepy."

Dean bit back a groan. There was an image he didn't need. Again. He knew what she slept in, thanks to Katrina's actions that morning. A long t-shirt and nothing else. Annabeth had nice legs. Ones he could see locked around his waist.

He ground his molars together, then swallowed, forcing the need away. "Did your mom get settled in all right?"

"Yeah. She went to bed too. I think she's asleep, though. She looked pretty worn out."

"I can imagine. A lot happened today."

"It did. Did you talk to Chief Wage?"

"Yes." Dean noticed the subject change. He hoped their reunion went well, and she wasn't avoiding things. "We're having breakfast tomorrow at Murphy's. Ms. Taggart works the breakfast shift."

"Good. I hope she rats them out. I'd like nothing more than to see Johnathan's smug smile collapse when he learns his alibi has disappeared," she said, her tone dark, then sighed. "Mostly, I'm ready to put all this behind me. It's sucking me in again and dominating my thoughts. I had a hard time shutting it off at work today."

"Do you have any personal time you can take?"

"Not too much. I just started at this practice in July. The ink is barely dry on my attending status. I think the senior partners at my practice would understand, but I don't want to push it. I might have to use some, though, in the next few weeks. We'll see how ugly things get between my parents. Mom said Dad wasn't very happy. And she's determined not to go back. He'll fight dirty in their divorce, so I might have to take a few days to help her get things sorted and to be moral support for her." She let out a soft snort. "I don't know why I should after the lack of support I got from her growing up. I guess I'm trying to be the bigger person. Pettiness is for children. Besides, she's making an effort to make amends, and that means something."

A soft smile curled Dean's mouth. "You sure you're only thirty? You sound a lot older."

She chuckled. "I'm sure. But you're right. Today, I feel about fifty."

"Well, if you need help with things, I know people." A thought struck him. A concerning one. "And actually, I think I need to call one of them right now."

"What? Who? And why?"

Dean took the phone away from his ear and put her on speaker. "My friend, Asher. Computer hacker—sorry, tech genius—extraordinaire. Don't call him a hacker. He doesn't like it. Anyway, what you said about your dad making your parents' divorce ugly and a comment he made before we left the house made me wonder something." He opened his contacts. Asher's name was at the top. "Your dad might try to freeze your mom out of their bank accounts."

Annabeth groaned. "You're right. He would."

"Did you know he conned your mom into signing her parents' farm over to him? She had no idea she'd done it."

"No, but it doesn't surprise me. He'd bring home papers every so often and ask her to sign them. Said they were updates to the will and to the family trust, adding businesses or taking out assets he'd sold. She'd just sign without reading anything."

Dean paused. "You never did that, did you?"

"No. He tried once to make me sign without reading. I refused and read the entire thing. He wanted to put himself on my bank accounts and put the account in the family trust. I'd opened that account specifically so I could have my own money away from him. I tore the papers up and left them on his desk."

"Good for you." Dean chuckled. "You okay if I put you on a group call with Asher?"

"Oh. Um, sure." He heard rustling and imagined her sitting up, putting her book down.

Business, Dean. Focus. He shoved thoughts of her in that

too short sleep shirt away and touched Asher's name, bringing him onto the conference call.

"Hey, man. What's up? You hit a problem with the car?"

"No. Asher, you're on conference with Annabeth."

"Oh, hello."

"Hi."

"What's going on?" Asher asked.

"I need your fingers," Dean said. He quickly outlined the situation. Asher was typing before he finished talking.

"Annabeth, what bank does your family use? Do you know?"

"There are several. Dad didn't like to keep all our assets in the same place. It gave him more influence and curried more favors when he spread the wealth around."

Asher snorted. "Nice guy." He cleared his throat. "Sorry."

"No, you're fine. I'll be the first to agree he's an asshole."

With a chuckle, Asher moved on. "Do you know your mother's social security number?"

"No. How about I just wake her up? Hang on."

Movement came over the line. A few moments later, Dean heard her talking to her mom.

"Mom? Hey, sorry to wake you. Dean's on the line with a friend of his. They have some questions."

"Oh." Katrina's soft voice sounded in the background. "Um, okay."

"Okay, guys?" Annabeth's voice grew louder, but a bit tinny as she spoke into the receiver. "You're on speakerphone now."

"What's going on?" Katrina asked.

"I had a thought, Katrina," Dean said. "Your husband might try to freeze you out of your bank accounts. I have a friend on the line who's going to check into it and see if we can't protect some of the funds."

"Oh, dear. I hadn't even thought of that. But yes, you're probably right. He might have done it already."

"Don't worry, Mrs. Swenson. I won't let you be penniless. I'm Asher, by the way."

"Hello, Asher."

"Hello, ma'am. I just need some information from you. Can you tell me your full name—maiden included—and your social security number?"

Katrina gave him what he asked for. Through the line, they all heard the click-clack of Asher's fingers flying over the keyboard.

"Hmm."

"What does that mean?" Dean asked.

"Well, he's frozen her cards. Reported them all stolen. You still have access to your money if you visit a bank branch. Although, you'll still have a hard time getting anything. It looks like he reported your ID stolen too. Let's fix that one right now."

"How are you able to do all this?" Annabeth asked.

Dean snorted, aware Asher had secrets no one knew about; not even Ford.

"I have—assets, we'll call them—I use all over the world. This is child's play."

"I'm glad you think so, Mr. Asher," Katrina said. "I wouldn't even know where to start."

"It's just Asher, Mrs. Swenson. That's my given name."

"Oh. What's your last name?"

"Horn. But you can call me Asher. Most everyone does."

"All right, thank you, Asher. Please, call me Katrina."

"Yes, ma'am," Asher responded, sounding a bit distracted. A few hard hit keys echoed over the line. "Okay. Your ID status has been restored. Let's work on these bank accounts. I'm opening you an account that's in your name only. Do you have a preferred bank? Actually, you know what, scratch that.

I'll pick something local to you there with Annabeth. It'll be harder for your husband to try to gain access."

Over the next few minutes, they sat in silence, listening to Asher type and mumble to himself as he worked. He removed the blocks on Katrina's card, then transferred the maximum amount the bank allowed from their joint checking account into her new account at a local bank.

"Are you sure this is a good idea?" Katrina asked. "Won't a judge get suspicious about me transferring money?"

"Nope. I'm printing bank statements for everything, both before and after I transfer the money. The paper trail is airtight. He can't claim you're stealing anything. Your name is on the account I transferred money from and you didn't take it all. Just keep meticulous records of what you spend in case there's any question about what portion of the money you're owed."

"Can I use the card for our joint account? I'd rather not deplete what's in the new one. Just in case he locks me out again."

"Tomorrow, you need to go see a divorce attorney and file for divorce. That will put a freeze on his ability—and yours— to transfer or remove money, except for normal living expenses. I'm also adding a note to your accounts that if the cards are reported stolen, they need to talk to you directly on a recorded line. When you talk to your attorney, make him or her aware of what he did and what you've set up with the bank to prevent it from happening again. FYI, you did all this through their chat function online and talked to Stacy."

Katrina gave a short chuckle. "Okay."

"Don't worry, Katrina. *Most* everything I did was above-board. I truly did go through the chat dashboard. No one will be able to dispute that the bank's system reset your card, because it did."

"What about that employee?" Annabeth asked. "Is she real?"

"No. But the process to reset the card and move the block is an A.I. bot, so it won't matter. It generates a name for itself and responses based on questions—"

"I think we get it, Asher," Dean said with a soft chuckle. "The computer did it and you helped it along."

"Ruin my fun… I happen to like tech speak." Asher snickered. "Okay. Well, you're all set for now. If something changes, call me. But please go see a divorce attorney tomorrow."

"I will. Thank you for your help."

"Any time. Dean, do you need anything else?"

"Actually, can you do a deep dive on a Donna Taggart? She works for Murphy's Diner in Medina."

"Yep. Anything in particular I should look for?"

"No. Just general stuff."

"Got it. Talk to you tomorrow." He hung up.

"Dean, I am glad you have friends in high places. Higher than my husband." Katrina breathed a sigh of relief. "I'm going back to bed now. Good night."

"Good night," Dean echoed.

"Night, Mom."

Dean heard Katrina move away, then a door close.

"Was what he did really aboveboard?" Annabeth asked. "Other than the fact he obviously hacked the system, I mean."

"I have no idea. Asher can do things with a computer I didn't think were possible."

"Where did you find him?"

"I didn't. He was already in Costa Rica when I got there. He's a friend of Ford's."

"How did he find him?"

"Military connections, I guess. Ford was a SEAL, like me, but he spent more time on the deep black ops stuff. Asher was an intelligence analyst before he quit and went down to Costa Rica."

She let out a low whistle. "I thought people like you guys only existed in books and movies. But I'm glad you don't. Thank you for getting my mother's life in order. And I'm sorry my dad's a piece of crap."

"Don't apologize for him. He deserves everything coming toward him in the next few weeks. Even if it turns out he didn't intentionally cover up anything, for what he did to your mom, he deserves it."

"I know. I just—" She stopped and blew out a harsh breath. "This is a mess."

"But it's manageable. And you've got me and my friends. We won't let you drown in it."

She was silent for a long moment, but when she finally spoke, Dean's heart started to race at her words.

"I wish you were here. Or I was there. I could use a hug." Her voice quieted. "You give good ones."

Dean tapped his phone screen, waking it up, then touched the FaceTime icon. He knew it probably wasn't wise, but he needed to see her.

A moment later, her face popped up on his screen. "Hi." She lifted a hand and waved, giving him a quick smile.

His was bigger. She was so pretty, and it was nice to see her smile. "Hi. I won't keep you. I just wanted to see your face. I know it's not a hug, but it's the best I can do for now."

She smiled again, brighter this time. "I'll take it. So, what are you doing after you talk to that woman tomorrow?"

"I'm not sure. Maybe fly home and meet my friend who's going to look at your sister's car." He still didn't like the idea of leaving her alone, but the threat now was minimal. Everything was out of her control and in his hands or those of the authorities. Jordan would probably welcome the help. Plus, Annabeth had her mom with her, so she wasn't by herself.

"Oh." Her smile dropped, then reappeared a second later. "Okay. Well, I guess that's that, then. Thank you for all you've done."

Dean frowned. Why was she acting like this was goodbye?

"I should go. I have an early morning."

"Anna—"

"Goodbye, Dean." Her gaze left his to look at the bottom of her screen. A moment later, her hand appeared in view, then his screen went black.

Dean tossed the phone on the bed with a growl. She hung up on him. What did he say?

THIRTY-FOUR

Warmth and the scent of coffee and bacon slapped Dean in the face as he walked into Murphy's Diner. His stomach grumbled. From the corner, Chief Wage waved. Dean headed his way and slid into the booth opposite him.

"It smells good in here." Dean picked up a menu. "So does your coffee. I need some of that." He'd had trouble falling asleep after his phone conversation with Annabeth. He still wasn't sure why she'd ended things so abruptly. Maybe she'd expected him to come back to Ohio when he was done here. That was his plan now. He couldn't leave things with her the way they were. Jordan and Wendy's car could wait.

He frowned. That was another thought that kept him up late. Why did he care? She was a client, essentially. He shouldn't get involved with her. Plus, they led completely separate lives in different parts of the world. Where was the future in that? But he'd be damned if he could stay away.

"Best eggs and pancakes I've ever had. Don't tell my wife I said that."

Dean chuckled, pushing his thoughts aside for now. "I won't."

A woman walked up, carrying a coffeepot. "Mornin'. You want coffee?"

"Please." Dean turned his cup over and scooted it toward her, noting the nametag pinned to her shirt. This was their target, unless there was more than one Donna working here.

"Do you need room for cream?" she asked.

"No."

She gave a quick nod and filled his cup. "You two ready to order?"

"Could you give us just a couple minutes, Donna?" Wage asked.

"Sure. Wave at me when you're ready."

He nodded, and she walked away.

"Is that her?"

"Yes."

"She's not at all what I expected." He'd been picturing a skinny woman with beady eyes. Donna Taggart had a little extra meat on her bones and a kind, grandmotherly face.

"I know. It's probably how she gets people to tell her things. She looks trustworthy, so they spill their guts." Wage shook his head and raised his coffee cup to take a sip. "And FYI, we're going to wait until after we eat to talk to her. I don't want syrup in my lap. Or the rest of that coffee she's carrying around."

"Me, either." Dean smiled and turned back to the menu.

A few minutes later, Wage waved Donna down, and they placed their orders.

"Can I ask you something?" Dean studied the chief over the rim of his cup after Donna walked away again.

"Sure."

"What do you know about Pierce Swenson?"

"Wendy's dad?"

"Yeah."

"Not much. I never formally met him. He was in the

station once to talk to the detective and the chief, and I saw him."

"What was your impression? Did he look like a heart-broken dad?"

"Honestly? No. He looked like Mr. Business. He had on a suit and a severe expression." He took another sip of his coffee. "You trying to figure out why he had the car shipped home instead of destroyed?"

"Yep. I *have* met the man, and he won't ever win father or husband of the year awards. There has to be a business angle behind his decision; I just don't know what."

"Have you looked into whether he was in business with the Cassidys?"

"No. It crossed my mind, but the Cassidys run a global shipping business. Pierce Swenson is a real estate developer. Unless the Cassidys were in the market for property, they wouldn't have any reason to do business with him."

"Maybe Swenson had an idea that would bring the two businesses together and make them both a lot of money. Their kids were dating, after all. Wouldn't it be wise for him to link the families in another way? To capitalize on the link between the kids?"

Dean frowned. Wage had a good point. "I guess I just had it in my head that the reason Swenson kept the car was more for blackmail purposes. His wife said he called it insurance." He lifted a shoulder. "To me, that means blackmail." He waved a finger. "See, this is where my inexperience as a P.I. comes into play."

"You're doing all right so far. How long have you been at this?"

"About a year. Mostly, I track down vendors who owe money to the local hotels back in Costa Rica. I've been back in the U.S. twice to follow a couple of cheating spouses for friends of friends. This is the first serious case I've taken on."

And it had him feeling a little out of his depth. It didn't help that he wanted to solve it for Annabeth. He constantly saw her face in every move he made, so it was doubly frustrating when he came up against a wall. He didn't want to let her down.

"I think you're on the right track. Eventually, all the puzzle pieces will make sense. Just keep adding them to the table."

"Easier said than done."

"I know. But trust the process. It'll get you answers."

He certainly hoped so.

Donna brought their breakfast, and he and Wage turned to less serious topics while they ate. It was nice to decompress for a bit and talk about sports. He discovered the chief was a fellow baseball fan. One thing Dean missed about living in Central America was going to professional baseball games. He could get the games online, thanks to Asher's skills, but it wasn't the same as sitting in the stadium.

Shoveling his last bite of bacon into his mouth, Dean pushed his plate away and sat back. "That was good."

Wage wiped his hands and nodded. "You ready to never be welcome in this diner again?" He smiled.

With a chuckle, Dean sat forward. "Yes. Let's see what she knows."

Lifting a hand, Wage motioned Donna over.

She smiled as she approached. "You two ready for the check?"

"In a minute. We have a couple questions to ask you. Do you think you could take a few minutes and sit down with us?" Wage asked.

Her smile faded, and a wariness crept into her eyes.

That was interesting. Dean watched her closely. What did she have to be wary of? She didn't even know what they wanted to ask.

"We're still a bit busy." She glanced around at the half-full diner. The breakfast rush was coming to an end. She had customers, but nothing pressing like when Dean arrived.

"We won't keep you long. I promise." Wage reached across the aisle and grabbed a chair from the middle table, pulling it closer. "Have a seat."

Her gaze bounced between them. Dean gave her a bright smile, hoping—as Stella said—he could use his charm and put her at ease.

Donna's mouth twisted. "I suppose I could for just a couple minutes." She set the coffeepot on the table and lowered herself onto the chair. "What's this about?"

"A cold case," the chief replied. "Well, not really cold. It was solved, but we're not sure it was solved correctly." He cast a quick look at Dean.

"Mrs. Taggart, fifteen years ago, you told the police that Johnathan and Will Cassidy were here late into the night studying," Dean said. "Some information has come to light that contradicts that."

She frowned at him. "Who are you?"

"Sorry. I'm Dean Adler. I'm a private investigator working for Annabeth Swenson."

Donna's tongue darted out, and she wet her lips; her eyes rounded. "Oh."

"Can you tell us what you remember?" Wage asked.

She lifted a shoulder. "That was a long time ago. Why is it important?"

"Because the Cassidys might have had something to do with Wendy Swenson's death." Dean wasn't telling her anything she didn't already know. "Were they here that night?"

"Yes." The conviction in her voice and her eyes told him that was the truth.

"But they weren't here as long as you said they were, were they?"

She looked down, raising a hand to scrape at a speck of dirt on the tabletop. "I'm not sure."

"Donna, look at me." Wage kept his voice soft.

She glanced up.

"What really happened? You're not in any trouble. Just tell us the truth, please."

She rolled her lips in, pressing them together. "No trouble?"

"No. We just want the truth."

"Fine." She blew out a breath. "They were here. They came in around eight, ate dinner and sat in that booth"—she pointed to the opposite corner, just a few feet away—"then drank sodas for a few hours while they studied."

"What time did they leave?"

"It was after eleven. Maybe eleven-fifteen or eleven-twenty?"

Dean looked at Wage, excitement building in his gut. Wendy's accident happened just after midnight.

"Did they say where they were headed?" Dean asked.

"No. But they followed Wendy out."

"What?" Dean frowned. "She was here?"

"Donna, why didn't you tell anyone that?"

She lowered her hands into her lap and stared at them. "Will asked me not to."

"Will did?" Dean looked at Wage, who looked equally surprised. "Will Cassidy asked you not to mention that Wendy was here? Did he ask you to say they were here later than they were too?"

After a long moment, she nodded. "He paid me."

"He approached you out of the blue and offered you money to lie to the police?" Wage asked.

"No." Her voice was quiet. She slumped in her seat, folding her arms over her ample chest. "After I heard what happened to Wendy, I told them if they wanted me to stay quiet about the fight I overheard, then they needed to leave me a big tip. Johnathan didn't want to. Said she'd just crashed and there was nothing to cover up. Will, though... he gave me this look, and I could see the gears turning in his head. He pulled out a wad of cash and handed it to me. Told me not to say a word about her being here and that they left that night around one. Johnathan protested again, but Will told him they were just covering their bases. He said he knew it was just a terrible accident, but that even a hint of impropriety could jeopardize their futures, so it was best if they had all their time accounted for."

Dean glanced at Wage again, frowning. Will was the one who paid her? He could see in the chief's eyes that similar thoughts were running through his head.

"What happened with Wendy?" Dean asked. "What did they argue about?"

"She came in all hot and bothered. Marched right up to their table and stuck her finger in Johnathan's face. Told him he needed to take responsibility for their baby. He gave her this dismissive look and told her no. That she needed to get rid of it. She smacked him and called him a callous asshole. Will stood up then and tried to calm her down. I couldn't make out all of what he said, but he ushered her toward the door. I did catch him say that he'd talk to his brother."

"Did she seem satisfied with that?" Wage asked.

Donna tipped her head side-to-side. "Enough that she left without any more fuss."

"What did the Cassidys do then?" Dean asked.

"Will walked her out, but came back in a few minutes later. They huddled at their table for a minute, talking, then left."

"When did Will ask you to keep quiet?"

"A couple days later. They came in for a late dinner."

"Okay," Wage said. "How much did he pay you?"

"Why does that matter?"

"Just answer the question."

She huffed. "Five hundred thirteen dollars."

The chief's eyebrows shot up. "You remember the exact amount?"

"Wouldn't you if something like that happened?" She pinned him with a look, then scooted her chair back. "I need to get back to work. Are we done?"

Wage glanced at Dean.

"One more question," Dean said.

She turned her glare on him. "What?"

"If you were asked to tell that story in court, would you?"

"Maybe. What's in it for me?"

"Staying out of jail on obstruction charges," Wage replied.

Her eyes widened, and she turned to him. "You said—"

"I know what I said, but that was before you admitted to impeding a death investigation."

She glared at him. "The charges won't stick. You never read me my rights, and you told me I wouldn't get in trouble for withholding the information."

"Not for back then. But now? If I reopen this case, you can bet I'll make the D.A. subpoena you."

She stood up and grabbed the coffeepot.

Wage tensed. Dean had a vision of him taking a coffee shower. But she didn't dump it on him.

"You play dirty, Tim Wage. Get out."

And that was their signal to go. Dean didn't trust she wouldn't use that coffee if they stayed. He lifted his hip and took out his wallet, tossing down more than enough money to cover the bill. "Thanks, Mrs. Taggart."

She just glared at him and stood back while he and the chief slid out of the booth.

Outside, Dean couldn't stop the smile that spread over his face. "They don't have an alibi."

"Nope. But"—Wage held up a hand—"let's not get ahead of ourselves, though. Just because they argued with her and followed her out, doesn't mean they did anything. We need physical evidence."

"Which I'm hoping we'll find in Wendy's car."

"You get me that, and I'll convince a judge to reopen the case."

"Deal." Dean held out a hand.

THIRTY-FIVE

Annabeth frowned and pulled her phone away from her ear, irritated. Dean wouldn't pick up; it just kept going to voicemail. She stabbed the end call button with her thumb. She didn't want to leave a message. Why hadn't he called to tell her how his meeting went this morning? It was mid-afternoon now. She rolled her eyes. He was probably on a plane back to Costa Rica. She didn't know why it annoyed her so much to think that he was leaving. He had no obligation or reason to stay. She shouldn't want him to stay. But she did. That annoyed her more than anything else. She didn't want to have feelings for the man. Or any man. Eventually, sure. But right now, she just wanted to focus on her medical practice and finding out what really happened to her sister.

With a huff, she shoved her phone into the pocket on her dress slacks and picked up her stethoscope. She'd have to try again later; she still had patients to see.

Pasting a smile on her face, she walked out of her office and down the hall to her next appointment. Inwardly, she might be upset and frustrated, but her patients would never know. These kids—and their parents—didn't need a distracted, angry doctor.

She moved from room to room, stopping between patients to check her phone. By the time she reached her last appointment of the day, he still hadn't called her back. Maybe he'd taken her goodbye last night to heart. She probably shouldn't have been so quick to react to his intent to go home. It wasn't like she'd expected anything else. Their kiss meant nothing. It was just a reaction to stress—a way to decompress.

Shaking off her thoughts, she reached for the exam room doorhandle, but her nurse's voice stopped her.

"Hey. There's a man hanging out by your car. I saw him through the window when I was restocking room three."

Annabeth's mind immediately went to Noah Reitman. He'd probably made bail. "What's he look like?"

"Tall, hot." Kim lifted a shoulder and gave her a sheepish grin. "He's wearing a leather jacket and has a beard."

Dean.

He was here? But why hadn't he called?

"Okay. Thanks."

"Do you want me to call the police?"

"No. I think I know who it is. It's fine."

Kim's eyebrows lifted. "Okey-dokey. If this is some juicy story, you need to share the next time we have lunch."

Smiling, Annabeth twisted the doorknob. "There's nothing to tell. I swear."

"Mmm-hmm." Grinning, Kim spun on her heel and walked away.

Somehow, Annabeth paid attention during her final appointment, when all she really wanted to do was run outside and demand Dean tell her what happened with that woman and why he was here. Thankfully, the child here to see her was only in for routine vaccinations. She was in and out in five minutes.

Once she typed up her case notes, she helped Kim clean up the last few things, then they walked out together.

"He's even hotter up close," Kim muttered as they entered the parking lot.

"Yep."

Kim sent her a quick side glance. "You're not going to tell me who he is, are you?"

"Nope."

"Spoilsport." Kim paused in the aisle. "I'm down there." She tipped her head to the right. "I'll see you tomorrow."

"Have a good night." Annabeth waved, then continued toward Dean.

He pushed off his car and walked toward her as she approached.

"Hi."

His low voice rolled over her, sending a delicious shiver down her spine. She stopped a few feet away and scowled, wishing her body would behave. "What are you doing here?" *Brilliant, Annabeth. Way to be friendly to the guy who haunted your dreams so spectacularly the last couple of nights.* She took a breath and tried again. There was no need to be rude. "Sorry. Hi. I've been calling you."

"I know. I was on a plane. I saw the missed calls when I landed. I figured it would be easier to come by."

"Oh."

He stared at her for several moments. Those pretty hazel eyes of his studied her face, but Annabeth couldn't tell what he was thinking.

"You hungry?"

"Yes." The truth was, she was famished. She always was after work.

"Good. I stopped at the grocery on the way here."

Her eyebrows winged upward. "You did?"

"Yes. I can't cook much, but I can handle some fancy grilled cheese and tomato soup."

Annabeth's mouth watered. It was chilly today, and that sounded great. "Okay."

He closed the gap between them, a small smile on his handsome face. Annabeth tipped her head back to see his eyes. He raised a hand and touched a strand of hair hanging near her cheek. The hair on her neck stood on end and her scalp tingled. She fought to hold his gaze and not close her eyes. He leaned closer, and she parted her lips, eager for his kiss.

His mouth landed on her forehead, lingering for a moment as he enfolded her in a hug. She buried her face in his neck and closed her eyes. This wasn't entirely disappointing. But as much as she liked the hug, she really wanted the kiss.

She rolled her eyes again. What was wrong with her? A moment ago, she'd been wishing her body wouldn't react to him.

He let her go and stepped back. "Come on. Let's head back to your place. I'm starving."

THIRTY-SIX

Dean put his car in park behind the open garage door at Annabeth's and scowled as he stared at her vehicle. What had he been thinking? Why had he stopped at hugging her? He'd seen the desire in her eyes right before he kissed her forehead. He'd felt an answering need coursing through his body, so why hadn't he done what they both wanted?

Unbuckling, he got out and snagged the grocery bags from the backseat. He was an idiot, that's why. In his mind, he was keeping things uncomplicated by just being her friend. But he wasn't. Not when she tied him up in knots and all he wanted to do was lose himself in her touch.

Dammit.

He shut the door with a little more force than necessary and locked the car, then headed for the garage.

"You okay?" She glanced at him, stepping back from her SUV, a briefcase in her hand.

Dean wiped his expression clean. "I'm fine. Just hungry."

She held his gaze for a second, then turned. "Let's go eat, then." She led him to the interior door and unlocked it. "I hope you don't mind my mother joining us."

He held up the bags as she let them in. "Already planned on it."

The first smile he'd seen from her spread over her face. "Oh. Good."

They stepped inside, and she set her briefcase down and took off her coat. "Mom?"

Dean put the bags on the counter, then removed his jacket, laying it over the back of a barstool.

"Hi, honey—oh! Dean. What a nice surprise." Katrina smiled at him as she entered the kitchen.

He smiled back. "Hello."

"Dean's going to make us dinner. And he has news."

"Oh, well, good. What are we having?"

"Grilled cheese and tomato soup. Annabeth, where are your pots and pans? And you have milk, right? I didn't buy that, but I'll need it for the soup."

She pointed to a cabinet, then crossed to the fridge and took out a half-gallon carton of milk.

"Perfect, thank you."

"You're welcome. Do you need help?"

"No. I can handle this." He bent down and opened the cabinet.

"Okay. I'm going to go change."

He straightened, a pot in one hand and a skillet in the other. "Go ahead. But don't take too long. This stuff cooks quick."

With a nod, Annabeth left the kitchen.

"So, you can cook?" Katrina sat down at the island and watched him work.

He chuckled. "Well enough I don't starve."

"That's good."

"It is. So, did you meet with an attorney today?" He opened the soup cans and dumped them in the sauce pot, along with some milk, and set the pan on the stove.

Her smile faded, and she nodded. "I found a woman who was willing to be a liaison for me with a firm in Massachusetts. She was really helpful. The firm back home filed an emergency financial restraining order. They were going to work overtime to file the divorce petition by the end of the week." Her smile returned. "I got an angry text from Pierce earlier asking what I was doing and why he was being served with a restraining order." She laughed. "I only wish I could have seen his face."

So did Dean. He'd probably popped that blood vessel that throbbed in his temple. "Don't delete anything he texts you. And don't take his calls. Everything needs to go through your attorney. Where's the cooking spray, do you know?"

"Probably up there." She pointed to a cabinet next to the stove. "And that's what she said. Trust me, I want to do this right. And you know, I don't care about the money so much. I just want my parents' farm back. Even if I sell it, that's not his, and I don't want him to have it." Her expression hardened. "I still don't know how he slipped that one past me." She scrunched her nose. "Though I guess it wouldn't have been all that hard. I didn't pay attention to things like I should have."

Dean found the spray and sprayed the skillet. He turned on the burner. "That still doesn't mean he had any right to do what he did."

"No. But things wouldn't be so complicated if I hadn't been so stupid."

"He's your husband, Katrina. You're supposed to be able to trust him."

"Trust who?" Annabeth walked back into the room in leggings and a long olive-green sweater. She'd piled her hair into a messy bun on top of her head.

Dean looked away and concentrated on making their sandwiches. He wanted to bury his nose in the long expanse of her exposed neck. See if it tasted as good as it looked. "Your dad.

Spouses should be able to trust each other. Your mom's beating herself up over trusting him."

"Oh. Yeah, Dean's right, Mom. Don't. Dad took advantage of you and of your grief."

"He did, but I didn't do anything to pull myself out of that hole, either."

"Well, you are now."

Dean chanced a look at her to see her lay a hand on her mom's shoulder as she took a seat next to her at the island.

"So, you guys want to know what I found out?" he asked, ready to change the subject. Glancing at them again, he laid their sandwiches in the hot skillet.

"Yes," Annabeth said.

"Johnathan and Will left the diner sometime between eleven and eleven-thirty the night Wendy died. And she was there right before they left."

"Seriously?" Annabeth said.

"Oh, you're kidding!" Katrina cried, drowning out her daughter.

"Nope, not kidding. The chief and I also learned that *Will* paid the waitress to lie. Not Johnathan. It sounded like he didn't think they needed to, but Will insisted."

Annabeth tipped her head. "That's odd. If Johnathan had something to do with her death, why wouldn't he want to buy an alibi? Why was it Will?"

"It could be he's just that cocky." He stirred the soup. It was close to done.

"Maybe. Or maybe he—" She stopped and let out a groan. When Dean looked at her, she had a hand on her forehead. "I can't believe I'm saying this, but maybe he didn't do it. Maybe Will did."

THIRTY-SEVEN

The sizzle of the bread frying in the skillet was the only sound that met Annabeth's theory. She stared at Dean, watching as the idea sank in. His eyes turned thoughtful, then he nodded.

"That makes sense," he said. "But is he capable of that? We know Johnathan is. He went after Brooke and tried to kill her. Or have her killed, anyway."

"Right. But they were always together back then. Will worshipped his brother. He might have done it, thinking he was saving him. A baby at eighteen is a big deal."

"Does it matter who did it?" Katrina's soft voice broke into the conversation.

Annabeth clutched her hands together on the counter, the reality of what they were discussing fully hitting her. She'd always thought Johnathan murdered her sister. Even if it was Will instead, it didn't really matter. With this new information, it looked like she really was murdered.

"So, what now?" she asked, her mood more somber.

"We see what my friend finds in Wendy's car." Dean

flipped the burners off and moved away from the stove, grabbing three plates and bowls from a cabinet. He set them down and lifted the skillet. "I called Asher on my layover." He looked back at Katrina. "The one we talked to last night?" At her nod, he turned back to the food. "He's going to look into Pierce. Chief Wage made a good point; one I've neglected to follow up on. Why was the car insurance? He thinks it might have to do with a business deal and not something personal. I was leaning toward personal, since his business and the Cassidys' don't really have much in common."

"We know the Cassidys," Katrina said. "They have a home on the island they stay at several months out of the year. Which you probably know."

Dean nodded.

"Pierce and Rich Cassidy would talk about their businesses sometimes at dinners and charity functions, but I don't remember them ever talking about a joint venture. But I didn't hang around them much. I wish I could be more help."

"Don't worry about it. If there's anything to find, Asher will find it." He lifted the saucepan and poured soup into the three bowls.

Annabeth got up and went to the pantry to get some crackers. She didn't know about him, but she and her mom liked crackers in their tomato soup. When she came back out, he'd spread the plates and bowls out on the small table in the breakfast nook and Katrina was sitting down. Annabeth and Dean scooted in around the table.

Opening the crackers, Annabeth took out several, then handed it to her mother.

"Thank you, sweetie."

"You're welcome." Settling onto her seat, she crushed up the crackers and stirred them in. The heat from Dean's body rivaled what came off her soup. She was sure it was all in her head—that he really wasn't that warm—but it didn't make a difference. Before long, she was sure she'd be as red as her soup.

Annabeth tucked her head and dug into her dinner. The sooner she finished, the sooner she could put some space between them.

The clink of spoons filled the silence as they ate. It seemed her mother and Dean were both as lost in their thoughts as she was. Which was fine. She didn't want to talk anymore.

Wolfing down her food, she finished first and got up to put her dishes in the dishwasher. She added the few utensils and cups in the sink, then turned to the skillet and saucepan Dean used.

"You don't have to do that. I can wash them."

Annabeth kept her eyes on the skillet in the sink as she ran a soapy sponge over it. "It's fine. I'm standing here. It won't take long."

He opened the drawer beside her, then closed it, then did the same to the next one.

"What are you doing?"

"Looking for a towel. I'll dry."

"Oh. They're in there." She pointed to a drawer in the island.

He turned and opened it, taking out a gray towel. Annabeth rinsed the skillet and handed it to him.

Katrina walked over and put her dishes in the dishwasher. "I'm going to head to my room and watch some TV, then go to sleep. It's been a long day."

"Oh, are you sure? We can watch something in the living room." Annabeth prayed her mom would change her mind. Being alone with Dean was not a good idea.

But Katrina nodded. "I'm sure. I need to—process everything." She patted Annabeth's arm. "I'll see you in the morning."

"Okay. Goodnight, Mom."

Katrina smiled and touched Dean's arm on her way out of the room. "Goodnight."

"Goodnight." He smiled at her.

Annabeth turned back to the dishes. Those dimples of his would be her undoing.

Hurrying through cleaning the saucepan, she handed it to him, then opened the cabinet beneath the sink to get a dish-washer tab. After stuffing it in the dispenser, she shut the appliance's door and started it.

"I think I'll follow in Mom's footsteps. You must be tired too. All that traveling."

Dean set the pot and towel down and walked closer.

Annabeth's eyes widened. Her butt bumped the counter as she shuffled back. Oh, she'd made a critical error. She should have put some distance between them. Now he had her pinned.

"We need to talk first."

"About what? Is there something about the case you didn't want Mom to hear?" Her eyes rounded for a different reason. "You found out something about Dad, didn't you?" She clenched her fists and steeled herself. "Just tell me. Nothing would surprise me at this point."

"It's not about your dad." He inched closer until, with one deep breath, their chests would touch.

Annabeth kept her breathing shallow.

"It's about us."

"There is no us."

"There should be."

Her breathing stopped altogether. Did he just say what she thought he did?

Any further thoughts she had on the matter disappeared when he laid gentle hands on her head and short-circuited her brain with his touch. His thumbs toyed with her cheekbones and his long fingers tunneled into her hair, sending shards of electricity over her scalp. She'd been wrong. It wouldn't be his dimples that were her undoing. It would be his hands.

"Dean. This isn't a good idea."

"No, I agree. I even told myself that on the way here. That I should have just called you and told you everything on the phone. That it was stupid to even fly here. I should have gone home. But I couldn't. Something—you—won't let me make rational decisions."

"Don't blame me for your penis-brain. I'm attracted to you, too, but I was well on my way to bed when you stopped me."

A quick burst of laughter shot past his lips. "Penis-brain? I guess you could call it that. But that's not why I'm here."

She lifted an eyebrow, not believing him. She could see in his eyes that he wanted to kiss her. It was easy to recognize when she felt that way too. Her body didn't care that her brain had misgivings. That she didn't want a relationship at this point in her life. It wanted him and was overriding all rational thought.

He smiled. "It's not. Not entirely. It has more to do with your wit. And your smile. And your determination to see justice for your sister." He leaned in as he spoke, his voice growing quieter. "And how you accepted your mom into your home without a second thought, even though the two of you don't have the best relationship. It's about who you are."

Oooh. There was that charm of his. But it wasn't charm. It was just Dean. She could see in his eyes that he meant what he said. His words weakened her mind's walls against him and her feelings and stoke the fire building in her belly.

Millimeters away, he hovered over her lips. An invisible string connected them, pulling her closer. She resisted, but with every second, her resistance lessened and the force pulled harder.

"That's why I'm here, Annabeth. I don't want to be anywhere else."

The force on that string tugged again. Hard. Annabeth's resistance gave way, and she kissed him.

Thirty-Eight

A firestorm erupted inside Annabeth's head at the first touch of his mouth on hers. This kiss was even better than the first one. She didn't know why. Maybe because this wasn't a test the waters kind of embrace. It was a, we're doing this on purpose and it means something, type of embrace. She wasn't sure what it meant, exactly, but she knew she wanted it to mean something. To lead to something. She didn't care anymore that she wasn't in the market for a man. With some pretty words and one touch of his lips, her misgivings had melted into a puddle at her feet. Annabeth knew she should be worried about that—about how fast she was giving in—but she couldn't bring herself to care. She was done keeping him at arm's length.

She clutched the front of his long-sleeved t-shirt, balling the soft cotton in her hands. What she really wanted was to feel what was underneath. But they were standing in her kitchen, and her mother was in the house. So, she let go and swept her hands up his shoulders to touch the coarse but surprisingly soft beard covering his firm jaw. The short hairs pricked her palms, then slid along them like silk as she moved her hands. A fierce need rose in her belly to feel it elsewhere.

Growling like a madwoman, she pressed closer and clutched a handful of his hair.

He let out a soft grunt of surprise, then dropped his hands to skim her back and wrap over her butt. With a quick tilt of his pelvis, she felt the hard ridge behind his fly. Annabeth moaned deep in her throat and lifted a leg to pull him closer.

Dean lifted his head. "Crap, woman." He gulped in air. "I meant what I said. I didn't come here for sex."

Annabeth didn't care. Their embrace had quickly wound her up to the point of no return. If they stopped now, she'd be an aching, angry mess all night. Even if she took care of herself, it wouldn't be the same.

She bit back a laugh. Now who had penis-brain?

"Before we go any further, you need to decide what you want. I know what I want."

His low words pierced the fog of passion clouding her mind. "What's that?"

"To give us a chance. I know our lives are different. Separate. But I can't imagine going back to my life, pretending you don't exist, and that I don't feel the way I do. I don't want to. But I understand if you don't want to get involved." A little of the passion died in his eyes with his last words.

An ache formed in Annabeth's chest at how the idea of them going their separate ways made him sad. It made her sad too. Hadn't she lamented just last night how it bothered her that he was leaving?

But wishing for something and actually getting it—and having to work to keep it—were different things. A simple roll in the hay and being in a relationship were too. She'd come to grips with the fact she wanted this man in her bed. But could she handle having him in the rest of her life too? Could they make this work? She didn't know the answer to that, but she knew herself. If she said no, and he left, she'd kick herself for the rest of forever.

She ran her hands through his hair again and tipped her head as she looked at him; a soft smile formed on her face. "It won't be easy."

"The good things in life rarely are."

"At some point, one of us will have to move."

"Yep."

"Some days, I come home all bitchy and just want to hide in my room with wine and a book." Those were the days she had really sick kiddos. She wished her job was all about vaccines and colds, but sometimes, it was so much worse.

"I'll buy the wine." He leaned in and nuzzled his nose along her neck. "But you won't need the book."

A heady, floating sensation hit her. She closed her eyes and tried to keep her feet firmly planted on the floor. "Okay."

His lips latched onto the pulse point at the base of her ear. She clutched handfuls of his dark hair and held him there. Strong arms surrounded her and lifted her off her feet. He lifted his head to look at her.

"Where's your bedroom?"

Annabeth tipped her head toward the living room and the stairs beyond, unable to force words past her throat. Dean turned and carried her the way she indicated. She continued to point until they reached the bedrooms, then he set her down and they tiptoed past her mother's room and into hers.

"We have to be quiet." Dean closed the door behind them and spun her around, pinning her against it. "Your mom's not dumb. I'm sure she'll realize something's up when I'm here in the morning, but let's not give her a play-by-play." He wedged a thigh between hers and kissed her neck again.

Biting her lip, she nodded. A low moan escaped.

Dean chuckled and backed up. "Let's start with a shower. The water can drown you out."

She sent him a dry look. "I only moaned. You're talking."

"Okay." He pulled her into his arms and kissed her, quick and hard. "No more talking." He hauled her into the bathroom and shut the door.

In the smaller, more confined space, nerves fluttered to life in Annabeth's stomach. Things felt much more intimate in here.

He leaned into the shower and turned the water on, testing the spray until it was the right temperature. Before Annabeth could say or do anything, he grasped the neck of his shirt and pulled it over his head, tossing it to the floor.

All the moisture in her mouth fled south. Dear Lord, the man was magnificent. His torso was like a work of art. Well-defined muscles rippled under sun-bronzed skin in the overhead lights. A line of dark hair split his perfect abs and disappeared into the waistline of his jeans. Swirls of intricate tattoos decorated his arms and chest.

She stepped closer, drawn to the designs. Some were just shapes, filler between the drawings. It was all incredible. She traced her fingers over the flag-draped tombstones, then to the sunburst shining over a humpback whale breaching the waves. His body told a story. One she'd ask about later.

His fingers curled around the hem of her shirt and inched it upward.

Much, much later. She raised her arms and let him draw the garment over her head. It joined his shirt on the floor. Annabeth reached behind her back and flicked open her bra. Dean's fingers hooked under the straps and drew it down her arms. It hit the tile floor with a soft plop. With just his fingertips, he traced the tight buds of her nipples. She tipped her head back and closed her eyes, letting out another quiet moan.

An instant later, her eyes shot open, and she yelped in surprise as his mouth closed over the tip.

He grinned against her flesh and looked up at her, his

mouth still on her breast. Lifting his head, he angled her face and leaned down. "She's going to hear you."

"Only if you keep doing that."

"Then we're screwed." His mouth crashed onto hers.

In a flurry of hands and heady kisses, they discarded the rest of their clothes. Dean opened the shower door and drew her inside. Warm water hit her skin, adding to the fire he stoked as he tucked her back to his front and let his hands roam. If she didn't melt into a puddle and swirl down the drain with the water, she'd be astonished.

He picked up the bottle of shower gel and squirted some on his palm, then rubbed his hands together before sliding them over her skin. Annabeth raised her arms and clutched at his hair. She tipped her hips back, pressing against the hard shaft sliding along her backside.

"If this wasn't our first time, I'd bend you over and take you right here." Dean nipped at her ear, then plunged a soapy hand between her thighs.

She yelped again and ground harder against him. "I don't care. Do it." Waiting was not her strong suit. In any situation, but particularly this one.

He groaned, then shifted to the side. Annabeth looked over her shoulder and pouted. "Spoil all the fun, why don't you?"

He turned his now silvery jade eyes on her. The passion burning in their depths made her shiver. The predatory glint made her core clench.

"Babe, I'm only getting started." He slid a finger into her channel.

Her eyes rolled back. "Oh," she panted.

While one hand worked the sensitive flesh between her legs, his other hand glided over her breasts, toying with her nipples until she quivered in his arms. With a quick pinch of that tiny bundle of nerves hiding in her folds, she sailed over the edge into pure bliss. He swallowed her shout of pleasure with a deep kiss, milking her for all she was worth.

When he shifted, bumping her hip with his rock-hard shaft, the fog lifted from Annabeth's brain. They were far from finished. She spun in his arms and lifted her right leg, hooking it behind his thigh. She rocked her hips, sliding him through the wetness coating her core.

"Annabeth." He tipped his head back, his jaw working as he fought for control. "Not here."

"Yes, here. You can take me on the bed later. I'm not a virgin who needs to be treated like a fragile flower. Now, you have about five seconds to bury this"—she grabbed his thick shaft and squeezed—"inside me, or I'm climbing you like a tree and doing it myself."

With a growl, his eyes opened. The man who stared back at her was more predator than human. A delicious thrill went through her, making her even wetter than she was before. He disentangled himself from her and opened the shower door to step out, then picked up his pants. A moment later, he had his wallet in his hand and had it open, removing a foil-wrapped square. She watched, mouth watering, as he sheathed himself, then stalked toward her.

Stepping into the shower, he took over the space with his larger-than-life presence. He held her gaze for a moment, the need spinning up between them, before he flipped her around, away from him and the heavy spray of water. His large hand landed on her back and pushed her shoulders down, and he used his foot to spread her feet wide.

Annabeth braced her hands on the wall as he moved in behind her. He couldn't move fast enough for her. Every cell in her body wanted to feel him deep inside, bringing her to a place only he could.

A sharp smack on her butt made her moan loud and long. Then he pressed the tip of his erection to her entrance and dipped inside. She pushed her hips back, trying to take him deeper.

He smacked her butt again. "Hold still."

She bit her lip and tried to do as he asked. But he wasn't moving fast enough. She pushed back again, but this time, he clamped down on her waist and held her there. She whimpered. "Please, Dean."

The words barely left her mouth, and he thrust inside in one smooth, quick stroke. She let out a shout and slapped at the wall. He filled her like no one else ever had. Touched every inch and created a friction so incredible, she was sure she'd burst into flames any second.

"You okay?" His voice was hoarse, and his fingers dug into her hipbones.

She gave a jerky nod. "Yes." She squirmed in his grip, desperate to move.

He must have been too. At her affirmation, he pulled back, then slammed into her again. Over and over, he repeated the movement, building the tension. Annabeth locked her elbows until she broke apart into a million shards of light. With a guttural groan, her body went boneless.

Dean wrapped his arms around her, hauling her to his chest so she wouldn't hit her head on the wall. She sagged against him. His grip was the only thing keeping her from sliding down the drain.

The water cut off, then the room tilted as he picked her up. She tried to tell him she could walk, but she couldn't make her mouth work. Honestly, she was surprised her brain functioned enough she could still breathe.

With her in his arms, he walked out of the bathroom and laid her on the bed. She glanced at him, surprised to see him still at full attention. A slight frown marred her forehead. "Did you not come?"

He shook his head, that dangerous predator still staring back at her.

Her eyes widened. Oh, boy. She was in for another ride. Her body heated again and that steady thrum of desire started back up in her belly.

He moved in, spreading her thighs. "It won't take much. Your pretty ass about did me in. But you came too quick."

She let out a soft giggle. "Sorry."

"Don't be. Now I get to watch you come again." He dipped his head and swiped his tongue through her folds.

Annabeth's hips bucked. "Oh!"

She felt more than saw him smile as he continued to bring her to the brink again. When she wasn't sure she could stand much more, he sat back, then shuffled forward on his knees and drove inside her. She locked her ankles behind his waist and stared up into his swirling steely-jade eyes as they went over the edge together this time.

THIRTY-NINE

Dean ran a hand over Annabeth's naked hip and stared at her relaxed features in the dim room. He'd awakened a few minutes ago when the room lightened with the pre-dawn light. Too comfortable to get up, he'd taken the opportunity to stare at the woman who'd captivated his mind and body. Everything about this woman spoke to him on a soul-deep level. From her pretty gray-blue eyes and soft, full curves to her keen intelligence and feisty personality. She was everything he could ever imagine he'd want.

But could he hang on to her?

God, he hoped so. He'd move heaven and earth to keep this woman in his life. Even if it meant moving back to the U.S. Which, honestly, it probably would. But he was okay with that. He liked his life in Costa Rica, but it was just a place. He had a sneaking suspicion that wherever Annabeth was, was now home.

He glanced at the clock. Six-thirty-seven. His gaze roamed her face again. He wondered if they had enough time for another round to start the day right, but then he remembered he was out of condoms. He'd only had two in his wallet, and they used the second one not long after the first.

No matter. He'd just lie here with her for the next few minutes. She'd set her alarm to go off at six forty-five. For the next eight minutes, he'd just relish the feel of her next to him.

Three minutes into his eight-minute snuggle, her phone rang. She came awake with a groan, and Dean sat up, grabbing it from the stand beside her head.

"Margot?" He read the name, then turned it around so she could see it.

"What?" She snatched it from his hands and answered it. "Margot? Are you—?" She stopped, a frown forming on her face.

Dean had no problem hearing the frantic voice on the other end. Margot blubbered in Annabeth's ear.

"Whoa, slow down." She glanced at Dean. The concern on her face made him lean closer. She didn't protest as he listened.

"He's gone! I've been up all night, trying to figure out what to do. What do I do, Annabeth?" Margot broke into tears again.

Dean leaned back to look at Annabeth. "Who's she talking about?" he mouthed.

She pulled the phone away from her mouth. "Her husband," she whispered, then turned back to her friend. "Start at the beginning, Margot. And slow down. I couldn't under-stand you before. What happened? Did you guys have a fight?"

Dean tipped his head into Annabeth's again.

"No. That's what's got me so upset. I don't understand. I came home from work to find a note from him saying he'd quit his job and was leaving. That he was sorry, and to tell the kids he loves them. Annabeth, he left divorce papers with the note! And he took half our money. There wasn't much there to begin with. I don't think I can cover all our bills on just my salary. Especially with the added daycare costs that there will be now. What am I going to do?"

Dean had heard enough. He sat up and scooted toward the edge of the bed in search of his clothes. Scanning the floor, he remembered they were still in the bathroom and that his suitcase was out in his car.

"Where are you going?" Annabeth whispered, covering the end of her phone.

"To get dressed and call Asher. What's his name?"

"Who's name?"

"Your friend's husband."

"Oh. Tad Gaultier."

He nodded and got up, walking away to get his clothes.

"Sorry, Margot. What did you say?"

He glanced back on his way to the bathroom to see her staring at his butt. A crooked smile crossed his face, and he picked up his pace, not wanting to distract her any more. He'd ogle her as she walked away too.

Donning his boxers and jeans, he reentered the bedroom and sat down on the edge of the bed.

"Margot. Margot! Please relax. Everything will be fine, I swear." She pulled the phone away from her ear and put it on speaker. Margot's voice filled the bedroom.

"How? How will it be fine? I have twin toddlers, a full-time job—more than a full-time job—a house I can barely afford on my own, two car payments, because the jerk left in something other than his car, an increased childcare bill, and now no husband. How will that be okay? Plus, this is my week for early rotation. I should already be on my way to work. I had to call in because the asshole left. Thank God, the kids slept in this morning. I can't handle them yet."

Annabeth's eyes met Dean's. A flash of apology shone in

them for a moment. His brow dipped, wondering why. She didn't make him wait.

"Margot, here's what you're going to do. For now, anyway. When we hang up—which will be in just a minute —I want you to call your boss. Tell him what happened and ask for some time off. Then I want you to get online and book yourself and your girls on a plane to Columbus. You can stay with me for a few days. We'll get it figured out, I promise."

"I can't fly there. One, the wreckage of my life is here. And two, since Tad took half our money, I can't afford the tickets."

"I'll pay for them. You call your boss. I'll email you the ticket confirmation. Please, Margot. You're right in that you can't do this alone."

"But—"

"No buts. Dean's going to call a friend of his. He'll track Tad down, and we'll find out what his problem is."

Silence came over the line. Dean closed his eyes as he realized what Annabeth said. When he opened them, she looked at him with apology shining in hers.

"Sorry," she mouthed.

"Beth, how does Mr. Hottie already know to call a friend to help me?"

Dean's mouth twitched at the nickname. He turned an amused stare on Annabeth.

Cheeks turning red, Annabeth cleared her throat. "Because he's sitting here. On my bed. In just his jeans."

Margot's squeal filled the room.

Annabeth rolled her eyes. "Well, at least I've distracted you from your problems."

The other woman groaned. "For a split second, yes. Let's keep doing that. Does he look as good without the clothes as he does in them?"

Dean couldn't stop the bark of laughter that broke free.

"Oh, crap. I'm on speaker, aren't I?" Margot's embarrassment was clear in her tone.

"Yep." A broad smile spread over Annabeth's face, and she chuckled. "So, back to business. Do you agree with my plan?"

Margot sighed. "I guess." Some of the wobble returned to her voice. "Because I sure as hell don't know what else to do."

"We'll figure it out, Go-Go," Annabeth said.

Dean got up and grabbed his phone. He mimed calling and mouthed, "Asher." Annabeth nodded, and he left her to convince her friend to follow her plan.

In the hall, he opened his phone app, then frowned as the hour registered. He was two hours ahead of Asher. It was only going on five there.

But Asher liked to run in the mornings. If he wasn't up yet, he would be soon. He tapped Asher's name and lifted the phone to his ear.

"Why do you people always call so early? Time difference is a thing." Asher's sleepy voice came over the line.

"You know you were about to get up." Dean grinned.

"Just because I'm up doesn't mean I'm awake." He yawned to punctuate his point. "What do you need?"

"Can you look up a name for me?"

"Sure. Hang on."

Dean leaned against the wall, tucking his free hand under his arm while he waited for Asher to get up.

"Okay. What's the name?" Asher yawned again. "And you owe me coffee when you get back."

"Deal. The name is Tad Gaultier."

Asher hummed, typing. "Who's that?"

"Annabeth's friend's husband. She just called, completely hysterical, because he up and left all of a sudden."

"You're at Annabeth's? At this hour?"

Dean sighed. It seemed Annabeth wasn't the only one spilling the details of their private life. "Yeah."

Asher snickered. "Well, okay then. Anyway, back to this Tad fellow. What am I looking for?"

"His whereabouts. Margot wants to know why he left. He didn't explain it. She'll also need his location for their divorce proceedings. He left her divorce papers, but I imagine she'll have things in the document she wants to change. This came out of nowhere from what she said."

"Okay. Give me some time. I'll see what I can find."

"Sounds good. Thanks, Asher."

"Yep." He hung up.

Dean stuffed his phone into his back pocket and poked his head into the bedroom. Annabeth wasn't where he left her, and the bathroom door was shut. He scrubbed his hands over his face. So much for a good morning.

FORTY

"Dean?" Annabeth strode into the kitchen, heels clacking.

Dean glanced up from his spot at the island, taking in her put-together appearance. It was a sharp contrast to the wild woman who'd been naked in his arms a short time ago. The juxtaposition turned him on. He wanted to strip her down and turn the restrained doctor into the tigress again.

She stopped, her eyes heating, then raised a finger to point at him. "Stop looking at me like that. We don't have time."

"Sorry, honey. I can't help thinking how much I want to peel that severe suit off of you and find the hellcat who blew my brains last night."

She blushed and shook her head. "Later."

"Promise?" He gave her a sexy half-smile, injecting some growl into his voice.

"Oh, dear God, you have to stop." She paused in front of the refrigerator and yanked open the door. "I have to go to work."

Dean slid off the stool and stalked toward her. Just because they didn't have time for what he wanted, didn't mean he was letting her leave without a good morning kiss. Margot's hysterical phone call interrupted his plan to kiss Annabeth awake.

He stopped behind her and wrapped his arms around her waist, burying his nose in her hair behind her left ear. "Hi."

She let out a breathy moan and tipped her head, giving him better access. "Hi."

Nipping at her skin, he let his hands roam over her abdomen and up to her breasts. Cupping them through her suit, he kissed her long and deep. When she sagged against him and clutched his hair, he pulled back, breathing hard.

"Why did you have to do that?" She turned her liquid blue eyes on him. Accusation shone through the desire humming there.

He grinned. "Just making sure you don't break your promise."

She growled and narrowed her eyes, pushing him away. "Go over there and stop tempting me. I'm already running behind."

Chuckling, Dean moved away. She grabbed a yogurt smoothie and a container of grapes from the fridge, then opened the freezer and took out a plastic container. Setting the items down, she paused near the coffeemaker. "Oh, bless you. You started the coffee."

"Yep. We both needed it." While she'd showered and dressed, he'd run out to his car and retrieved his suitcase. After donning a shirt, he made coffee. He'd take a quick shower after she left.

Grabbing a travel mug, she poured herself a cup, then pulled a lunch bag from inside the pantry and filled it with the items she'd removed from the fridge and freezer.

"I need you to do something for me today."

Dean lifted his mug and looked at her over the top. "What's that?" He took a sip of the dark brew.

"Can you go to the store and get some things for Margot's

kids? I told her to just pack a suitcase of clothes and their car seats and not to worry about the rest."

Dean frowned. "What else is there?"

She blinked, then laughed. "Oh, so much. Babies have a lot of gear. A lot."

He lifted an eyebrow. "I have a tiny rental car, remember? I can't get that much in it."

She rolled her lips in and just gave him a look.

He groaned. "I guess I'll make more than one trip if I have to. What do I need to get?" He hated shopping. With a passion. This would be doubly worse, because he had no idea what to get. Baby stuff was as foreign to him as Mars.

Her bright smile soothed a bit of his angst about having to go shopping. "I'll make a list." She spun around and dug a small notepad and a pen out of a drawer.

Dean sipped his coffee while she wrote. When she flipped to the second page, he frowned. Finally, she finished and ripped the sheets off, handing them to him.

He glanced at them. Most of it made sense, but there was just a lot. And not all of it was gear. There was a grocery list on the second page. "Does it matter what brand I buy for any of this?" He glanced at her, watching her walk across the kitchen to her purse.

"No. Just don't get anything that feels cheap. Kids are hard on stuff, and I don't want to have to replace things after a day." She came back to where he sat. "Here. Take my debit card. I wrote the pin on the top of the first page." She held it out.

Dean glanced at it, then at her. "You're sure you want me to buy all this?"

"Yes. Babies—toddlers—need a lot of stuff. I don't know how long they're staying, and I want them to be comfortable and safe while they're here."

He sighed and took the card, looking at the list again. "Okay. But what will you do with all this when they leave?"

She shrugged, zipping up her lunch bag. "Some of it I'll keep in case they visit again. Like the gates and the other safety stuff. The food, obviously, we'll all eat. The other gear, though, I'll probably donate somewhere. Women's shelters always need baby stuff."

"Good point." He got up as she picked up her lunch bag and headed for the door. After she shrugged into her jacket, he snagged her around the waist and pulled her close. "You're a good friend, Annabeth."

A melancholic smile teased her lips. "Margot's the best friend I've ever had. And she's always been there for me. I'm only returning the favor."

He hummed and kissed her. "You're still a lovely human being." He dropped another quick peck on her lips. "Now, scoot. Before you're late for your first appointment." He let her go and spun her around, giving her a swat on the butt.

She tossed a naughty smile over her shoulder. "Do that again later?"

Dean's pants tightened at the thought. "Go. Before I do it now."

Laughing, she grabbed her purse and hurried out the door.

As the door closed, Dean adjusted himself and shook his head. Semi-aroused was going to be his new state of being.

Finishing his coffee, Dean took a quick shower and scarfed down some breakfast, then headed out. Navigating out of Annabeth's neighborhood, he turned onto the main road and was soon pulling into the parking lot at one of the big box stores. Before going inside, he opened his car's trunk and stared at the space. It had more room than he thought. Plus, he had the backseat and the front passenger seat.

With a nod, he shut the lid and locked the car, then went

inside. Grabbing a cart, he headed for the baby section. He'd get all that stuff first, then get the groceries Annabeth wanted.

What seemed like miles and miles of shelving stared back at him, holding every piece of baby equipment imaginable and in every color. He frowned. He didn't know if Margot's twins were boys or girls.

He called Annabeth.

"Hey, I'm about to head into a room."

"Sorry. I'll be quick. Are Margot's kids boys or girls? There are a lot of choices here." He eyed the shelves with trepidation again.

She chuckled. "They're girls. Identical twin girls. You don't have to buy everything in pink and purple, though. Gender neutral would probably be better. Then whatever I donate, anyone can use."

"Okay. Sounds good. Wish me luck."

Annabeth laughed again. "Consider it practice." Her laughter cut off. "I mean, um, in case you ever, um, you know."

It was Dean's turn to chuckle. "I get it. And for the record, I do want kids someday."

"Oh, um, that's good. I need to go. See you tonight." She hung up.

Dean narrowed his eyes and frowned at his phone. That was interesting. She hadn't said she wanted kids too. He'd figured she would with the job she had. A person should probably like kids if they were a pediatrician. But maybe she only liked other people's kids. He made a mental note to ask her about it later. He'd always imagined himself as a dad. If she didn't want kids, then he needed to do some thinking.

Putting his phone away, he forced himself to think about the task at hand. He took Annabeth's list from his pocket and looked it over, then glanced at the shelves. Swiping a hand over his face, he let out an exasperated sigh. "Okay. You can do this.

You're a damn SEAL. Shopping for baby stuff should be easy."

List in hand, he marched up to the first set of shelves. They were full of safety gear, like outlet covers and cabinet locks. He glanced at his list, then picked out middle-of-the-road options for the things Annabeth had listed.

Moving on, he added sippy cups and chunky spoons to the cart as well as several sets of plastic plates and bowls. Turning the corner, he found himself in the diaper aisle. "Holy crap." He eyed the rows of colorful boxes, then glanced at his list again. Annabeth had written down the brand and size. He just had to find it.

He stopped in front of the teal packages and scanned them for the size. His gaze landed on the five, and he reached for it. As he pulled it off the shelf, he saw a different kind in the same brand, also in a size five. "There's more than one type?" He groaned. "Hell."

A woman who'd entered the aisle a moment ago let out a soft laugh. "Do you need some help?"

Relief rushed through him. Judging by the baby seated in her cart, she knew her way around the diaper aisle. "Please."

"Is this your first child?" She sent him a sympathetic look as she walked over.

"No. I don't have any kids. My"—for a split second, he debated what to call Annabeth, then just went for it—"girlfriend's best friend is coming to town, and she needs most everything for her daughters. It's a long story. I have a list." He held up the notes covered with Annabeth's writing. "She has size five diapers down, and the brand, but there's more than one type." He gestured to the shelves. "Is one better than the other?"

"How old are the kids?"

"I'm not sure. Toddlers. They're twins."

"I'd get those." She pointed to the second kind. "They

don't leak. Like, at all. The others are better for when they're little and don't move around as much."

"Perfect." He put back the ones he held and grabbed the others. No pee dribbling on the floor sounded like a great idea.

"Did your girlfriend write down what kind of wipes to get?"

Dean glanced at the list, then turned it so she could see.

She nodded and turned around. "That's these. And I'd definitely get the fragrance-free ones. Some kids can be sensitive to perfumes, and since you don't know, it's better to be safe than sorry."

"That sounds good."

She set them in his cart. "What else is on your list?"

He handed it to her, welcoming the help. He hated shopping. So much.

"Most of this is pretty straightforward. Except for the baby gates. Don't get the pressure ones for the top of a staircase. They're too easy to push down. I know a woman whose baby did that and fell down the stairs. You want the kind you can screw into the wall."

"Is that on the packaging?"

"Yes. Here, I'll show you." She snatched a box of diapers off a shelf and put them in her cart, then turned around and led him to a different aisle. Stacks of baby gates lined a lower shelf.

"You want that one for the top of the stairs." She pointed to one.

Dean picked it up and put it in his cart.

"And that one's good for the bottom." She pointed to another one.

He added it to his cart. "What about for the kitchen doorway? I need two. One for either side of the island." Annabeth had listed those separately.

"Just a cheap gate will work." She picked up a wooden gate and handed it to him. "It's just a barrier."

He eyed it, wondering if it was big enough to go between the island and the wall. It said forty-two inches on the packaging. He pictured the opening, then shrugged. It was probably wide enough. If not, he'd return them and find something else. "Okay." He reached past her and grabbed another, then set both in the cart. "Thank you for your help. I'm lost."

She offered him a bright smile. "You're welcome." She held out his list. "Most everything else on there is self-explanatory. Playpens are over by the cribs and strollers. I think you have most everything else except that and toys. And the toys have age ranges on them. Probably anything between twelve and twenty-four months would be appropriate."

Dean took the list and thanked her again. "I really appreciate the help."

"Not a problem. I hope everything works out for your friend."

"Me too." He smiled and lifted a hand in farewell as she turned her cart and headed off.

Feeling more accomplished now that most of the hard stuff was in his cart, he headed over to the baby furniture. It only took him a moment to find the playpens. He picked out two that were moderate in price and slid them onto the bottom rack of the cart. With that done, he found two booster seats near the high chairs and stacked them beside the diapers.

Eyeing the cart, he shook his head. He'd need a second cart for the groceries.

FORTY-ONE

Annabeth let herself in after work and smiled as she saw her mom at the stove in the kitchen. "Hi. That smells good."

Katrina glanced over and returned her smile. "I needed comfort food. Dean was nice enough to go out this afternoon and get me what I needed to make chili." She glanced at the door leading out of the kitchen, then back at Annabeth. "You need to hang on to him. He went back out after shopping all morning for those things for Margot and her daughters. He's a good one."

Smiling, but not commenting, Annabeth walked deeper into the kitchen. "Where is he, anyway?"

"Upstairs, trying to install that baby gate."

"I think I'll go help him."

Katrina gave her a knowing look. "You do that."

Annabeth's cheeks heated. She'd tried to be quiet last night, but she knew she'd failed. She needed to work on that.

Without a word, Annabeth left the kitchen. Her footsteps slowed as she entered the living room, taking in the piles of baby gear now decorating the space. When she gave him the list, she didn't think about how much room it would all take up. Part of it was the packaging. Everything was still in boxes and bags.

She passed by it all and put a foot on the first step, looking up.

Oh, dear Lord.

She grabbed the handrail and locked her knees. Dean crouched at the top of the stairs, a drill in one hand, a screw in his mouth, and an intense look of concentration on his face as he attached a bracket to the wall.

Annabeth cleared her throat. "Hi. Want some help?"

He looked down and smiled, flashing his dimples and making her clutch the railing a little harder. He took the screw from between his teeth. "Sure. You can hold stuff while I mount brackets." He picked up the instruction sheet at his feet. "This thing looks simple, but it has a lot of small parts, and my big fingers get in the way. I got one on." He pointed to the bracket on the wall near the floor. "But it wasn't easy."

"I know. Manufacturers don't always think about the people using their products when they make the stuff." She walked up the stairs and surveyed the array of parts strewn over the carpet.

"Hold this bracket there while I put this other screw in, would you?"

Annabeth leaned down and moved the bracket into place, lining it up with the marks he made on the wall. He screwed it into place, then shifted, turning to do the other side.

"So, did you find everything I sent you out for?"

"Yeah. A lady in the diaper aisle took pity on me and helped me pick out a few things."

Annabeth laughed. "You needed help?"

He glanced at her, arching an eyebrow. "Have you ever been in the baby section? There's a lot of crap there. And that brand of diapers you told me to buy had two different styles. I hope I bought the right ones. The lady said the one kind was better at controlling leaks, so I bought those. She helped with these gates too. I didn't know there were different kinds for the top of the stairs versus what you just put in a regular doorway."

"That's why I wrote them separately on the list."

"But you didn't explain that. I don't know anything about babies, Annabeth. I have a sister, but she's not that much younger than me, and none of my friends have kids."

She picked up the bracket and put it on the wall over the pencil marks. "Yet you want your own?"

"Someday." He walked closer to it on his knees. "Do you?"

She pressed her lips together and sucked in a breath through her nose. The question sounded casual, but she knew he'd noticed she hadn't replied earlier when he said he wanted kids. She'd been blindsided by the image of a tiny, dark-haired baby nestled against his bare chest and too stunned to respond. She knew she'd need more time than she had right then to process that, so she'd just ended the conversation.

But now, she'd had time to think about it. The image still rendered her speechless, but she liked the idea.

"I want kids, yes. It's just not something I think about much right now. I haven't had a man in my life since college."

"Oh. Were there many of those?"

"Men?"

He nodded, not looking at her. He picked up the bracket screws and set one in the hole in the metal.

"Dean, are you trying to ask me how many men I've slept with?"

"Maybe." He tossed her a crooked smile. "Or maybe I'm hoping to figure out where I stack up." He attached the screw.

She gaped at him. He had to ask that? "Uh, the top. Miles above anyone else. And there have only been two others. I dated a guy in undergrad, then had a brief relationship during med school."

"What happened? Why didn't either of them work out?"

Annabeth waited until he attached the second screw to talk. "The first relationship ended because we graduated and just weren't committed enough to try a long-distance thing. The second I broke off. I got taken in by a pretty face. He just wanted to cheat off of me. At the time, school was grueling, and I was too tired to see the signs. It was Margot who figured it out. I don't know how long I'd have stayed with him if she hadn't pointed out a few things." She grabbed the bottom bracket off the floor and held it to the wall.

"Tell me more about her husband. Has he ever done anything like this before? Not the divorce thing, but just taking off with no notice." Dean put in the first screw.

"No. Never. Tad's practical. And a planner. He was in med school with us. When he and Margot started dating, he wrote out this plan for when they would get engaged, then married, then have kids. The twins were a surprise, though."

"Is that why he left? Because they threw off his plan?" He attached the second screw.

"No. Tad loves those babies." She shook her head and dropped her hand. "That's why this makes no sense."

"Well, if there's anything to find, Asher will find it." Dean stood and picked up the gate.

"I hope so. I just can't imagine why he took off like that." And she didn't want to speculate. It wouldn't give her any answers and would just make her wonder more, which would make her more frustrated.

She bent down and lined up the bottom of the gate with the bracket. "So, how about you? How many women have there been besides me?"

His lips curled up. "More than two."

Annabeth rolled her eyes. "Not an answer, Dean."

He chuckled. "Four. And they've all been relationships. I don't do one-night stands." He held her gaze.

Annabeth read the meaning behind the look, and her inner self did a little dance. She hadn't been looking for a relationship; and when she welcomed him into her life, she hadn't been hoping to start one. But now that he was here, and they had, she wanted to continue things and see where they went. Her body, it seemed, had won over her mind. "Good. I don't, either."

His gaze heated. An answering heat pooled in her core. She wished her mom wasn't downstairs. She'd be open to getting rug burn on her back and knees.

Dean let out a low grunt. "Later. We'll make sure this isn't a one-night stand later."

She bit her lip and nodded.

He swooped in and kissed her hard, then backed up. "Let's get this thing finished. Before I forget we aren't alone."

Forty-Two

Dean stepped out back and shut the sliding glass door, welcoming the relative peace and quiet of the backyard. Margot's kids were loud. He didn't mind the rug rats running around, but he needed a minute to let his ears stop ringing.

Scrubbing his hands over his face, he inhaled a deep breath and let it out slowly. Twin sixteen-month-olds probably weren't the best introduction to small children.

The sliding door opened, and Dean glanced back to see Annabeth smiling at him from the doorway.

"Too much?"

He gave her a sheepish smile. "Was it obvious? I just needed to take a quick break from the yelling. How do two tiny humans make so much noise?"

She stepped outside and shut the door. "It's a new environment. Their routine has been wildly disrupted. It's not surprising they're protesting bedtime." She walked over and straight into his arms. "They'll calm down soon. Sleep will eventually overcome even the strongest-willed child."

"Hmm. Is that the doctor's opinion?"

She laughed. "It is."

He leaned down and pressed a kiss to her lips. Need ignited in his veins. Dean lifted his head. "Once everyone goes to bed, you want to take another shower?"

Annabeth stood on her toes and pressed her body to his. "Only if you promise to spank me again."

It took everything he had not to back her up to the wall and test how distracted everyone else inside was. Instead, he clutched the back of her head and kissed her again.

The crack of a branch and a soft curse, followed by leaves rustling, doused his desire. He lifted his head and looked back, staring at the trees,

"Did you hear that?" He put some space between them, still staring at the rear of the yard. It wasn't completely dark yet, but the light was low enough he couldn't make out anything in the shadows.

"Yeah. What was that?"

"I don't know." He took his phone out and turned on the flashlight, aiming it toward the trees. Annabeth's house bordered a thin wooded area that hid a stream and separated her property from the homes on the other side.

Something moved, and the shrubbery jostled. A quick "Ow!" sounded. It was enough to jolt Dean into action. "Hey!" He ran through the grass toward the tree line. "Who's there?"

Whoever it was took off running. Dean glanced over his shoulder. "Call the police." Annabeth nodded, and he turned around, dashing after the intruder.

Using his phone to light the way, Dean ran into the woods. He caught sight of a hooded figure running away. "Stop!"

The man—and he was sure it was a man—turned left and splashed through the stream, heading for the next street. Jumping the creek, Dean ran the twenty yards to the edge of the woods and exited into the neighbor's backyard. The hooded figure hopped the low fence that rimmed the property and separated it from the woods. He dashed across the grass, dodging children's outdoor toys, then jumped the fence again into the side yard. Pocketing his phone, Dean followed. They raced between the houses and onto the street.

A car whizzed by, nearly hitting Dean. Its horn blared. He ignored it and kept going. Ahead, the man darted between two more houses. Running faster, Dean ran up the sidewalk and turned into the yard. A black hole met him. Cursing, he took out his phone and shined his light into the abyss. Fences on either side greeted him. At the rear of the properties, he could see the backyards of the houses behind the two he stood between.

He jogged forward, listening to hear movement in either yard. All was quiet. At the end of the fences, he glanced both ways. The yards were empty.

"Dammit!"

Turning around, he started back to Annabeth's, keeping his head on a swivel. He could hear sirens now. Maybe the police would have better luck. He wasn't so sure, though. Whoever the man was, he bolted that way deliberately. There was no hesitation when he turned. Dean would bet the man had left a car parked nearby.

He took the long way home, not wanting to compromise any evidence in the woods. He also hoped he'd catch the guy walking to a car on the outskirts of the neighborhood. But the sidewalks were empty. When he turned onto Annabeth's street, two squad cars sat in front of her driveway with their lights on.

Dean jogged up the driveway and went inside through the front door. Katrina spotted him first.

"Oh! There you are. Did you find the guy?"

"No. I lost him between some houses on the street behind

us." He looked at the officer who'd taken note of his arrival. The man walked over.

"You the boyfriend?"

"Yes, sir. Annabeth and I were out back when we heard someone in the woods. I ran after him, but lost him between the second and third houses on the left side of the road behind us."

"It was a man?"

"Yes. Black hoodie, dark jeans, dark shoes. I never saw his face. He took off and didn't look back."

"Okay." The officer radioed that information to dispatch. "Do you know why someone would be watching the house?"

"There could be several reasons. It could be a reporter, trying to dig up information on a story about Johnathan Cassidy. It's also possible it could be someone trying to find out what we know about Annabeth's sister's death. Or it could be unrelated to either of those and be Margot's estranged husband, or even someone spying on Katrina for her soon-to-be ex."

The officer blinked and tapped a finger against his leg. "Okay, then. Miss Swenson said something similar. You guys are sure in the thick of things."

Dean's mouth flattened. "Tell me about it," he muttered. A thought occurred to him. "Has Noah Reitman made bail?"

Frowning, the officer tipped his head. "I don't know. Why?"

"You know who he is, yes?"

"Of course. He's been a pain in the department's backside for years."

"He attacked Annabeth in her garage last week, trying to get the story of her sister's death out of her. It could have been him hiding in the woods."

The officer pursed his lips, then nodded. "I'll check."

"Thank you."

"Dean?" Annabeth walked inside with another officer.

"Excuse me," Dean mumbled and walked toward her.

She hurried into his arms. He kissed the top of her head.

"You didn't catch him, did you?" She tipped her head back.

"No."

She scrunched her nose. "I wonder who it was? And what they wanted?"

He didn't know, but he was extra glad he'd come back here after he talked to Donna Taggart instead of flying home.

The next hour passed in a blur as the officers took their formal statements and swept through the woods. Since no one was hurt, they did a brief canvass, then said a unit would come out in the morning and check for further evidence in the daylight. They'd also discovered that Reitman made bail several days ago. It was possible the lurker in the woods was him.

Thankfully, Margot's twins slept through the ruckus, leaving the house quiet once the police left.

"I'm going to bed." Katrina waved on her way upstairs. "Goodnight."

"Me too. It's been a day." Margot followed her.

"Night," Annabeth called.

Dean lifted a hand, then looked at her. Light bounced off her toffee-colored hair and highlighted her face. She was so damn pretty.

He felt lust stirring in his gut, pushing away the adrenaline and worry of the last hour or so. Lifting an eyebrow, he leaned closer. "You still game for that shower?"

A slow, sexy smile spread over her face. "That sounds like a nice, relaxing distraction. You still promise to spank me?"

He spun her around and smacked her butt. "That's just the start."

FORTY-THREE

"Fas!" Emily yelled, laughing.

Dean chuckled and spun the toddler around faster in a circle. Margot was busy making the kids dinner, so he was keeping little Emily and her sister Lily occupied. He'd been taking turns with the girls, flying them around the room like an airplane. Lily liked the dips, but Emily liked the speed.

"I'm really glad you did this before they ate."

At the sound of Margot's voice, he gathered Emily close and turned to smile at the girl's mother. "Yeah, after dinner might be disastrous."

She laughed. "Definitely. Their food is ready." She glanced down at Lily, who sat by the couch with a plastic phone in her hand. "Come on, Lily-billy. It's time to eat."

The little girl got up, phone still in her hand, and ran toward her mother. Margot picked her up, then headed for the kitchen. Dean followed with Emily.

"Fas? Fas!" Emily screeched in his arms, protesting the end of their game.

"We'll play again tomorrow, Miss Emmy. It's time for your dinner."

The girl shrieked and shook her head. "Fas."

Margot sent him a look. "You've started something."

He sighed. "Yeah."

Together, they wrangled the girls into their booster seats. Lily went easily, but Emily didn't settle until the plate of chopped chicken and peas landed in front of her.

"Distraction is the best technique for a stubborn toddler." Margot grinned.

Annabeth walked out of the pantry with a box of pasta, a jar of spaghetti sauce, and a loaf of French bread. "Don't lie. You bribe them all the time."

"Which is a distraction." Margot's smile widened.

Annabeth chuckled and put her load on the counter. "True."

Dean shook his head. He was learning a lot about young children—and these two women. Their banter was lively, but never mean. "So, I take it we're having spag—" His phone buzzed in his pocket, and he stopped. "Sorry." Digging it out, he glanced at it. "It's Jordan. On FaceTime." He looked at the women. Annabeth nodded for him to answer it. He swiped the icon. Jordan's face and upper body appeared on the screen. Behind him, he could see Max's garage. "Hey, what's up?"

"A lot."

"Oh?" Dean walked over to Margot and Annabeth, so they could see. "Jordan, this is Annabeth, and her friend Margot." He pointed to them in turn.

"Hello." Jordan offered them a friendly smile.

They waved back.

"So, what did you find out?" Dean asked.

"That someone seriously screwed up—or covered something up—all those years ago."

Annabeth sucked in a breath.

The front door opened and closed. "Hello?" Katrina's voice carried from the front of the house.

"In here, Mom," Annabeth yelled.

"Hang on," Dean told Jordan. "Katrina just got back." She'd had a late-afternoon meeting with her attorneys.

Katrina walked in, the smile on her face fading as she took in their dour expressions. "Is everything okay?"

Dean nodded. "Jordan's on the phone. He found something in Wendy's car."

"Oh." She walked forward, scooting in next to her daughter.

"It's not just Wendy's car I have news on. Asher and Ford are here too." He shifted the phone to show the other two men in the garage with him, then walked toward Wendy's mangled car up on jacks. "I went all over this thing. There were cuts to her brake line and her power steering. And they weren't even disguised. They were completely obvious. Any rookie mechanic could have found them and been able to tell you, 'Yep. A knife did that.'" He shook his head.

Katrina covered her mouth. Annabeth put a hand on her shoulder and pressed her lips together.

"I also found dried blood."

Dean frowned. "That we knew was there. It's all over the seat. And the door."

"Not there." Ford came into view. "It was on the power steering line. Whoever cut it nicked themselves. I called our local police, and they sent a crime scene unit over at my request to swab it. I called in a favor and had it sent to a private lab. It'll still take a couple weeks to get a DNA profile back on it—if they can get one—but it's faster than the national lab here."

"Wow, that's great," Dean said. "Did you find anything else?"

"Not on the car. But Asher found some stuff on Pierce." Ford moved as Asher stepped forward.

Dean glanced at Katrina and Annabeth. They both stared at the phone screen, frowns on their faces.

"A month before Wendy's death, Cassidy Global filed a lawsuit against Swenson Development. A week after her death, they dropped it."

Katrina closed her eyes and tipped her head back. Annabeth muttered under her breath.

"What was the lawsuit for?" Dean asked.

"They alleged Swenson defrauded them on a deal for a warehouse. From the way the lawsuit sounded, they were also looking at criminal embezzlement charges. He was looking at some serious problems."

"Okay," Margot said. "But how would he know that Johnathan tampered with Wendy's car? Who in Medina looked the other way?"

A short silence met her question, then Ford spoke.

"Asher, can you check financials for the officers and crime scene technicians involved in Wendy's case? See if any of them had a sudden large deposit?"

Asher's eyebrows rose, and he rocked back on his heels, crossing his arms. "Maybe. That far back, I'm not sure what I'll find. Banks are only required to keep financial records for five years, and most don't keep anything after seven."

Dean uttered a curse. "This has been our problem all along. It's just been too long. A lot of the records are gone." He swiped a hand down his face and sighed. "Okay. Where was the lawsuit filed?"

"New York," Asher replied.

"Can you contact the police there and see if they have anything on any possible criminal charges and what might have happened with those?" Dean asked.

"Already did. They're looking."

"Good." Dean let out a low groan. "Is there anything else?"

"Yes and no," Asher said. "Margot, I checked into your husband. Did you know he opened several credit cards in the last few months and maxed them all out?"

She gasped. "What? No. How much?"

"A hundred and fifty thousand dollars."

She groaned. "This is a nightmare. Do you know what he bought with it?"

"No, but I can guess. They're big purchases at places like Walmart, Target, and Best Buy. I'm thinking large electronics."

"We don't have any new electronics."

"Does your husband gamble?" Jordan asked.

Margot's frown deepened. "Not that I know of. Why?"

"Because he could be buying the electronics, then selling them to get cash to pay his bookie. My dad did that. Screwed my mom over big time, because he put the cards in her name. There were some in mine too. Those got wiped, though, when he was convicted of fraud. I was only ten when he opened the accounts in my name. Hers eventually got erased, too, but it took some time."

"Did you check my name and the girls' names?" Margot asked.

"I did yours, but not your daughters'. I'll do that today," Asher said. "I'll also put a freeze on their credit, so he can't open any in their names. Do you want me to freeze yours too?"

She bit her lip. "Should we?"

"Not necessarily. I can put a monitor on it. You should have that, anyway."

"Let's do that, then. I don't know what's going to happen in the next few weeks to months, and I might need to take out a loan."

"Sounds good. I'll keep an eye on it."

"Okay, thank you."

"Not a problem. Also, your husband isn't currently using

his credit cards or his debit card. I haven't been able to find any trace of him since he accessed your bank account on Wednesday."

Margot rolled her eyes. "He won't need to for a little while. He took out about ten thousand in cash."

"Have you talked to an attorney?" Ford asked.

She nodded. "Before I left Texas. They have a copy of the divorce papers and are working on things."

"Good. I'm sorry this is happening, but I hope it gets resolved quickly for you. My team and I will do everything we can to help you."

She nodded, moisture gathering in her eyes. "Thank you."

Annabeth wrapped an arm around Margot's shoulders and gave her a side hug.

Margot sniffed and wiped at her face. "If you find him, you might want to put a freeze on all my money, so I don't get on a plane and go strangle him. He better have a damn good reason for this."

Dean agreed.

A yell and the sound of plastic hitting the floor drew his attention.

"What was that?" Ford asked.

"Our resident holy terror." Dean chuckled and turned the camera so his friends could see Emily. She'd dumped her food on the island top and thrown her plate and spoon on the floor.

Margot sighed. "Well, at least she's still eating."

FORTY-FOUR

"I'm heading out."

Annabeth looked up as her nurse, Kim, poked her head into the office. "Okay." She smiled at the woman. "Have a good night."

"I plan to. The hubby's taking me out for our anniversary."

"Congratulations. That's great."

"Yep. Fifteen years. Seems like a lifetime. How are things going with you and the biker?"

Annabeth frowned. "Biker? What biker?"

"Bearded, leather-jacket man. He's not a biker?"

"Oh, you mean Dean. No. He just likes leather and his beard." She did too. She crossed her legs beneath her desk, remembering the feel of that beard on her inner thighs just last night.

A knowing smile lit Kim's face. "You're blushing. That's good. Is this a fling or something more?"

Annabeth twiddled her pen. "Hopefully, something more. We've kind of talked about it, but it's still pretty new."

"Well, I wish you good luck. I hope he's as nice as he is

gorgeous, and that someday, he's taking you out for your fifteenth wedding anniversary too."

Annabeth chuckled. "He is. And I hope so too." She'd spent some time thinking about where things were heading with Dean. They'd had the kids talk last week, but since then, hadn't broached the subject of a long-term relationship. She knew she wanted to make it work. He was like no one she'd ever met. It was nuts how fast her mindset had shifted. She went from completely against a relationship to not being able to imagine her life without him in the span of a week. It was wild, but it didn't feel wrong. On the contrary, it felt extraordinarily right. And also a little scary. She had gone from nothing to the verge of being in love in just days. It would be scary for anyone. In the quiet moments over the last week, she'd tried to sort out her emotions as well as work through the changes to her life that would be necessary if things worked out with him. They'd touched on the subject of one of them moving, but hadn't said anything else. She'd been contemplating what that might look like. It was something they needed to discuss before things went much further.

"Good. Well, I'm off. Have fun with your not-biker."

"I will." Annabeth raised a hand and smiled. "Have a good night."

"Yep." Kim waggled her fingers and left.

Hurrying through the rest of her paperwork, Annabeth shut down her computer, then donned her jacket and grabbed her purse. Locking up, she exited into the parking lot and headed for her car. She was glad it wasn't dark yet. That would change in another month or so. She hoped they put her sister's case to rest by then. She was tired of looking over her shoulder.

Safely ensconced in her car, she locked the doors, then texted Dean that she was on her way home. He'd been coming to meet her every day and follow her, but today, he'd texted just as she finished with her last patient and said he was stuck in the tailback from an accident on the highway. She'd opted not to wait on him. No one had been hanging around her office, so she felt safe enough.

Pulling out of the lot, Annabeth kept one eye on the road ahead and another on the cars behind her. If any of them acted even remotely suspicious, she was heading for the nearest police station. Just because she felt safe enough to drive home without Dean on her tail, didn't mean she was stupid. This murder business was serious, and she was taking it that way.

Because of the accident, Annabeth decided to take the surface streets home. It added fifteen to twenty minutes to her drive, but that was better than the freeway backup. Hopefully, Dean could make it to the next exit and get off soon, if he hadn't already.

Humming along to the radio, she glanced in her mirror. The black BMW sedan, three cars back, changed lanes. She knew that car.

Annabeth pushed the button on her steering wheel to activate the voice commands. "Call Dean."

"Calling Dean," the voice assistant said.

The phone rang through the car, and he picked up a moment later.

"Hey, babe. I'm off the freeway and headed back to the house. You home?"

"Not yet. There's a black BMW behind me. Isn't that what Reitman drives?"

"Christ. Yes. Is it him?"

"I can't tell. He's too far back. I'm not even sure the car is following me. I know other people besides him drive that kind of car, but I'm paranoid." She glanced in the mirror. The car was still in the other lane, but only two cars back now.

"Make a few nonsensical turns. See if it follows."

"Okay. Hang on." At the next intersection, Annabeth turned right. The BMW cut across the lanes and followed her.

"Well, crap. I think he is." She made another right-hand turn into a neighborhood. The car followed.

Heart thumping in her ears now, she turned again, this time seeking an exit to the main road. She might need to go around the block. And she hoped this wasn't one of those neighborhoods with a bunch of dead-end streets.

"Where are you? I'll come to you."

She caught sight of a street sign and read him the name. "I'm trying to get back out to the main road, though."

"That's fine. Keep driving."

Annabeth drove around the block, finding the road she came in on. At the stop sign, she saw the black car coming up behind her. She glanced to her left. There was a line of traffic coming, but she didn't want to be a sitting duck. In the smallest possible space she thought she could make it out onto the road safely, she turned. A dark blue Range Rover blew its horn at her, but she didn't care. She stepped on the gas and drove on. A quick glance in her mirror showed the black BMW pulling out well behind her now.

"I'm on the main road again. At the next light, I'm going to turn around to go back the other way. I'm headed away from home right now."

"Okay. That car still following you?"

"Yes, but it's further behind. I might be able to lose it."

"If it's Reitman, it won't matter. He knows where you live."

She hadn't thought of that. It didn't fill her with comfort. Or make sense. "Why is he following me, then? He could just wait at my house."

"I don't know. Maybe he's hoping he can catch you when you stop somewhere. I'm heading for your neighborhood, and I'll wait on the main street into it, then follow you the rest of the way. Make sure he doesn't try to run inside the garage when you pull in."

Memories of the first time he cornered her in there surfaced, and her scalp tingled with remembered pain. She suppressed a shudder. She didn't want that either. "Okay."

Twenty-five nerve-wracking minutes later, she turned into her neighborhood. Dean's little silver car sat waiting at the curb when she made the turn. He pulled in behind her and followed her home. Annabeth took shallow breaths, not relaxing until the garage door closed behind her car.

Her hands shook, and she leaned forward, resting her head on the steering wheel for a moment. She gulped in air until she felt steady enough to get out. The interior car light came on as she opened the door. Dragging her briefcase and purse across the seat, she climbed out and shut the door. Halfway to the interior door, it opened, and Dean walked through.

"You okay?"

She nodded and let him enfold her in his strong arms. "I'm fine. A little shaky, but no worse for wear. Did you see the car?"

He nodded. "He must have recognized me. He turned around at the first intersection, then left."

"Was it Reitman?"

"I think so. I only got a partial plate when he turned around. But the first couple letters were the same. I'll call the detective assigned to your case here in a few minutes and report it. How about we go inside?"

"Yes, please."

He took her hand and led her in, helping her out of her jacket and taking her things. Annabeth walked straight to the cabinet next to the fridge and grabbed a glass. She filled it with ice-cold water and took a sip. The chill helped push away some of her fear, taking the shakes with it. She sipped on the water as she listened to Dean report the incident. When he was done, she glanced around, noting the quiet.

"Where is everyone?" The house hadn't been this silent in days.

"Your mom decided to go out for the evening, and Margot took the kids to get a few groceries. The girls were wound up after they ate, so she wanted to burn some energy off of them. They should be back soon, though."

"Oh, okay. I guess we should think about dinner. Or did you already eat?"

He shook his head. "I was waiting for you. We could do Indian, again. Or throw something together here if you'd rather not go back out."

"I'd rather stay in. Being followed once today is enough." She ran her fingers through the hair by her face and blew out a breath.

Dean sauntered closer and put his hands on her hips, then turned to lean back against the counter. He pulled her into his body. "How about we grab some finger foods—fruit, cheese, maybe some peanut butter and some pretzels—and the carton of ice cream in the freezer and go upstairs?"

She bit her lip. "I should probably say hello to Margot and my mom, though. When they get back. It's a bit early to stay in my room all night."

"We can come down later." His eyes heated. "Cheese and peanut butter won't replace all the calories I intend to burn."

Her stomach did a flip as her mind conjured up all the ways he could burn those calories. "If you're trying to distract me, it's working."

That dimpled smile she'd come to love appeared. "Good. I told you that you wouldn't need a book." He pushed her back. "You get the fridge stuff; I'll find the peanut butter and pretzels."

Smiling, Annabeth reached for the fridge door.

Her phone rang.

"No," she groaned. Letting go of the handle, she crossed to

where Dean left her purse and fished out her phone. She frowned at the Boston area code on the screen.

"Who is it?" Dean asked.

"I'm not sure." She slid her finger over the screen and answered it, making sure to put it on speaker. "Hello?"

"Annabeth? It's Stella."

"Oh, hi." Annabeth frowned and looked at Dean. "How are you?"

"I'm fine. Listen, um, so I have something to tell you, and I don't want you to be upset. I—well, I lied to you. I had my reasons, which I've come to recognize were completely selfish. None of what happened back then matters now."

Annabeth's frown only deepened. "What are you talking about?"

"I have Wendy's diary."

All the air left Annabeth's lungs.

"I didn't tell you when you were here because I wanted to look at it again. She wrote some things about me—" She stopped and sighed. "Well, they didn't show me in my best light. But none of what happened then can affect me now except to embarrass me. There are some things about Johnathan and Will you should read. I put it in the mail this afternoon. It should reach you tomorrow. I sent it to your practice. I couldn't find your home address online. Your number was listed, but not your address."

"Oh, okay. Thank you."

"I'm sorry, again. I know I shouldn't have lied, but—"

"No. It's all right. I'm just grateful you did the right thing. Thank you, Stella."

"Of course. I hope it helps. And I swear, I don't have anything else of hers. I only took the diary because I didn't want anyone else to read what she wrote about me. And you know, she had a lot of dirt on a lot of people. I'd read the whole thing if I were you."

"Okay. I'll definitely do that. And I won't share what she said about you."

"I appreciate that. Will you let me know when you find out what happened to her? Despite what she wrote and our sometimes—fractious—friendship, I cared about your sister."

"I know you did. And yes. I'll let you know."

"Thank you."

They said goodbye and hung up.

Annabeth turned wide eyes on Dean. He stared back at her, equally surprised.

"Well, that was unexpected."

"Yeah. I wonder what it says?"

"I don't know, but it's bound to be interesting. Hopefully, between that and the evidence Jordan found in your sister's car, it'll be enough to reopen her case."

She nodded. For the first time in years, Annabeth had real hope they could prove her sister was murdered and put the person responsible behind bars.

FORTY-FIVE

Dean cracked one eye open as Annabeth flopped over onto her other side. That was the third time she'd changed position in ten minutes.

He pushed up on his elbow. "Are you okay?"

She rolled onto her back to look up at him. Her eyes glittered with the reflection of the small amount of light coming in through the window.

"I can't sleep."

"I can tell." She'd slept fitfully all night, which meant he had too.

"I'm sorry." She sighed. "I can't stop wondering what's in that diary." She rolled her head side-to-side on her pillow. "I've believed for so long that she didn't just crash, that it's hard to believe we're on the cusp of figuring out what exactly happened. I mean, I know she didn't write about the crash, obviously. But if she had an argument with Johnathan the evening before and wrote about that, well, it proves motive."

"It does. But what should really be keeping you awake is whether the DNA Jordan found will match one of the

Cassidy brothers. That's what will truly convict them. Motive is great, but you can't convict someone on motive."

She sighed again. "I know. But—" She stopped and shook her head. "I don't know. It's just different, you know? Knowing what my sister was thinking and feeling. And knowing how Johnathan reacted. Even thinking about it makes me want to punch him."

Dean chuckled. "Punching people is bad. And you have such dainty hands, you'd probably break every bone in them." He lifted her hand and kissed her fingers.

"I don't care. I'd welcome the pain if I got to break his nose." She growled. "Sorry. I'm not a violent person, but he just—" She stopped and growled again, louder, then flapped her free hand. "But, anyway, let's change the subject."

"You want to keep talking? Babe, it's three-thirty."

"I'm awake, so yes. Let's talk about us."

The thumb he'd been running over her hand stilled. "Us?"

"Yes." She sat up and turned on the bedside lamp. "What happens to us when this ends? When we get all the evidence and all the players have been arrested. You don't live here. I don't live there. What happens?"

Dean blinked in the light as his eyes adjusted. That same thought had been swirling through his head. He'd entertained it, but never given it full brainpower. "Well, we have a couple of options. One, is we continue seeing each other, but long distance."

She wrinkled her nose. He didn't much like that idea, either.

"Option two is one we sort of mentioned; one of us moves. My life is easier to pick up and change, so it would probably be me." He could build a private investigation business here just as easily as in Costa Rica. He could also put his mechanical skills to work and find a job as a mechanic. He'd have to get a few qualifications, but it wouldn't be too difficult.

"Or I could look into starting a practice down there. They have a nationalized system, but doctors are able to practice privately. I could do both. Your area is rural, isn't it? I looked up Golfito when it was mentioned on the news."

Dean blinked, too stunned to speak. Finally, he was able to hang on to a thought long enough to force some words out. "You want to move down there?"

She lifted a shoulder. "Why not? I can be a doctor there as well as here. It'll take some work, but it's doable. And I'll probably do more good in a rural setting than in my suburban practice. There is no shortage of healthcare options for the people around here." She laid a hand over his. "I don't want you to have to leave the place that healed you."

He did love it down there. But was it home?

Dean glanced away, thinking about how he felt about the place he'd laid his head for the last year. He was certainly more comfortable there than anywhere else. Arizona wasn't home. Not anymore. Sure, his mom and sister were there, but he didn't have a burning desire to live near them. And even Costa Rica he could live without.

The heat of Annabeth's hand registered, along with something else. It punched him in the face and left him reeling. Home wasn't a place; it was people. That's why he loved Costa Rica so much. His friends—they were family. But no place or person held a candle to where he was right now. To the woman who had invaded his thoughts from the moment he laid eyes on her and steadily worked her way into his heart and soul.

"I'm sorry. Is it too soon? I know we've only known each other a few weeks. But I've never felt like this."

Hearing the worry in her voice, Dean looked at her. "No,

honey. It's not too soon." He raised a hand and cupped the side of her face. "I love you. Home to me is wherever you are."

Her pretty blue eyes went wide, and her mouth dropped open. She stared at him for a moment, then launched herself at him. He caught her with a laugh.

"I hope that's not too soon to say." He pushed her hair back to stare into her eyes.

She shook her head, tousling her caramel hair. "No." A slow, confident smile slid over her face. "I love you too."

He answered her smile with one of his own and threaded his fingers into her hair. "So, what do we do now?" He chuckled. "I've never been in this situation."

"You've never been in love?" She touched his face, tracing the edge of his beard.

"Not really. And definitely not like this."

Her smile turned satisfied. "I like that idea. That I'm the first. You are for me too. My undergrad boyfriend—I thought I loved him, but if I had, letting him go wouldn't have been so easy. I can't imagine saying goodbye to you."

He nuzzled her neck. "Good."

She let out a breathy moan, and Dean felt himself stir. Knowing where this was headed, he gently pushed her back, laying her on the bed, then reached for the condoms in the nightstand.

"I'm going to make love to you, like a man who loves his woman does."

"Oh, it's different, is it?" She gave him a crooked smile.

"Damn straight."

Forty-Six

Annabeth let herself sink into the mattress while Dean ran gentle fingers over her body. He left a trail of fiery goosebumps in his wake and stoked the embers flaring to life in her core. They'd made love every night for over a week, including just hours ago, but this time felt different. He made her feel cherished every time they were together, but now she knew she was loved. Words shouldn't matter, but they did.

She still could scarcely believe he'd said he loved her. Or that she'd said it back. But once he did, the thoughts that had been swirling through her head all week coalesced into a giant, flashing neon sign that said, "I love you too!" and she hadn't been able to hold the words back. Their time together this week—not just in bed, but simply talking—and seeing him with her mother and Margot's girls told her all she needed to know about him. He was one of the good ones. Her heart had recognized that from the beginning. It had just taken her brain a little longer to catch up.

His soft beard teased the skin of her ribcage as he kissed her breasts, pulling her back to the present. She bit her lip, holding in the moan that wanted to break free. A little whimper escaped. Dean nipped at the skin just below her nipple, then drew the tip into his mouth. She speared her hands into his hair and held on tight. He tugged and played with her breasts, sending heat through her body and making her wet.

The beard trail continued down her abdomen and over her hipbones, nipping at the skin there before he snacked on her inner thighs. An ache grew in her core, growing stronger the closer he got to her center. By the time his wicked tongue darted out to touch her there, she was wound tight enough to pluck. And he played her like a master. Annabeth clutched his hair, riding him like a demon until she came undone with a wild moan of pleasure that included his name somewhere in it. Her core still pulsed when he rose up, sheathed himself, then drove home with a quick stroke.

Annabeth moaned again when he held himself above her, fully seated but not moving. She tried to raise her legs, but his strong hands held her knees to the side. The sensation was enough to bring her back to the top. In an instant, she shattered.

Dean's low chuckle broke through the fog in her brain a moment before his mouth covered hers and swallowed the rest of her moans.

"I hope everyone else in the house is a sound sleeper. You surprised me with those. I wasn't quick enough to silence you."

She skimmed her hands up his arms, tracing the lines of his muscles. "Sorry. Couldn't help myself."

"I'll try to be more ready next time."

"You do tha—oh!" He'd moved, creating more delicious friction. "Yes!" She tried to lift her hips, but his hands kept her pinned. Angry he wouldn't let her participate, she grabbed fistfuls of his hair. "This isn't fair."

"Nope. Hang on, babe."

Hang on, she did. Really, she had no other choice as he slowly withdrew, then equally slowly, seated himself deep within her body again. Over and over, until she clutched a pillow to her mouth to stifle the moans. When she was sure she couldn't take anymore or she'd break into hundreds of millions of tiny pieces, he let go of her knees. Bringing her legs up, he put her feet over his shoulders, then leaned forward and pounded into her at a bruising pace. She clutched the pillow tighter, biting it. With her other hand, she held onto the back of his head, which was now buried in the crook of her neck. She was folded like a pretzel, but she didn't care. It felt too good.

With a grunt, Annabeth felt him stiffen and his pace faltered. He reached between them and ran his fingers through her soaked folds. It was all she needed to follow him into bliss.

Every bone and muscle in her body liquified as she floated back to earth. Her legs slid off his shoulders, falling open as he sat up. With a few more circles of his hips, drawing out their pleasure, he withdrew and flopped down beside her.

"*That* is how a couple in love makes love," he said through his harsh breathing.

"Oh, okay," she panted. "I'm just never walking right again. Good to know."

He chuckled. Getting up briefly, he disposed of the condom in the bathroom, then climbed back into bed with her and rolled her into him, tucking them both under the covers. "Get some sleep, pretty lady."

She hummed against his chest, already well on her way there.

When the alarm buzzed a few hours later, she groaned and rolled, slapping at it. She didn't want to get up. Her dreams were delicious. But work called, so she sat up and pushed the blankets away.

Dean groaned. "We have to stop these middle of the night sex sessions. I'm getting too old."

Annabeth chuckled. "You're not that old. You're younger than me." She remembered that from when he showed her his ID. She had a few months on him.

"Old enough."

She rolled her eyes and got up. "You can go back to sleep. I'm taking a shower."

He lifted his head. "Hmm? Can I join you?" That cocky smile that showed off his dimples appeared.

"No. We'll be late if you do." She pointed a finger at him, then hurried into the bathroom and locked the door. His low laughter followed her, making her smile.

Annabeth had another reason for not wanting to shower with him. She was quite sore. Last night had been—well, epic—and she'd enjoyed it immensely, but she needed more than a couple of hours to let her body recover this time.

After a quick spritz in the shower, Annabeth left the bathroom and went into her closet. She pulled a light blue pantsuit from a hanger and paired it with a flowered top. Stuffing her feet into a pair of brown ankle boots, she went into the bedroom. Dean was gone, but she smelled coffee.

Wandering downstairs, she found him in the kitchen. Margot was there, too, with Lily.

"Hi, sweet girl." Annabeth smiled at her and gave her hand a quick shake. Babies and toddlers had the softest skin.

"Lily doesn't feel very well." Margot kissed her forehead.

Annabeth frowned. "No?"

"No. With all the upset and travel, I'm not surprised. She'll be okay. Low grade fever and a sniffle. Hopefully, she'll be on the mend before Emily gets it. Two sick at once is not fun."

"I can imagine it's not." Annabeth poured herself some coffee in a travel mug. "Is there anything I can do?"

"No. I'll let you know if I think she needs a prescription. Right now, it's just looking like a virus."

"Okay, sounds good."

Bustling around the kitchen, Annabeth packed her breakfast and lunch. She and Dean waved to Margot and Lily and left.

"So, what do you plan to do today?" Annabeth glanced at Dean's profile as he turned out of the neighborhood and onto the main road.

"This morning, I plan to research what it takes for you to move to Costa Rica."

She blinked. "Oh."

"Unless you weren't serious?"

"No. I was. I guess I just thought I'd do it all." She smiled at him. "I appreciate the help." Anticipation surged through her veins. Moving down there seemed daunting, but she didn't regret voicing the idea. It would be an adventure. One she'd get to live with him, and that was all that mattered.

"You've got enough on your plate, so it's no trouble. Besides, I feel a bit superfluous at the moment. Until test results come back and we get that diary later today, there isn't much for me to do. I'll probably help Margot keep Emily occupied too."

"Good idea. If Lily's like most sick toddlers, she'll be grumpy."

"That's what I figured."

The rest of the drive passed quickly as they made idle chitchat. Dean dropped her at the door, then waited until she unlocked the building and went inside. She waved at him from the doorway, relocking it behind her. He lifted a hand and drove off.

Walking down the hallway, Annabeth flipped on lights as she went. She was the first one here. Her partners and the rest of the staff would be in soon. She hoped this morning went by fast. The mail couldn't get here quickly enough.

But it didn't. The morning appointments dragged. Even though she was booked solid, the number of patients she had to see before lunch felt like it never went down. When she only had two left, she walked out of a room and to the desk where she typed up notes, eyeing the mail tray. It was still empty.

Flattening her mouth, she logged into the computer, typed out her notes and filed the prescription for the little girl with strep throat, then picked up the chart for her next patient. She tried not to look at the mail bin as she walked past. Staring at it wouldn't make things magically appear.

Outside the exam room, she paused, shoving the thoughts of her sister and her diary away so she could focus on her patient. It was still there, niggling at the back of her mind, but it wasn't shouting now. She stepped into the room and greeted the family waiting for her.

Ten minutes later, she walked out, pleased with how well she'd compartmentalized things. She had one more patient to go, then it was lunchtime and the mail would arrive while she ate. Again, she did her best to ignore the empty mail bin and went about charting.

Her final patient of the morning was a newborn. Annabeth leafed through the notes Kim left on the chart and frowned. She didn't like what she saw.

Rapping her knuckles on the door, she walked in. The four-week-old boy sat in his mother's arms, grunting and red-faced.

"Hello." She set the chart down, speaking to the parents. Her gaze stayed on the baby. He didn't look well at all. "I've looked at the notes the nurse left. Can you lay him on the table?"

The mom stood up and put the baby on the exam table.

Annabeth raised her stethoscope to her ears. "How long has he been grunting?"

"Just this morning. He had a fever and a stuffy nose yesterday."

"How high was the fever?" Annabeth grasped the baby's hand. It was warm now. Kim had noted a temperature of one hundred point seven on his chart.

"About a hundred. Just under. We called the nurse line last night, and they said to monitor him and take him to the doctor in the morning. He was taking fluids fine and his fever stayed low. It wasn't until after breakfast he started to make that noise."

"How did you take his temperature?"

"With one of those forehead thermometers."

Annabeth glanced at the baby, her mouth twisting. In a baby this young, she would have preferred a rectal temperature. Her office also used the forehead method and it could be off by as much as a degree. In a baby this young, that was significant. "Okay." She put the stethoscope earpieces in and pressed the bell to the baby's tiny chest. His ribs pulled inward as he breathed. Annabeth had a feeling about what she'd hear, and she already knew she was sending this infant to the hospital.

A deep wheeze greeted her ears. She moved the bell around, listening. He had some congestion low in his lungs as well as a wheeze.

Straightening, she removed the stethoscope from her ears and looped it around her neck. "He's very sick. His lungs have a lot of congestion, and I think he needs to go to the hospital."

The boy's mom covered her mouth and gasped. Her husband gripped her hand.

"I'd like to test him for RSV and flu. It's a nasal swab done here in the office. While the nurse does that, I'll call for a transport."

"He really has to go?" The dad asked. "It just seems like a mild illness."

"In older children, even older babies, and adults, it could be just a mild illness. It could be a cold and not RSV or flu. But your son is too young to have the ability to fight off any of that alone. Hopefully, the swabs will come back negative, his lungs will clear with a little support and he'll only spend one night in the hospital for observation. It's better to be safe when they're this young. They can turn bad very quickly at his age."

The man nodded, looking more resigned to what was happening. "Okay. Thank you, doctor."

"Of course." She picked up the chart and walked to the door. "My nurse will be back in shortly to run the tests. If you have any questions, please ask."

Hurrying down the hall, she found Kim. "Hey, room four needs an RSV and flu swab done. I'm calling for a hospital transport."

Kim grimaced. "I had a feeling that was coming. Do you want me to get a rectal temp on him too?"

"Please."

"On it." She backed away from the counter, then paused. "Oh, the mail came."

"Oh, great. I'll check for my package after I call the hospital. Thanks."

"Yep. I saw it there. It's in the bin." With a quick smile, Kim hurried off.

Annabeth reached for the phone. Two phone calls and fifteen minutes later, little Waylon had a transport vehicle on the way, and the emergency room team was aware of his condition. She walked away from the desk and turned to the mail bin.

It was empty.

FORTY-SEVEN

"Oh, come on." Uttering soft curses under her breath, Annabeth walked over to the mail bin and glanced under the desk. Sometimes, the staff put bigger parcels there to get to the envelopes. But there was nothing today. With a sigh, she glanced at the receptionist. "Allie, do you know what happened to the package in the mail for me?"

Allie looked over, a frown marring her pretty face. "No. Tammi gathered everything up a little while ago. Maybe check your office?"

"Okay, thank you." Changing direction, Annabeth walked down the hall, forcing herself not to run. It was like the universe wanted her to wait to solve her sister's murder. Every time a new lead showed up, it was hurry up and wait.

Huffing out a breath, she entered her office. In the middle of her desk was a padded mailer. She let out a sigh of relief and moved around to sit in her chair. Tearing the package open, she peeked inside.

A wave of nostalgia hit her at the sight of the mint-green notebook inside. The memory of Wendy sitting on her bed, tongue poked into the corner of her mouth as she wrote inside the diary with one of her colored pens, hit Annabeth hard. Tears welled in her eyes as she withdrew the notebook from the package.

"Oh, Wendy." She traced the word "Diary" and the year written underneath on the front in her sister's handwriting. Sniffing, she opened the cover and started to read.

August 14th

>*Well, here I am again. Back in this damn school. I cannot __wait__ until this school year's over and I move to Boston. Harvard will be amazing. Especially compared to this dump. I hate it here so much. But it's still better than being at home. I about told Dad where to shove it last night when he yelled at Mom for not having dinner ready. I mean, is he really so incapable of picking up the phone and ordering takeout himself? She was busy helping me and Annie pack the last of our stuff and lost track of time. I wish she would grow a spine and tell him to take a long walk off a cliff. I only kept my mouth shut because I need him to not revoke my trust before I turn eighteen and gradu-ate. That's my college money. Why Grandpa had to put him in charge of it and not Mom—his daughter! —is beyond me. She's not dumb. Just a wimp. But I'll mind my p's and q's until school's out and then he can kiss my butt. Once I have that money, he'll have no control over me ever again.*

>*Enough about my idiot father. Stella's my roommate again. She's about the only good thing*

about this place. Well, that and the dorm monitor, Miss Blumenthal. That woman comes off like a total busybody, but most nights, she has her TV up so loud, watching her shows, she doesn't know what goes on in the building. Makes it easy to sneak out to see Johnathan.

And I decided I'm going to do it this year. The big IT. Sex. Johnathan wanted to last year, but then Carlie Jeffries got an STD from her boyfriend and it freaked me out. I know Johnathan's been with other girls, and I don't want to get anything. Plus, Misty said sex is painful the first time. Like, she cried. No thanks. But I'm going to be an adult. It won't hurt forever. So, I think that'll be my birthday present to myself. Lose my virginity. I might do it before, though. I'm not sure. The longer I put it off, the more I'll psych myself out. We'll see.

Annie's rooming with Olivia Martinelli again. I'm glad. That girl's nice, but she's bolder than Annabeth. I love my little sister, but she can be boring. Olivia livens her up. Maybe I can get her to help me find Annie a boyfriend. Hmm...

Smiling, Annabeth turned the page. She had tried, but failed. Annabeth just wasn't that interested in the boys at school. They'd all wanted more than she was willing to give.

August 16th

Ugh! I got Mr. Cartwright for political science. Miss Michaels was supposed to teach it. I was really looking forward to that class. Why did he have to transfer from civics? He's the worst! At least the rest of my classes are okay. And Stella's in two of my classes, which is great. We can do home-work together. I don't have any classes with Johnathan, though. But, whatever. I'll see him at lunch and after school. IF I can pry him away from his brother. Now, there's someone who needs a date. Even more than Annie. If he wasn't so weird, I'd set them up.

Annabeth was glad she hadn't. She wouldn't have said yes, anyway. Like Wendy said, he was weird.

She flipped through the diary, reading each entry and getting well into September before a knock on her door brought her back to the present. She looked up.

"Um, you going to come see your next patient?" Kim asked.

Annabeth glanced at her desk clock. "Holy crap!" She set the journal down and pushed back from her desk. "Yes, sorry. I lost track of time."

"I figured." Kim tipped her chin at the desk. "What's that?"

"My sister's journal." Annabeth took the chart Kim held out.

"Your sister? Didn't she die a long time ago?"

"Yeah. It's—" She broke off and shook her head. "Never mind." Fluttering a hand, she headed for her first patient of the afternoon.

The next few hours dragged by; even more so than the

morning. All she wanted to do was read more of her sister's journal entries. She'd learned several things she hadn't known. Like, Miss Michaels and Mr. Bourne were secretly dating and that Miss Spencer was insanely jealous. She'd also learned that Miss Blumenthal snuck extra desserts from the kitchen and that two of Wendy's friends sold essays to other students. There was nothing untoward about Johnathan, though. So far, all she did was gush about how great it was to have a boyfriend, especially one so desired by the other girls.

Annabeth couldn't help but roll her eyes as she packed up for the day. He was only sought after because he was handsome. If they really knew him, they'd run the other direction.

Tucking the journal into her purse, she locked her office and headed out. Dean waited just outside. Excited, she increased her walking pace and got in.

"Hey. You look peppy. I take it Wendy's journal arrived?"

She nodded and leaned over the console to give him a quick kiss. "It did." She opened her handbag and removed the diary. "I read some at lunch. Nothing too interesting so far. But it's filled with things a lot of people probably wouldn't have wanted to see the light of day back then."

"Oh?" Dean pulled away from the building and exited the parking lot.

"Yeah. Cheating, secret relationships, weird quirks about people. Wendy noticed a lot that others missed."

"Well, maybe she'll have noticed something that would interest us now."

"Hopefully. I hope you don't mind, but I plan to ignore you the rest of the night."

"No, go for it. We need answers."

Forty-Eight

May 17th

Why does life hate me? I have worked hard all year to keep my grades up, to be a good student, and a good friend, and a good daughter all so I could finish school, keep my trust fund, and FINALLY get out from under my dad's thumb. I was even going to dump my cheating-ass boyfriend. I would be free. One hundred percent, completely free. But now, I'm not. My master plan didn't include being a mom at eighteen. Oh, God. That feels weird to even think. But it's true. And I don't know how it happened, either. We used protection. I didn't even think it was the right time of the month. Apparently, it was, and our protection failed, because I'm pregnant. I haven't told anyone yet. Not even Stella. She's noticed something's off, though. She keeps asking if I'm *okay. I snapped at her today and told her to stop asking. That it was just stress. I guess that wasn't a total lie.*

I've been thinking about what to do. My dad will tell me to get rid of it. In fact, when he finds out, he might try to force me to do that. I don't want to, though. I just can't. I'm not ready to be a mom, but I don't think I could live with myself if I had an abortion. I can support a baby with my trust fund. If I invest it right, I'll never have to worry about money. What I really want, though, is for Johnathan to step up and take responsibility. To be the dad to our baby that I never had. Ideally, we'd get married and make our child legitimate. Even if we divorce later, at least our baby will carry his name. In our circle, that's a must. Illegitimate children live life on the sidelines. I don't want that for our baby. This kid is a Swenson and a Cassidy. It should have <u>everything</u>.

Now, I just have to find the right time to tell him and convince him we need to get married.

Annabeth shook her head and flipped the page. If Wendy's pregnancy had happened in her twenties, there's no way she would have thought these things. But Annabeth knew where she was coming from. She'd had the same ideas when she was a teenager too. They'd both seen some of the kids around town who had fathers from wealthy families, but their mothers were the men's mistresses, or they were products of relationships that just didn't work out. Those kids didn't live the life she and Wendy did growing up.

Now, though? Annabeth wouldn't give a rat's ass. If she got pregnant and the dad turned out to be a Class A jerk, she'd wash her hands of him and raise her baby alone.

May 20th

He called me a liar! The bastard! Oh, I've never been so mad! Told me I screwed someone else—some poor local—and now I want to foist his baby off on him! I can't even write any more. I'm too pissed off!

"Whoa." Annabeth let out a low whistle at the line of choice names she called Johnathan that followed. He deserved every one of them too. Shaking her head, she turned the page.

May 25th

Johnathan's still refusing to marry me. He still wants me to get an abortion. I won't. I'm not even giving the baby up for adoption. I'll raise it and make sure the world knows Johnathan Cassidy has a child and that he refuses to take responsibility. If he doesn't change his mind in the next few days, I'm going to announce my pregnancy right after the graduation ceremony. With everyone there. Dad can't take away my inheritance because I'll have met all the requirements. Johnathan's not going to pretend this child doesn't exist. I won't let him. And he's about to find that out. My life won't be the only one to get turned upside down by this kid. I've got other ammunition too. I know what really happened to his mom. Drunk Johnathan is a chatty Johnathan. I hate to take down Will, too, but it's his own fault for letting Johnathan sucker him into so much.

"Oh my God." Annabeth sat up and turned the page. "What? No." That was the last entry. What did she mean? What really happened to their mother?

Scrambling off the bed, she ran out of the room and downstairs. "Dean! Mom!" She rounded the banister and went into the living room. They looked up, along with Margot, who shushed her.

"The girls just went to sleep."

"Oh, sorry." Annabeth looked at the clock. She hadn't realized the time. "You guys need to hear this."

"You finished the diary?" Katrina asked.

"Yes. And the baby wasn't the only secret Wendy kept." Annabeth sat down next to Dean.

"What do you mean?" He frowned at her.

She held up a finger. "Listen." She flipped open the notebook and read the last passage.

Dean let out a soft whistle when she finished. "Whoa."

"What supposedly happened to their mom?" Margot asked.

"She died of cancer. That's what Wendy told me once." Annabeth lifted the journal. "Now, I'm not so sure."

Dean leaned forward and clasped his hands between his knees. Annabeth could see the wheels turning in his head.

"What are you thinking?" She sent a curious look his way.

"About what Stella said. How Will was—off?"

She nodded.

"If he knew that she knew Johnathan told her the truth

about how their mom died, that gives him motive if he was involved in that. I know we kind of floated the idea before. That it could be Will who's responsible for Wendy's death. What if that theory is right? What if Johnathan didn't do it, and it really was Will? I mean, Johnathan's a narcissist, we know that, right?"

The three women nodded.

"But think about Will. His odd mannerisms and behavior. What if we're not dealing with a hothead in Johnathan, but a sociopath—a true sociopath—in Will?"

"So, what are you saying?" Margot sat forward. "That Will's the one who killed Wendy? What about Johnathan and how he went after his fiancée? Where was Will then?"

"At home, getting arrested," Dean said. "And Johnathan wasn't the one who was going to do the killing. He hired a group of mercenaries and hid out on their yacht while they did the dirty work. My guess is that even if they'd brought her aboard the ship, so he could face her, he wouldn't have been the one to kill her. He might not even have watched."

Annabeth ran a hand through her hair. "So, what do we do now?"

"I need to make some phone calls and do some research. See if I can figure out what really happened to their mom. It'll give us leverage with them. Other than that, we just have to wait for the lab to analyze what Jordan found in Wendy's car. Once we get that information, if it comes back as a match to Johnathan—even as a partial—we'll know one of them was involved, and I can get Chief Wage to reopen her case. I need to call him back too. I left him a message asking about who could have leaked information to Pierce, but he hasn't gotten back to me yet."

Blowing out a breath, Annabeth sank into the sofa cushions, hugging Wendy's diary to her chest. Her mind reeled. Was everything she thought for the last fifteen years wrong?

FORTY-NINE

Music blasted into Annabeth's ears as she scrubbed her bathtub. Humming along, she swished the soapy smear around until the porcelain sparkled. Not that it hadn't before, but she needed something to keep her busy. Dean was off trying to dig up information on the Cassidys. Annabeth had thought about offering to help, but she didn't have the patience to wade through online resources. She also had a feeling he was going to call that techie friend of his again, Asher, and get him to do things that probably weren't legal. She'd rather be able to deny knowledge of that. Just in case.

So, she'd donned some old clothes and set about cleaning. Margot took the twins to the park to get them out of the way. Katrina offered to help and was downstairs tackling the kitchen.

Turning on the faucet, Annabeth rinsed her sponge and the tub basin. She pushed to her feet with a groan as her knees protested. The tile was hard. Moving to the shower, she sprayed it down, then started scrubbing grout lines.

When she finished the bathroom, she grabbed some clean linens from the cupboard and remade the bed, then popped into the laundry room to put the sheets she'd stripped off earlier and washed into the dryer. She tossed a load of towels into the washer and went downstairs.

Taking out an earbud, she rounded the corner. "Hey, Mom? I'm done upstairs. How's the kitchen—" She stopped halfway through the living room. Her mother sat on a barstool at the island, staring into the kitchen. "Mom?"

Slowly, Katrina turned her head. Annabeth's eyes widened as she saw the tears staining her face.

"Hey, are you okay?" She started toward her mother. It wasn't until she got past the wall and saw the man standing by the stove that the fear in Katrina's eyes also registered.

Annabeth froze. Her heart flip-flopped with fear, then some of that turned to anger as she recognized him. "What are you doing here, Mr. Reitman? You're not supposed to be anywhere near me."

His eyes shifted back and forth and sweat dotted his forehead. Some of her fear returned as she realized he was tweaking. It made the handgun he held that much more dangerous. All it would take was one jerk of his hand and either she or her mother could be shot.

"You should have just given me the story." He brought the gun up and aimed it at her.

"No!" Katrina yelled. The barstool scraped the floor as she stood up.

Annabeth held up a hand, urging her mother to stay put. "Noah. Please. Put the gun down. We can talk now. How about that?"

"No. The time for talking is done. Someone else promised me a bigger story."

She frowned. "Who?"

"Me."

Annabeth whirled around at the new voice. All the air left her lungs. "Will?"

FIFTY

Annabeth thought furiously as Will Cassidy walked closer. He shouldn't be here. He'd been wearing an ankle monitor the last time she saw him. And how did he know Reitman?

"What's going on? Why—how—are you here? Where's your ankle monitor? How do you know him?" She pointed at Noah, giving voice to her thoughts.

"Oh, don't play dumb, Annabeth. It doesn't suit you. Your boyfriend outlined it all last night. He's quite right. Johnathan doesn't have the stomach for killing."

"How did you—who told you that?"

"Parabolic microphone," Reitman said. "I hid in your bushes with it and listened."

Annabeth made a note to have her landscape trimmed if she made it out of this. Shrubs were great, but not when they hid people stalking her.

"Your little visit to the Vineyard made me curious."
She turned back to Will.

"After we ran into each other, I did some digging of my

own. Your dad's still very upset that you snuck that car off the farm."

"You talked to my dad?"

"Yes. At first, he told me to go away. But then I reminded him that we both had a lot to lose if he didn't cooperate. There's no statute of limitations on murder, and he helped cover one up."

Katrina let out a short, pain-filled wail. Annabeth sucked in a harsh breath through her nose and swallowed back the sudden lump in her throat. It was one thing to suspect her sister was murdered and that her dad had a hand in it, but quite another to hear it confirmed. And to look into her killer's eyes.

"He told me who your boyfriend was and what you guys were doing in town. It only took a phone call to a private investigator of my own to find out that Dean was an associate of the man who Brooke hired to keep her safe. Another search uncovered the police report you made against that man." Will pointed at Reitman. "When I found out his profession and the legal troubles he was in, well, it all just fell into place. Tweakers in danger of spending years in jail make good spies, did you know that?"

"I'm not a tweaker."

Annabeth glanced at Noah. He shifted on his feet as he glared at Will.

Will just arched an eyebrow and ignored him. "Anyway, now that I know what you know, it's time I left the country. And you're going to help me."

"What? The hell I am. You killed my sister. The only place I'm going to help you go is to jail."

He smiled a toothy grin that didn't reach his eyes. Those remained cold and emotionless. Like their conversation was no more serious than what the weather would be like tomorrow.

"You will help me leave the country, or your mom dies.

Right now." He took a pistol from beneath his jacket and aimed it at Katrina. "What'll it be, Annabeth?"

Eyes round, Annabeth turned to stare at her mother. Katrina stared back with teary eyes. The weary set to her shoulders said she expected to die. Even though she knew it might mean her own death, Annabeth couldn't let that happen. She looked at Will. "I'll go with you, but you let her go."

He scoffed. "No. She comes too." He looked at Noah and tipped his chin.

The other man hurried forward and grabbed Katrina's arm, pulling her forward.

"No!" Annabeth lurched toward them.

Will grabbed her arm and yanked her back. "No, no. She's my insurance that you cooperate. And so I don't have to kill her. That just creates a mess, and I don't have time to clean it up now. If I leave her here alive, she'll tell, even if she promises not to." He gave Annabeth a shove. "Let's go."

FIFTY-ONE

Dean sat back and rubbed his eyes, which were dry from staring at the library's computer screen for so long. He'd found an obituary for Linda Cassidy, but it didn't list a cause of death. Asher was working on digging up more information, but he doubted they'd get much. Too much money had been exchanged and too much time had passed.

His phone buzzed in his hip pocket. He lifted it out, seeing Asher's name on the screen.

"Hey, I was just thinking about you. Did you find something on Linda Cassidy?"

"No. Listen, Will left Martha's Vineyard. The feds don't know where he is. He got on a ferry and left."

"What?"

The older woman seated two computers down cast a look at him. Dean logged off his computer and got up. "What do you mean, he left? He had an ankle monitor on." He kept his voice low as he walked through the library to the exit.

Asher scoffed. "You and I both know those things are ridiculously easy to fool."

Dean pushed through the front doors. "How did they know he was gone, then?"

"One of the feds made a surprise visit to his house. Will put the bracelet on one of the staff and paid the guy to sit in the house."

"Geez. When did he leave?"

"Last weekend. On a hunch, I pulled the reports on your background and Annabeth's. Someone ran them both nine days ago. In fact, yours was run twice."

"What? Who ran them?"

"Last week, it was a private investigator named Ken Amsted. Before that, it was Medina's Police Department."

Dean's mouth flattened. He honestly wasn't surprised that the chief checked him out. He'd have probably done the same thing. "What do you know about Amsted?"

"He's a P.I. to the rich. My guess is either Pierce or Will hired him. You need to watch your back. I don't like that Will's disappeared. Maybe he sensed the walls closing in and ran. Or maybe he wants revenge. I don't know enough about him to guess."

"Okay. I'll keep an eye out. So, you haven't learned anything about Linda Cassidy?"

"Not really. She had cancer, that much is true. I found medical records of her illness. Non-Hodgkin's lymphoma. But if that's what actually killed her, I can't tell you. Ford said Brooke told him that Johnathan told her she fell at home."

Dean let out a low whistle. "Someone's lying somewhere if what Wendy said in her journal is true."

"Yep."

"All right. If you learn anything else, let me know. No matter what time. I'm serious. Things feel like they're coming to a head."

"I agree. Talk to you soon."

"Yep." Dean hung up, then immediately called Chief

Wage. He wasn't upset about the background check, but he'd like to know the man's reasoning. Plus, he wanted to know what he'd discovered about the leak in the department.

"Medina Police Department, Chief Wage's office." The receptionist's pleasant voice came over the line.

"Hello. This is Dean Adler. I need to speak to the chief."

"I'm sorry, he's not available. May I take a message?"

Dean ground his molars together. He'd bet that was double speak for the chief didn't want to be bothered. "If he's there, could you please put me on hold and ask if he'll speak to me?"

"Sir—"

"Please. It's important."

She hesitated, then sighed. "One moment."

Music played in his ear. He paced down the sidewalk, willing the chief to hurry up.

The music stopped, then crackling sounded.

"Adler?"

"Hey, Chief. Sorry to bother you. I have some questions."

"If this is about the leak, it's a dead end. It was a retired officer who died last year. I talked to his widow. She said he took the bribe to pay off their house after she lost her job, so they wouldn't end up homeless."

"Okay, that answers one question. My other question is, what were you hoping to find by running a background check on me? A quick check of my license would let you see I'm legit."

A beat of silence passed. The hair on Dean's neck rose. It only tingled more when the chief spoke.

"How'd you find out about that?" Suspicion and something else colored the man's voice. Dean wished he could see his face.

"Does it matter?"

"I guess not." Wage huffed. "You weren't the first person

to come looking for information on Wendy Swenson's death. We had a swarm of reporters who came asking. And another P.I."

"Ken Amsted?"

Wage stuttered. "How the hell did you know that?"

"Doesn't matter. Did you give him or any of the others copies of the police reports?"

"The basic version, yes. But I gave you all the notes on the case. The stuff that didn't make it into the official report."

That gave Dean pause. "Why?"

"Because your background and your friend's involvement in the McGinty case made me think you were looking into this for the right reasons. I meant what I said. This case has haunted me from the beginning. I wanted to know why it got so badly screwed up."

Dean's mouth pulled as he chewed on the corner of his mouth. "Okay."

"Okay? That's it?"

"Yep. I get why you did it. I like that you have some integrity too."

"Gee, thanks."

Dean chuckled. "That didn't come out quite right. It's been a long week. Anyway, I'm close to getting you the evidence you need to reopen the investigation."

"Really? That's great. I can't wait to finally put this case to rest and let that young woman rest in peace."

"Me too."

"All right. Keep me posted."

"I will." Dean hung up, then tapped his phone on his hand, thinking. He glanced over his shoulder at the library, debating whether to go back in and search for more news articles and police records. He'd gotten about all he could from public sources and the databases he had subscriptions to.

What he really needed to do was talk to people again. That meant going back to Martha's Vineyard.

Pursing his lips, he sucked in a quick breath. He didn't want to leave Annabeth here alone. With the way things were shaping up, maybe he could convince her to take a few days off of work and come with him. His only other option was to call in reinforcements from Costa Rica. Someone needed to stay with her.

He doubted she'd go for a trip, but he figured he'd try anyway. Lifting his phone, he thumbed through his contacts and found her name, then put it to his ear. It rang several times, then rolled to voicemail. Frowning, he left a quick message, then tried Katrina. They'd been gearing up to do some cleaning when he left. Maybe Annabeth was up to her elbows in water or something.

Katrina's phone rolled to voicemail too. An uneasy feeling skittered through Dean, pricking his skin. He tried Margot.

"Hey." He could hear the smile in her voice. "What's up?"

"Are you home?"

"No. I'm still at the park with the girls. We're getting ready to go, though. Why?"

"I can't reach Annabeth or Katrina."

"Oh. They're probably just busy. Annabeth had her hair in her 'I'm serious' bun. She only does that when she plans to deep clean. Do you want me to try calling, though?"

"Would you? I'm going to head that way."

"Sure. I'll call now and can keep trying while we walk home. Do you want me to have her call you if I get a hold of her?"

"Please. Thanks, Margot."

"Sure. And try not to worry. They probably are just deep into something and either didn't hear their phones or they can't answer them right now."

"Yeah. Probably." He still wasn't convinced. Not with

what he knew now about Will. Saying goodbye, he hung up and jogged to his car.

The miles whizzed by as he wove through the city streets to Annabeth's. About five minutes from home, his phone rang. His relief was short-lived when he saw it was Margot and not Annabeth.

He pushed the button on the steering wheel to answer. "Yeah?"

"They're not here." There was an edge to Margot's voice that put him on alert.

"Did they leave a note?"

"No. Dean... their purses are still here. And their phones."

The curses that flew from his mouth filled the car. He hoped Margot didn't have him on speakerphone where the twins could hear. "I'll be there in a couple minutes." He hung up and pressed his foot down, changing lanes.

Three long minutes later, he turned into the driveway. Margot met him at the front door.

"I've looked all over the house. They're not here, and there's nothing to say where they went."

"Would they take a walk?" He could see them leaving their purses behind if they just went out for a stroll. Maybe not their phones, though.

"I don't think so. There's a sink full of dirty water and dishes. They'd have either finished it or drained it."

"Maybe the dishes are soaking."

"I looked at them. It's the glassware that was on top of the cabinets. It only really needed rinsed."

Dean strode toward the counter and the two phones sitting on the white marble. He tapped the screen on Annabeth's. "Do you know her passcode?"

Margot shook her head.

"Damn. She wears a watch that's linked. We could use her phone to track it."

"Oh, no."

Dean frowned. "What?"

"It's on the nightstand upstairs in her bedroom. I saw it when I was looking for her. I bet she took it off while she cleaned."

He let out an exasperated breath and tipped his head back, staring at the ceiling. "Okay. Tracking her is out, even if we can get into her phone. I'm going to see if any of the neighbors saw anything."

She nodded, and he ran outside and across the street. They had a good view of the front of Annabeth's house.

Knocking, he waited. A moment later, the door opened, and a woman in her forties offered him a curious smile.

"Hi. I'm Dean. My girlfriend lives across the street." He pointed at the house. "Did you happen to see if she and her mother left a short time ago?"

The woman frowned and shook her head. "No. Sorry. I've been out back until just a few minutes ago."

Dean's shoulders sagged.

"But my husband was in the garage. Hang on." She turned. "Dan?"

A man came around the corner. "Yeah, hon?" He frowned when he saw Dean.

"This is Annabeth's boyfriend. He wanted to know if we saw her leave with her mom. Did you see anything while you were in the garage?"

Dan's frown deepened. "I didn't see her leave, no, but there was a car that pulled up out front."

Dean's gaze sharpened. "Did you see who was in it?"

"No. I was on my way inside with my drill to hang a shelf. I saw it pull up as I went in. When I came back out a few minutes later, it was gone."

"What kind of car was it?"

"A white Ford Explorer."

"You didn't catch the license plate, did you?"

"Just that it was out of state. Illinois, I think. What's going on? Is everything all right?"

"I hope so. What time was that?"

"Um, an hour ago. Maybe a little more?"

"Okay. Did you notice anything else out of the ordinary?"

"No."

"Great." Dean backed up and lifted a hand. "Thank you."

The couple frowned at him, and the husband opened his mouth to ask more questions, but Dean didn't stick around. He turned and ran to the house beside them. Maybe someone else got a better look.

At the fourth house he went to, the one to the right of Annabeth's, his heart skipped as he saw the doorbell camera. He rang the bell.

A tinny male voice came through the speaker. "Hello?"

"Hi, my girlfriend lives next door to you. Annabeth Swenson? I need to ask you a quick question. Are you home and able to come to the door?"

"Um, yes. Just a moment."

Dean tapped his foot. They could have accomplished the same conversation much faster if the man had just opened the door and cut out the wait time.

The front door swung open. "Yes?"

"Your doorbell camera"—Dean pointed at it—"would you mind showing me the footage?"

The man frowned. "Why?"

"It's a long story. I just need to see if Annabeth and her mother left with someone."

The man's frown deepened. "I've never seen you around. Are you some stalker of hers? I won't—"

"No." Dean held up a hand. "Look, I think she's in danger. I need to know if she left with someone. Can you please pull up the footage?"

Tipping his head, the man studied Dean. He must have liked something he saw or heard, because he took his phone from his pocket and opened an app. "What time?"

"I'm not sure. About an hour ago? The neighbor across the street said he saw a white Explorer pull up outside."

The man tapped the screen a few times, then turned the device around. "That it?"

A white Ford Explorer filled the screen as it drove past. "Possibly. Can you back it up a bit and play it?"

"Sure." He did as Dean requested, then turned up the volume.

The vehicle was out of frame, but the audio still played. He heard a woman's voice, but couldn't make out what she said. A moment later, three car doors slammed, an engine started, and then the SUV drove past.

Dean clenched his teeth, wishing the houses on this street didn't all have recessed porches. He'd have had a clear view of the area in front of Annabeth's if the camera wasn't tucked away. "Can you pause it when the vehicle is right in front of your house?"

"Yeah." The man turned the phone around and fiddled with the video, then handed it over.

Squinting, Dean tried to make out faces inside the car. He zoomed in. In front, a man's profile was clear, but he didn't recognize him. In the back window, though, what he saw made his heart stutter. It was Annabeth.

FIFTY-TWO

Streetlights whizzed by; bright streaks against the night sky as Will drove down the highway. Annabeth's butt was numb from sitting in the car for so long. They'd been on the road for at least eight or nine hours now. She didn't know where they were headed; Will wouldn't say. But they were going west. They'd passed through Indiana and into Illinois, then Missouri, stopping only long enough for gas. Twice, he'd thrown some gas station sandwiches and chips at them. When they had to pee, he'd turned off the highway and made them go into the woods. Annabeth had contemplated running away, but she didn't want to leave her mother alone; plus, she didn't know where they were or how close help was. She only had a vague idea of where they were now, which was somewhere near Arkansas, but without looking at a map, she couldn't be sure.

She cast a glance at her mom, who rested her head against the doorframe, feigning sleep. Annabeth knew she wasn't asleep, because every once in a while, a tear would slip out of her eyes. Her own had long since dried up. Now she was just pissed.

More miles ticked by; the drive monotonous until Will turned off the interstate. Annabeth sat up, paying more attention. Where were they going?

For over an hour, they went south. After they crossed into Arkansas, Will turned off the highway and onto a narrow county road that wound through the hills. Eventually, he slowed and turned down a gravel driveway.

"Where are we?" She glanced outside, seeing only trees.

"Somewhere no one will think to look."

She rolled her eyes. "Why do bad guys always say that? It's rarely true. Someone's going to find out where we are."

He cast a look at her over his shoulder as he pulled to a stop outside a cabin. "Maybe. But I'll be long gone by then." He tipped his head toward the door. "Let's go."

Annabeth looked at her mom again, silently telling her to behave for now. They hadn't been allowed to talk to each other during the ride, so she didn't know what was running through her head. She hoped now that they were stopped for the night, Will would put them in the same room and they could hatch an escape plan.

Getting out, Annabeth followed Reitman toward the house, while Will walked behind them, a gun trained on their backs. Noah unlocked the door and let them inside.

A musty, stale smell hit her. No one had been here in a long time.

Noah flipped a light switch and led them in. "The bedrooms are back there." He looked at Will, his gaze flicking to Annabeth and Katrina, then back.

"They can stay out here for now. We need to escape-proof one of the rooms. Get on that."

A flash of something lit Noah's eyes. Anger, maybe? But he nodded and walked away. His movements were jerky, and he couldn't keep his arms still. Annabeth tipped her head, recognizing the signs of a meth addict coming down from a high. If he didn't have drugs with him, pretty soon, he was going to crash and sleep for a day. Somehow, she needed to make sure that happened. It would be easier to get away if they only had one conscious captor.

"Sit down." Will gestured to the dusty sofa.

Annabeth waited for her mom to move, then followed, sitting next to her. She looked at Will. "Now what?"

"We wait."

"For?"

He walked closer and crouched in front of her. Those dark eyes that always slightly creeped her out studied her now. "You ask a lot of questions. Your sister did too." His expression hardened. "It's what got her killed."

Annabeth narrowed her eyes, not intimidated, even though she knew she should probably be scared. But she was just angry. "Why did you do it? She wasn't your girlfriend. It wasn't your baby."

"No. But Johnathan was going places. I couldn't have Wendy ruining it all."

"Why did you even care? He treated you like crap."

Will pointed the gun in her face. The first true feeling that she might die hit her then, sending butterflies through her stomach and a shiver up her spine.

"You don't know what our relationship is like. He's my brother, and he loves me."

She stared down the gun barrel, still defiant through her fear. "No. He doesn't. If he did, he would treat you as an equal. Not as a lackey. Did he tell you to get rid of Wendy? Or did he want you to just get her to see reason and abort the baby? Or at the very least, keep her mouth shut? Did she refuse, and that's why you decided to make sure she stayed quiet?"

His jaw worked. "Annabeth."

"And what about now? He's in jail; denied bond because he was deemed a flight risk. How can you help your precious brother now?"

The back of his hand whipped across her cheek. She let out a quick yelp and covered her face. Her eyes watered, but she glared at him.

"Shut. Up."

"Or what?" Her eyes flashed fire. "You'll kill me like my sister? That won't go so well for you this time. It won't take fifteen years for someone to figure out what you did and track you down. Dean's probably already looking for us."

Katrina laid a hand over hers. "Annabeth, please."

Her soft, broken whisper did nothing to help cool Annabeth's temper. But she didn't want to make her mom any more anxious than she already was, so she clamped her lips together and resorted to glaring at him.

"If your boyfriend ever wants to see you alive again, he'll be wise enough to stay put and give me what I want when I ask for it."

"And what's that?"

"Wendy's car and the evidence he has against me." A cold, mirthless smile spread over his face. "It's the only way you and your mother live."

They'd see about that. If she got her way, sometime soon, they'd be sneaking off into the woods. Even if they followed the road back to civilization, it was wooded enough here they could easily hide from him if he followed.

"How did you do it? She found you two at the diner. You walked her out."

His smile died. "How do you know that?"

"A witness."

"Who?"

She shrugged. "Dean didn't say," she lied. "Just that someone saw her yelling at Johnathan, and then you walking her out of the diner. So, how did you cut her brake and steering lines and she didn't notice?"

The cold smile returned, but there was an evilness to it now. "I told her it looked like her car was leaking and offered to check it out. By then, I'd convinced her I would talk to Johnathan on her behalf, so when I asked if I could check things out to make sure she could get back to school safely, she trusted me. I used her jack, lifted the car and cut the lines. I was back in the diner in five minutes."

Annabeth fought to keep the triumphant smile off her face. It was his blood Jordan found on the brake line. She just wished she'd been able to record that confession. At least she wasn't the only one who heard it.

"You know what I still don't understand, though?"

He sighed. "This is growing tiresome."

"Last question." She crossed her toes. It probably wouldn't be. Maybe now, but not for good. "Why were you so willing to kill for Johnathan?"

His eyebrows slammed together, and the angry look returned.

She held up a hand. "I know. He's your brother. But there's more to it, isn't there?"

His expression smoothed out. He still wasn't happy, but he didn't look quite so furious now. "Johnathan protected me. Our mother—she wasn't well. Even before she developed cancer, she wasn't well. In the head. Always quick to anger. Johnathan took the beatings, even when it was my fault."

The entry in Wendy's journal about her knowing what really happened to Johnathan and Will's mother flitted through Annabeth's mind. A sinking feeling settled in her stomach. "She died of cancer, right?"

He shook his head. "It contributed to her death, but no. She fell."

Annabeth swallowed hard. Not sure she wanted to know the answer, she still had to ask. "How did she fall?"

"I pushed her. She beat Johnathan with a candlestick because she was too weak to use her hands. Broke his nose and a finger. So, I pushed her. And she fell down the stairs." He looked away, remembrance on his face. "She didn't die right away."

Katrina let out a soft whimper and looked away, gripping Annabeth's hand tightly.

"I waited. And watched." Will turned his head to look at them. "It didn't take long. Maybe twenty minutes. Then I went to bed." He shrugged. "Bitch got what she deserved."

Annabeth clutched Katrina's hand. Some of her fear returned as Will's psychopathy became completely clear. He'd been a killer from a young age. Her earlier bravado seemed a bit foolish now. She'd have to be careful—and meticulous about what she said and did—if she wanted to get them out of here alive.

"What do you plan to do about your brother?" she asked quietly.

His eyes went frosty again, but not because he didn't care. This chill was different. He was angry. "Nothing, for now. He messed up. I told him we just needed to leave the country. Use the money we embezzled and flee. But no. He wanted the whole pie." He paused, shaking his head. "We didn't need the company. We had enough. If he'd left Brooke alone and just let her go, we'd be safe somewhere the government couldn't extradite us. Until I'm safely away, I can't think about getting him free. That will take some planning." That calculating smile returned. "It's not quite as easy as getting your mom to open the door."

Katrina choked on a soft sob.

Annabeth leaned in. "It's okay," she whispered to her.

Noah reappeared, then. "I put some bolt locks on one of the doors. I think there's plywood in the shed I can nail over the window. Gramps left a bunch of stuff in there."

Will gave a short nod. "Good." He looked at the ladies. "Let's go see your new accommodations, shall we?"

Fifty-Three

Images moved over Dean's laptop screen as he went through the highway traffic cam footage. Asher had hacked into their system and set him up with the feed a couple hours ago after the police reluctantly put out a notice to local law enforcement to be on the lookout for the SUV. According to the officers who responded, the face in the car window Dean was sure was Annabeth's wasn't clear enough for them to make that determination, so they didn't want to cause a ruckus over something that could be nothing. He had a feeling it had more to do with the popularity of that car than anything else. Finding it wouldn't be easy; there were just too many of them.

So Dean called Asher and asked him to do what he did best.

Sitting back, he stretched and worked his neck. The last couple of hours had made him think the police were right. He'd seen literally hundreds of Explorers, a good half of them white. A couple had Illinois plates, but he'd been able to see all the drivers except one, and that one appeared to be a single occupant.

All of this could be pointless, too, if they'd stayed off the interstate system. Unless he could pick them up close by, he wouldn't know where to look next.

His stomach growled, reminding him he hadn't eaten since breakfast. Maybe food and another cup of coffee would help keep him focused while he reviewed footage from the southern cameras. Getting up, he took two steps away from the island when his phone rang. He glanced at it. The number that appeared didn't look familiar. With a frown, he picked it up. "Hello?"

"Is this Dean Adler?"

"Yes." His frown deepened. "Who's this?"

"I have someone who'd like to say hi."

Shuffling came over the line, then the sweetest sound met his ears.

"Dean?"

"Annabeth! Honey, are you okay? Who is that? Where are you?"

"All good questions." The male voice was back.

"Who are you? What do you want?"

"I think you know who it is. And I want Wendy's car and all the evidence you've collected."

Dean's heart thumped as he realized he was talking to Will Cassidy. And that he had Annabeth hostage. He forced his pulse to calm so he could think clearly. "I don't have it."

"But you know where it is. Have it shipped to the Little Rock, Arkansas airport under your name. It needs to be there Wednesday. Text me the arrival time at this number once you have the shipment scheduled. I'll text you an address, then, on where you should bring it after it arrives. It needs to be at the new location by Wednesday before midnight, so factor that in when you set up the shipment. Any later and you'll never see Annabeth or her mother alive again. And I don't think I need to tell you not to involve the police?"

"No." His voice was hard. He had something else in mind.

"Good." Will hung up.

Anger simmered in Dean's gut. He clutched his phone, determination seeping in. He now had everything he needed to track and take down that piece of scum.

Tapping the screen, he called Asher.

"Hey, you find something on that highway footage?"

"No. Will Cassidy just called me. He's got Annabeth and her mother. He wants Wendy's car and the evidence we collected. By Wednesday. He said to ship it to the Little Rock, Arkansas airport, then pick it up myself and bring it to him. He said he'll text me an address after it arrives."

"Well, hell. Wednesday? That's cutting it close. I don't think I can get the stuff back from the lab and get it to the U.S. in that time frame."

"Then don't. Fake it. He'll never know. I also don't intend for him to get away, so there's no point in derailing the investigation by pulling the evidence."

A brief pause came over the line. "You have a plan. What is it?"

"Send the car. But send some of the others with it. He said no police, but he didn't mention my friends."

Asher's low chuckle told Dean he knew what he was thinking. "Sam and Edie okay? Sending Ford would not be a good idea, and someone with more persuasion skills than me needs to stay behind and keep him here."

"Yeah. Max is good at that. Okay. How's Ford coping?"

"Crotchety as ever. I think Max and Sam might stage an intervention soon if he doesn't snap out of it. If they don't, I will. He's a bear."

Dean could imagine. The idea of leaving Annabeth—or her leaving him—hurt. Just having her missing right now had punched a hole in his heart. He didn't want to do life without her. "Well, let me know if there's anything I can do."

"You just focus on your own problems right now. Ford will be fine. I'll talk to the others. We'll get things sorted on our end, and I'll let you know when the shipment is on its way. In the meantime, you need to get yourself to Little Rock."

He did. But he needed to stock up on a few things first.

FIFTY-FOUR

Gravel crunched under Dean's tires as he turned off the state highway and onto a Mountain Hollow Road. He glanced at the GPS. This was the right place, according to the address he received an hour ago. He still couldn't believe Cassidy's arrogance. It was only a little after three p.m. He'd told Dean not to deliver the car until after dark. If that was what he wanted, he should have waited to give him the address. Now he had time to do some recon on the location. Or to call the cops and set up a sting. Not that he was going to. He and his friends could handle Will just fine.

The tree cover closed in around him as he drove up the road. He'd googled the location before he set off and saw that it looked like an abandoned farm. He was going to drive by and get a feel for the property and just how abandoned it was. He doubted Will would be so stupid as to give away the place where he currently was—though considering he'd given him an address and then hours to deliver the car, he could be wrong. But even if he wasn't, Dean would bet he wasn't too far away. This location was a wildly random and specific place.

Dust billowed out behind his car as he wound around the

twisting curves. A mile and a half up the road, the trees gave way to a fenced pasture full of tall grass and weeds. A weathered and leaning barn stood to one side. At the end of a long drive was a two-story farmhouse with its windows broken out and vines growing up the walls and into the eaves. It, too, leaned. Cassidy definitely wasn't staying here.

Continuing up the road, he drove another mile, noting a few occupied homes and an overgrown lane running alongside the property before turning around. When he went past the farm this time, he slowed, studying trees and light poles for cameras. Past the property, he pulled off and got out, walking back to take a closer look. Walking both sides of the road and venturing into the trees, he didn't find any surveillance equipment. That didn't mean there wasn't any up by the house or the barn. Out here, at least, though, they were in the clear.

Dean jogged back to his car and went back to the lane he saw, turning down it. Again, he parked and got out, walking the trail until it ended at a stream. "No trespassing" signs were posted about every hundred feet. There didn't seem to be any cameras on this side, either.

The lack of surveillance bugged him. What was Will's plan? Dean knew the man wasn't dumb. Even as a fifteen-year-old kid, he'd executed a murder and gotten away with it. Had possibly gotten away with one years earlier if Dean's suspicions about what happened to Linda Cassidy were true. What was his intent here? Or was he just so cocky he didn't think he needed to keep an eye on things?

Whatever his reasoning, Dean would be prepared. He'd already talked to Sam and Edie about what they might possibly do. When he picked them and the car up in a little bit, they would finalize things. Will wouldn't get away with Wendy's car without leading them to Annabeth and Katrina.

~

A plane streaked overhead, deafening Dean as he stepped out of the flatbed truck he'd rented to tow Wendy's car. He headed for the cargo terminal.

Inside, a man in a grease-stained shirt with his name—Bobby—emblazoned on the front and a ball cap looked up from the computer. "Can I help you?"

"I'm here to pick up a shipment. Dean Adler."

Bobby switched screens and typed Dean's name into the computer. "Yep. It's here. Where you parked?"

"Out front." He hooked a thumb over his shoulder at the door.

"Pull up to the main doors. We'll bring it out. You got chains or straps, right? We don't provide those."

"I'm good."

"Okay." With a nod of affirmation, the man disappeared through the door behind him.

Dean blinked. That was an—interesting exchange. Leaving the office, he went back to his truck and pulled it up to the main doors as asked. Leaving it idling, he hopped out. The big bay door opened, and he could see Bobby on a forklift, picking up a crate. The machine beeped as he backed up, then the engine revved; the high-pitched whine echoed off the steel building as he drove toward Dean. In moments, he had the crate deposited on the flatbed.

Dean hopped up onto the trailer and picked up a strap. He let out a sharp whistle to get Bobby's attention. The man looked up.

"Help me strap it down?"

Bobby nodded and shut off the forklift. Dean tossed him one end of the strap. Together, they tied the crate down, then Dean signed the paperwork.

"Thanks for the help." Dean touched his temple in a quick salute of thanks.

"You're welcome. Have a good day."

"You too." Dean opened the driver's door and climbed in. Starting the engine, he drove out of the lot, heading for his hotel. Sam and Edie would meet him there. Their flight landed in just a few minutes. It was plenty enough time for him to pack up and check out.

Parking at the rear of the hotel lot, Dean went inside. Ten minutes later, he walked off the elevator and left his key at the front desk. His friends knew to come to the flatbed waiting in the parking lot.

Half an hour later, a gray Dodge SUV rolled in. Dean recognized Sam behind the wheel. As they pulled up, he hopped out of the truck cab.

Three doors opened, and Dean paused, surprised. It was only supposed to be Sam and Edie. He had a fleeting thought it might be Asher, then Jordan's mop of light brown hair appeared.

"Hey, friend."

Dean scowled. "Why are you here? This is dangerous." Any other time, he would be excited to see his friend, but not today.

"I told him that too." Edie slammed her car door, scowling at Jordan. "He wouldn't listen."

Jordan tossed her a crooked grin, which only made her frown harder.

Dean looked at Sam. "Why didn't you leave him in Costa Rica?"

"He stole my keys and disabled my vehicle. Refused to fix it until I agreed to let him come. We didn't have time to argue. Plus, he'd already bought a ticket. He heard Asher giving us the details, then booked himself onto the flight."

"Seriously, Jordie?"

Jordan closed his door and walked around the hood. "You might need me."

Edie snorted. "No. And you seriously let him call you Jordie? Are you a Trekkie?" She grinned.

Jordan rolled his eyes. "Shut it, *Edith*."

She scowled.

"Children." Dean patted the air. "Focus, please."

"Sorry," Jordan said.

Edie crossed her arms and looked at him expectantly.

"What's the plan?" Sam asked.

"I scoped out the location just a little while ago. It's an abandoned farmstead in the hills. No cameras that I could see, but I didn't venture close to the house or barn. Keep your eyes open."

"You get firepower?"

"Yes." Dean opened the door to show Sam and the others the bags sitting behind the seats. "We get away from people and I'll pass it out." He looked at Jordan. "I wasn't counting on you, so we'll need to stop somewhere on our way north and get you some body armor."

Jordan wrinkled his nose. "Okay."

"You can always stay here." Dean gestured to the hotel, sensing his friend's hesitation now.

"No. I meant what I said. You might need me. I can stay with the car. Give me a radio, and if you need a quick getaway, I'm your man."

Dean nodded once. That might not be a bad idea. And Jordan was as good at driving as he was at mechanical things. "Okay. You still need body armor. Let's go."

"I'm riding with you." Sam walked around to the passenger side, passing Edie the car keys as he went. "You can give me more details on the location while we drive."

Edie huffed and glared at Jordan. "You better not drive me nuts, Jordie."

He tossed her a saccharine smile. "That'll be a short trip, Edith."

She whipped around and looked at Sam. "You suck, Brackley."

He grinned and got in the truck cab.

Dean's mouth twitched, and he glanced at Jordan. The man's gray eyes sparkled with amusement.

"Do you want me to drive?" Jordan asked as she stomped past.

"No. Get in the car."

With a quick, devilish smile at Dean, Jordan hurried after her.

Dean chuckled and climbed into the truck. "They're going to kill each other."

"Why do you think I wanted to ride with you? You could have filled me in on the place when we got there. All they've done since we got in the car is bicker. They've bickered every time they've been together since he arrived in Costa Rica. She took one look at him and decided he was public enemy number one."

Dean laughed. "Why?"

Sam shrugged. "Probably because when Max introduced them, he said—and I'm quoting Max, who was quoting Jordan here—'Edie? That's short for Edith, right? That was my grandma's name.'"

Dean laughed harder. "Oh, God. Did she attack him?"

"No. Max said her eyebrows slammed together, and she told him never to call her Edith, then stormed away."

"One day, she'll be less touchy about her name."

"It wasn't the name that bugged her. Your friend isn't exactly ugly. I don't think she likes feeling—things."

Dean tipped his head. "True." Edie was standoffish. She welcomed very few people into her inner circle. "Let's just hope they can work together long enough to rescue Annabeth and Katrina."

"She'll shove her misgivings about Jordan away. At the end

of the day, she knows what's important." Sam glanced away for a moment, then turned back. "How are you holding up?"

"Fine." Dean shifted. He didn't want to think about how he felt, let alone talk about it. If he wanted to do this right, he needed to keep everything compartmentalized. "And I know you're just trying to help me by getting me to let it all out, but I can't. Not right now. I need to stay focused."

Sam studied him for a long moment. Dean felt a bit like a bug under a microscope. Of all the team, Sam knew him best. They'd worked together; been under fire together. That forged a deep bond.

"Okay. I won't push. But if you want to talk, I'll listen."

"I know, and I appreciate it."

Sam gave a short nod. "Tell me about this farm."

FIFTY-FIVE

"Sweetie, what are you doing?"

Annabeth popped up above the bed to look at her mom, who sat against the wall. "Looking for anything I can fashion into a weapon. We've been here three days. I'm sick of this room."

"You've already scoured every inch of this place. Don't you think you'd have found something already?"

"Well, I can't just sit here." She wiggled back under the bed. Maybe she could pull one of the springs free. It wouldn't be much of a weapon, but it would be something. She poked at the interfacing covering the bottom of the box springs.

"Can you at least stop scratching at the wall? They'll hear you."

Annabeth frowned. "What?" She wriggled out. "I'm not scratching at the wall. I wasn't touching anything except the bottom of the bed."

Katrina sat up, brows furrowed. "Then what—?" She glanced around.

Annabeth stayed still, listening. A few seconds later, she heard it. Her gaze darted to the window. "It's outside." She got to her feet and hurried over. The glass was still covered in plywood, but there was a sliver of the outside visible at the bottom. "Hello?"

"It's probably just an animal."

Annabeth peered into the slit. It was dark out, so she couldn't even see a shadow. She huffed, her breath fogging up the glass, and sat back on her haunches. "Yeah." She'd seen small glimpses of a few animals since they'd been here. And racoons were notorious for getting into things, especially at night.

Katrina got up and came over to sit on the floor beside her. She wrapped Annabeth in a hug. "I know you're frustrated. I am too. Eventually, though, they'll have to move us. It'll give us more opportunity to get away. And I want you to run. Don't worry about or wait on me."

"Mom—"

"No. I've lost one daughter to this dirtbag. I refuse to lose another. You get away and you make him pay for what he did to your sister."

Annabeth lifted a hand and covered her mother's arm. Closing her eyes, she rested her head against Katrina's. A tear slipped out.

She saw the logic in her plan. Annabeth was younger and stronger. She could cover more ground and quicker. But it hurt to think of leaving her mom behind. They'd grown closer since she'd moved in. Especially in the last few days. There wasn't anything to do except talk, so they'd filled the time learning things neither of them knew about the other. Hearing the things Katrina went through as a child, the mental manipulation and emotional abuse she'd suffered her entire life—well, it explained a lot. She had a new respect for her mom's resiliency.

Spurred on by the desire to not lose what they'd found, Annabeth put her mind into overdrive, hoping to find a solution. What her mom said about being moved had the gears turning faster than ever. She let her thoughts swirl; then finally, something stuck.

"How good of an actress are you?"

Katrina frowned. "What?" She narrowed her eyes. "What are you thinking?"

"You said they need to move us for us to have an opportunity to escape. I want to create the opportunity."

"Oh, Annabeth. It'll come, eventually. We just need to be patient."

"Eventually isn't good enough. The longer we wait, the more time Will has to plan and prepare."

Katrina sighed. "Fine. What do you want to do?"

"I was thinking you feign an illness. We just need to get the door open."

"And then what? You fight off Will and Noah?"

Annabeth grinned. "Here's where being a doctor comes in handy. I know the effects of illicit drugs on the body, and I think we only need to worry about Will right now."

"Why?"

"I think Noah's passed out. I heard the two of them arguing last night. Noah crashed hard Sunday night after we got here. When he woke up Monday evening, he left and scored another hit. Last night, he was all over the place, pacing. It was driving Will mad, and he told him to do something about it. I heard him leave, then come back about an hour later. Since then, I've only heard one set of footsteps. I think maybe he went and got a sleep-aid of some kind."

"Okay, but Will's still bigger and stronger than you."

"I have a plan. Do you trust me?"

"Of course I trust you. But—" She paused and pressed her lips together.

"But what, Mom?"

"I don't want you to get hurt."

"I won't. So long as Noah stays asleep, we'll be fine."

"And if he doesn't?"

Annabeth lifted a shoulder. "We'll deal with that if it happens."

Again, Katrina huffed a sigh. "I still don't like it, but I'm not going to dissuade you, am I?"

"No."

"Okay, then. Explain your plan."

"I want you to fake being unconscious. I'll claim I think you're having a heart attack or something. I'll get him in here, get him to carry you out. When his back is to me, I'll attack him and keep him distracted while you grab a cord—lamp, telephone, whatever; I don't care—and wrap it around his hands and arms. We only need to secure him long enough to do a better job. Then I can use his phone to call for help."

Katrina glanced at the door, her brows pinched together. She worried her bottom lip between her teeth.

"Mom." Annabeth grasped her arms. "We can do this. I'm sick of letting a Cassidy have control over my life. It's time to end this."

Her words had an impact. Katrina's spine straightened, and her expression cleared. "You're right. Okay. Let's do this."

Before Annabeth could say more, commotion in the hallway drew their attention. They shared a glance, then hurried to the door, pressing their ears to it.

"Reitman!" Will yelled for Noah, then knocked on a bedroom door down the hall. "Reitman, wake up! I need to leave now. You need to keep watch here."

There was a short pause, then Will's curse floated down the hall. He banged on the bedroom door again, then Annabeth heard it open. Will's voice sounded again, but it was more muffled. He'd gone into the room. A few moments later, she heard him curse again, the sound louder as he walked back into the hallway. His footsteps grew closer, then stopped right outside the door. She looked at her mom, whose eyes were wide.

"Step back," Annabeth whispered, pulling her away.

The bolts holding the door closed slid open with a soft scritch, and the door swung inward. Will stood in the doorway, a dark glare on his face.

"Let's go." He motioned them forward.

"Go where?"

"Out." He reached behind his back and pulled a handgun from his waistband, and pointed it at Katrina. "Come on."

Hands raised, Katrina looked at Annabeth. This was not good. Annabeth had wanted to be in control of the situation when they made their escape attempt. She wasn't even sure Will had control right now. But they had little choice except to go with him. She gave her mother a small nod.

Katrina walked forward, and Annabeth followed. Will grabbed Katrina's arm and pulled her to him. She let out a yelp of surprise, and Annabeth took a step forward.

"Ah, ah, ah. Stop." Will dug the pistol into Katrina's side and pinned Annabeth with a harsh look. "I will shoot her and leave her here to die."

Annabeth clenched her jaw and glared.

"Good girl. Let's go. You walk in front."

Doing as he asked, she turned into the hall and headed for the living room.

"Get the keys on the coffee table."

She spied the key ring and picked it up.

"Outside. You're driving."

Her heartbeat sped up. This could be their chance.

She led them outside and unlocked the white SUV.

"Get in and start the engine."

"Annabeth."

Katrina's soft voice made her turn. She saw the message in her mother's eyes, but she couldn't heed it. She couldn't leave her behind. So, she turned away and did as Will asked. With the car running, he shoved Katrina into the backseat and got in beside her.

"You will go exactly where I tell you, or you both die. Understand?"

Annabeth nodded.

"Good. Go to the road and turn right."

She put the car in gear and started forward. At the road, she turned, then glanced in the mirror at him. His attention was on the road and not on her or her mom, but the gun was still trained on Katrina's side.

"So, where are we going?" She caught his eye in the mirror as he looked at her.

"To get your sister's car. You better hope your boyfriend delivered it on time."

Annabeth's heart skipped. Did that mean Dean was here too? She wasn't sure Will knew who he was dealing with. He seemed so confident, but if he was like his brother, that confidence led to some holes in his thinking process and made him cocky. He probably saw Dean as just a private investigator. It wasn't out of the realm of possibility, though, that he knew Dean was more than that. Her dad knew he was involved because of Johnathan's actions against Brooke. But would Will think to check into how Dean got involved? Or go deeper into his background than what he currently did for a living? She hoped he'd just assumed it was someone Brooke hired, and that he hadn't bothered to check into Dean's past. If he hadn't, then this would all be over very soon.

FIFTY-SIX

"Sam." Dean spoke into his throat mic. "You in position?" Sam was hunkered down in the woods with a rifle just beyond the house, watching things.

"Yes. Property is quiet."

"How about you, Edie?" The lone female on their little team was in the tall grass in the pasture by the barn. She, too, had a rifle.

"Same. All quiet."

"Maintain position and wait for my signal."

After a chorus of "Copy," Dean dropped his hand from his neck.

"You sure about this?" Jordan looked at him through the window from the driver's seat.

"Yes. You know what you're supposed to do?"

"Block the driveway after the bad guy arrives."

"And stay in the car." He gave Jordan a pointed look.

"Yeah, yeah. You better get going, so I can hide." He held out a slim case.

Dean took it and backed away from the car. "Be careful, Jordie. And stay in the damn car."

Jordan lifted a hand, then drove off. Dean rolled his shoulders, trying to rid himself of some of the unease plaguing him. He was edgy. A lot of it had to do with the stakes. They'd never been higher.

He jogged over to the flatbed and climbed in. Rumbling up the drive, he slowed near the house and turned the truck so it blocked the driveway beyond. He wanted to be able to roll out the passenger side and hide behind the engine block if need be.

Removing his throat microphone, he stowed it in the glove box. He left the earpiece in, so he could hear the others. Opening the case Jordan handed him, he removed the thick-framed black glasses he bought when he bought the rest of the gear the other day. It held a hidden infrared camera. Dean wasn't taking any chances. He wanted Will to go down without a shred of doubt.

Impatience had him wiggling his leg and tapping his fingers on his thigh. He recognized the nervous behavior and forced himself to stop.

"Get your head in the game, Adler." He pulled a breath in through his nose, closing his eyes. Where was that calm emotional center he'd used so much on the SEAL teams? It had gotten him through BUD/S training and all his missions. Why had it disappeared now?

Taking another breath, he felt himself calming. Sorting his thoughts, he threw up walls, blocking out the fear of losing Annabeth so he could focus on saving her.

"Incoming."

Jordan's voice sounded in his ear. Dean's eyes snapped open. He touched a small button on the back of one arm of his glasses to activate the camera.

"White Ford Explorer. Just passed me."

"Any others coming?" Sam asked.

"No. I only see the one vehicle."

"Copy."

A few seconds later, Dean spotted the headlights coming down the road. They neared the drive, and the car slowed, then turned.

"Crap." Edie's voice came through the earpiece. "Annabeth's driving. I see two figures in the backseat, but can't make out who they are."

Dean's walls cracked. Hastily, he slapped some mortar on and regained his focus. He really hadn't thought Will would bring Annabeth and Katrina along.

The car rolled toward him, coming to a stop about ten yards away. The headlights hit the cab, illuminating him. He got out, waiting to see who emerged.

Annabeth got out first. Her gaze flicked to him, then to the back seat. Will got out, hauling Katrina with him.

"Why are you here?" Will asked, pressing a gun into Katrina's side and glaring at him.

"I'm delivering Wendy's car."

"I said to bring it here. I never told you to stay."

"My bad. Maybe be clearer next time." Even if he'd told him to stay away, he still would have come.

The distinct click of a gun hammer being pulled back echoed in the damp midnight air.

"You're not really in a position to be a smart ass. Maybe I should show you how serious this is."

Katrina whimpered and tried to pull away. Will yanked her back.

Dean held out his hands, his heart picking up its pace. "You're right. I'm sorry. It's just instinct to mouth off. Ask my mom; she'll tell you."

Will's shoulders relaxed a bit, which let Dean's heart settle down. He needed to get Will away from the women and take him down. Sam and Edie were just backup in case he took off. This wasn't a military op, where they had permission to take out their targets. Will needed to remain alive no matter how much Dean wished him dead.

"Step away from the truck." Will tipped his head, telling Dean to move.

Bingo. Triumph made his heart skip. Time to make him nervous. He walked forward.

"Stop." Will removed the gun from Katrina's side and pointed it at Dean. "That's far enough. Walk to the side."

The sharp retort of a rifle rebounded through the night and a muzzle flash lit up the pasture to Dean's left. Will let out a shout of pain as the pistol flew from his hand. He dropped to the ground, holding the now bleeding appendage.

"Yeah! Get it, girl!" Jordan's voice sounded in Dean's ear.

"Shut it, Jordie. Sam, move in," Edie replied.

"Moving," Sam said.

Dean ran forward and pounced on Will, rolling him onto his stomach and pulling his good arm up behind his back.

Will groaned. "You didn't come alone? I said no cops. Sweet Jesus, my hand hurts."

Dean glanced at it. In the shadows from the headlights, he couldn't see much other than the blood glistening. "I didn't call the cops. I called my friends. You gave me days to plan. For someone who's gotten away with murder for fifteen years, you're not too bright. You didn't need that car to flee the country." He looked up, searching for Annabeth and Katrina. They were huddled together a few feet away.

"My plans changed." He groaned again. "Do something about my hand, would you?" He tapped his foot on the ground and moaned.

The crunch of gravel under tires had Dean reaching for the gun behind his waist. He swiveled on the balls of his feet to face the newcomer. His shoulders slumped as he recognized the car.

Jordan parked and got out. "I totally should have followed you into the military. That was awesome. Mr. Fancy Pants Bad Guy didn't stand a chance."

Dean huffed a short laugh that was more a sigh of relief than anything else. "It wasn't quite as easy as it looked."

"Speak for yourself. I could have hit him at another hundred yards." Edie walked up and aimed the flashlight attached to her gun at Will's hand. "Good luck ever using that again."

The comment seemed to galvanize Annabeth into action. She stepped away from her mom and came over to crouch next to Dean. He looked into her eyes for a long moment, taking in her beautiful face. Leaning forward, he captured her lips in a quick kiss, then pressed his forehead to hers. "Hi."

"Hi," she breathed, then pulled back. Holding his gaze for another second, she looked at Will. "I'll stop the bleeding. But only so you can stand trial for what you did to my sister. Death is too good for you. I want you to rot in jail for the rest of your life." She glanced up. "Someone find me a first aid kit." Then she pointed at Edie. "Give me your belt for a tourniquet. And I need something that can soak up blood. The basic kit in most cars doesn't carry enough gauze."

"We have a trauma pack," Dean said. He looked back at Jordan. "Jordan, can you get it? It's in the back of your car."

The other man nodded and jogged away, returning a few moments later with a backpack.

Annabeth dug through it, taking out an actual tourniquet and several packs of gauze.

"Everything good?" Sam asked, walking up.

"Yes," Dean replied.

"No," Katrina said. "What about the other man?"

Dean frowned, his senses going on alert. "What other man?"

"Noah Reitman is back at the house where we've been captive the last few days," Annabeth said while she examined Will's hand. "He's strung out on drugs."

"Do you think he's still there?"

"Maybe. He took meth, then couldn't sleep, so Will made him get something that would calm him down. He's been out for close to eighteen hours."

Will screamed as she pressed a heavy bandage to his hand. Dean wrinkled his nose at the mangled mess illuminated by the flashlight Edie aimed at it. The bones were shattered and two of his fingers hung by flaps of skin. Edie was right; he'd be lucky to regain use of his hand. She was a damn good shot.

"When the police get here, we'll make them aware."

"I'll call it in," Sam said.

Ten minutes later, the first of the sirens split the night. Soon, flashing lights bounced off the trees. Two sheriff's cars turned onto the driveway and came to a halt behind Jordan's SUV. The cop that emerged from the driver's seat took one look at their attire and put a hand on the butt of his gun, even though they'd put all their guns away in the vehicles.

"I need to see everyone's hands."

"None of us are armed anymore, deputy." Dean put a knee on Will's arm and held up both hands.

"Where are the guns?"

"In the SUV." Dean pointed to the car. "There's another over there somewhere, but I doubt it works now." He tipped his hand in the direction Will's gun flew when Edie shot it from his hand.

The man looked at his colleagues, then strode forward, assessing the scene. "Tell me what happened. Start from the beginning."

Dean took a breath and dove in. By the time he recounted

the whole story, the paramedics had arrived, and the deputy's eyebrows were at his hairline.

"Okay, then. We'll need the video footage from your glasses, and for y'all to come down to the station. I'm sure our detectives will want to have a word."

Grimacing, Dean glanced at the others. They were in for a sleepless night.

Fifty-Seven

Annabeth stared at the half-empty cup of lukewarm coffee in her hands, running a finger over the rim. Fatigue pulled at her mind, but the hard plastic chair in the waiting area at the local sheriff's office was not conducive to sleep. She wanted to go to a hotel and sink into a nice warm bed and Dean's arms.

A door opened and closed, and a man walked by. Her mother, who sat next to her, shifted in her seat, crossing and uncrossing her legs. She was in the same boat as Annabeth; exhausted, but too uncomfortable to fall asleep.

Annabeth let out a breath and tipped her head back against the wall. She shut her eyes. The station noise receded as her mind floated, stuck between wakefulness and sleep. Memories from the last few hours ran through her mind on a reel, interspersed by images of her sister. It was finally over. Wendy could rest in peace.

"Annabeth?"

She jolted upright when Dean said her name and touched her arm. Blinking, she looked at him.

"Hey." He gave her a soft smile. "You ready to go?"

"They're letting you leave?" She'd been sure he and his friends would all get arrested. The deputies hadn't been too pleased with their stunt.

"Yes. They've asked us to stick around for a few days, but that's it."

"And Edie? She's been released too?"

"Yep. The detectives watched my glasses cam footage. It clearly showed Will threatening us. I'm glad I sprung the extra for audio. It caught everything."

"Everything?" Katrina sat forward, breaking into the conversation.

Dean nodded, a slow smile spreading over his face. "Everything."

"It's really over?" Tears thickened her voice, breaking it. "My Wendy's killer is going to jail?"

"Yes. For probably the rest of his life." He reached out, laying a hand over her hands in her lap, and squeezed.

She smiled at him through her tears. "Thank you."

"You're welcome. And I didn't do it alone. Thank *you* for finding the courage to come forward. We wouldn't have been in the position to catch him if you hadn't turned over the car."

Annabeth wrapped an arm around her mother's shoulders and hugged her. "It was a group effort."

"It was." Dean patted Katrina's knee, then stood. "Come on. Let's go find a hotel and get some sleep." He glanced down the hall.

Annabeth looked over and saw the others coming. They didn't look as tired as she felt. Except Jordan. He walked with a weariness that said he hoped someone else was driving.

"You guys ready?" Sam stopped a few feet away.

Annabeth took a moment to study him in the light. He'd been imposing in the dark, but here, where she could see his size, it was like looking at a mountain. He had three or four inches on Dean and Jordan and close to a foot on Edie. It was the muscles bulging beneath his black long-sleeve shirt that made him look truly mountainous, though.

"We are." Dean helped Katrina to her feet.

"I talked to the deputy at the desk while I waited on you guys." Jordan tipped his head toward the main desk. "She said there's a cluster of hotels just down the road and called ahead to one. They're expecting us."

Edie glanced over, then looked at them and rolled her eyes. "She's watching you."

"Hmm?" Jordan turned, then lifted a hand and waved, smiling.

"Oh, please." Edie huffed. She tossed her long red braid over her shoulder. "Let's go." She stomped away.

Sam looked at Dean and lifted an eyebrow, a crooked smile on his face.

Dean returned it and shook his head. "You heard her. Let's go."

The group filed toward the door, catching up to Edie.

"So, what happens to Will now?" Annabeth asked. "Obviously, he'll stand trial for kidnapping us, but what about Wendy? And his mom?" She'd related the story of what Will told them about his mother to the detective who interviewed her.

"His mom?" Jordan asked.

She quickly summarized what she knew.

"He is one sick puppy." Edie wrinkled her nose.

"I don't know about his mom." Dean held the door for her and Katrina to pass through. "But he'll be extradited to Virginia eventually, to stand trial for Wendy's murder. The courts will sort it all out. He won't see the outside of a jail cell, maybe ever again."

It hit her then. Well and truly. She'd known it was over, but it hadn't completely sunk in. But now? Now she felt vindicated. She'd been right. She'd. Been. Right.

All the worry and anger she'd carried for so long melted away with the knowledge that Wendy's killer would get what he deserved. A joyous laugh bubbled free. She looked at Dean, then her mom. "We did it."

A bright smile wreathed Katrina's face. She pulled Annabeth into a tight hug.

"Thank you, sweetie. For not giving up. I'm so proud of you."

Moisture gathered in Annabeth's eyes. She gave her mom a squeeze. "I love you, Mom."

"I love you too." Katrina gave her another squeeze, then pulled back. She wiped the tears off Annabeth's face. "No more of those. Unless they're happy tears."

Annabeth's head bobbed, and she smiled, wiping at her eyes. "They are."

"Good." Katrina stepped back. She turned her head, and Annabeth saw her smile at Dean. "I mean that, young man. Don't make her cry sad tears. I seem to have found a backbone through all this, and I will not be afraid to call you out if you hurt my baby."

"No, ma'am." Dean held up his hands, a smile teasing his lips. "Only happy tears. I promise."

She arched an eyebrow and tipped a finger at him, then smiled before walking ahead.

Annabeth chuckled and watched her go.

"You sure you can handle her?" Dean took her hand. "She's not the same woman we brought back from Martha's Vineyard."

"No, that's for sure. I think the bigger question is, are you ready to have both of us in your life? We're a package deal." She could hardly believe the turn her relationship with her mom had taken. But it was true. After the last couple of weeks —and especially after the last few days—they were closer than ever.

Dean tugged her into his side and wrapped an arm around her. They followed the others into the parking lot at a slower pace. "Yeah, I think I can handle the two of you."

He looked down at her. Annabeth raised her head.

"Putting up with each other's families is something couples in love do."

Annabeth blushed, remembering what else he showed her that they do. "You seem to have a lot of ideas about what couples in love do. Are there more?"

He shrugged. "I'm sure I'll think of some." He grinned, then leaned down and kissed her. "I love you."

She hummed and smiled. "I love you too."

Fifty-Eight

Four weeks later...

"Oh my God. Annabeth, this pie is divine." Edie groaned and shoved another bite of apple pie into her mouth.

"You should try the cake." Jordan shoveled in a huge bite of Katrina's pumpkin coffee cake and moaned as he rolled his eyes up.

Annabeth laughed, looking over the table at her new friends. A warm breeze ruffled the tablecloth spread over the long table set up in Max's backyard. She glanced around, scarcely believing the turn her life had taken in the last couple of months. If someone told her she'd be celebrating Thanksgiving in Costa Rica with her mother, her sexy new boyfriend, and all their closest friends, she'd have shut the door in their face, then buried her feelings in a pint of mint chocolate chip ice cream.

Well, almost all their closest friends. Ford was in the U.S. with Brooke, which Dean and the rest of his little group were happy about. He'd apparently been a little crabby before he went after her.

But most of the gang was here, enjoying the oasis that was Max's backyard and an amazing Thanksgiving feast.

A high-pitched squeal filled the yard, then Max's booming laugh. Annabeth looked over to see him swing Margot's daughter Emily into the air and give her a soft toss. Her sister Lily watched while stuffing fistfuls of cake into her mouth.

She nudged Dean, who sat next to her. "He's having fun." She broke off a piece of pie and lifted her fork.

"Yeah. Max needs a family."

Annabeth's fork froze in front of her lips. Something in his tone made her think that was more than an innocuous comment. She cocked her head. "Are you playing matchmaker?"

Dean shrugged, then gestured to them with one hand. "Look at them. And look at her." He peered past her and nodded at Margot.

She glanced over. Margot sat with Lily, but she watched Max and Emily, a wide smile on her face.

Annabeth sighed. "She's still married. And even once the divorce is final in a few months, I doubt she'll want to get involved again anytime soon. Especially with a man fifteen years older than she is."

"Age is just a number. I mean, have you met a bigger kid than Max?"

Annabeth chuckled. "No."

"See? I rest my case."

She laughed harder. "Just... don't push it, okay?"

He nodded, his expression turning a little more serious. "I won't. I do think they'd be good together, but I get it." He watched Max and Emily for a moment. "Has she heard from Tad at all?"

"No. I don't think she will, either. That divorce decree was pretty thorough. He gave up all rights to the girls, turned everything over to Margot—except his student loan debt, thank goodness—and cited irreconcilable differences as his reason for the divorce. Her lawyer said they could contest it, but that it could take a lot longer for it to go through, since they'd have to track him down to approve the changes or for enough time to pass that a judge would grant the divorce on desertion grounds."

"Is she doing that? Contesting it?"

"No. She said she just wants to put it all behind her and focus on raising the girls."

"Well, she'll get a completely fresh start here."

"That's for sure." Margot and Annabeth had started the process to obtain medical licenses in Costa Rica. They'd both enrolled in an intensive Spanish course and were gathering what they'd need to submit their applications. Margot had quit her job in Texas and moved to Ohio. She and the girls were living with Annabeth until her divorce went through and she could sell her house. In the meantime, she'd found a job at a pediatrician's office in a neighboring suburb.

"I can't wait until you're down here full time." Dean leaned closer, his voice turning suggestive. He nuzzled her neck at the base of her ear.

Flutters erupted in her belly. She couldn't wait, either. Being apart more often than not was killing her. He'd had to come back down here not long after they were cleared to leave Arkansas. Sam needed him at the bar. She understood Dean couldn't leave his friend in a bind just to spend time with her. So, they called, and texted, and FaceTime'd. But this was the first they'd been together since he left the U.S. It had been all she could do to bake that pie and leave his house for this feast. She'd wanted to stay naked in the bedroom, like they had since she arrived. Annabeth was glad Max had a big house and offered to host Katrina, Margot, and the girls. It meant she and Dean didn't have to tiptoe around or be social. In between bouts of intense lovemaking, they'd talked and really gotten to know each other. With every passing minute, she fell a little more in love with him.

"It'll happen soon enough." She turned her head and speared him with a look. "But right now, you should pay attention to your friends." She sent a furtive glance across the table. She could feel Jordan's eyes on them.

Dean flattened his mouth and sat up.

"Hi." Jordan waved. "Remember us?"

"Funny."

"Leave them alone," Katrina said. "They're in love, and it's sweet. I'm happy to see my baby happy."

"Thanks, Mom." Annabeth smiled at her, glad to see her mom happy too. Like Margot, she was putting the past behind her and moving on. It helped that her dad had been arrested in connection to Wendy's death. The feds had also opened an investigation into his business. He was facing some serious fraud charges. Katrina had been called to answer some questions, and the police had picked her life apart as well, but so far, she'd been cleared of any wrongdoing. Annabeth hoped things stayed that way.

"I feel like I'm living in some sappy romance movie." Edie scrunched her nose and shook her head. She swiped her fork over her plate, scooping up the last bits of pie. "First Ford and now Dean. Who's next?" She glanced down the length of the table. "How about you, Sam? You got a girl lurking in the shadows we don't know about?"

"No."

Annabeth chuckled at his direct, one-word response.

"Asher?"

The dark-haired computer wunderkind shook his head. "Maybe you should look in the mirror."

Edie scoffed. "Yeah, right. With who? One of the surf bums who comes to my shop all the time?"

"No." Asher cast a glance at Jordan.

Edie froze, her eyes going wide.

Jordan picked that moment to look up from his cake. He frowned, seeing her expression. "What?"

"Nothing." She stood up. "You want more cake? I need more pie." She grabbed his plate, not waiting for an answer.

"Uh, sure." His frown deepened as she hurried away; then he looked at Dean. "What was that about?"

"Nothing." Dean hid a smirk.

Annabeth stifled a laugh. The poor man looked so confused. For that matter, so had Edie.

Max joined them then, carrying a giggling Emily. He lowered her toward a chair in a wide, swooping arc, making airplane noises as she descended. The girl landed on her bottom as he made an explosion sound. He sat down next to her.

She stood up on the seat and held her arms out to him. "Fas!"

"In a little bit, Em. How about some cake?" He picked up a fork and scooped up some of the mushy cake from Lily's plate. Emily ate it, sufficiently distracted.

Margot chuckled. "You're all sweaty."

"She's worse than my drill sergeants in basic." He wiped his forehead on his shirtsleeve. "There any of that pie left? It looked good."

"There was," Annabeth replied. "But you might want to run. Edie went to get herself more."

"Oh, uh-uh." He stood up. "She better not eat it all."

Annabeth laughed as he ran away from the table and skirted the pool to go inside. Settling back into her seat, she looked around the table again. Contentment settled over her like a thick, soft blanket on a chilly day.

She glanced heavenward, feeling Wendy's presence, and knew her sister had a hand in getting her here. Smiling, she put a hand over her heart. *Thank you, Wen. I love you. Rest in peace.*

About the Author

Ashley started writing in her teens and never stopped. Her first novel, Smoky Mountain Murder, came out in 2016, and she has since published two more series and has plans for more. When not writing, you can find her with her nose stuck in a book or watching some terrible disaster movie on SyFy. An avid baseball fan, she also enjoys crafting and cooking. She lives in Ohio with her husband, two kids, three cats, and one very wild shepherd mix.

Website: https://ashleyaquinn.com

goodreads.com/ashleyaquinn
amazon.com/Ashley-A-Quinn/e/B07HCT4QST

ALSO BY ASHLEY A QUINN

Foggy Mountain Intrigue

Smoky Mountain Murder

Smoky Mountain Baby

Smoky Mountain Stalker

Smoky Mountain Doctor

Smoky Mountain K-9

Smoky Mountain Judge

The Broken Bow

A Beautiful End

Wildfire

In Plain Sight

Close Quarters

Scorched

Light of Dawn

Pine Ridge

Sweetness

Loner

Shark

Katydid

Homespun

Wagner Brigade

Ford's Fight

Dean's Dilemma

Jordan's Journey